THE HERO

by Teiran

Bad Dog Books

2007

The Hero

by Teiran

First published 2007
First revision 2010

ISBN: 978-90-79082-20-9
Published by Bad Dog Books

www . baddogbooks . com

Cover art by Satinka
Cover design by Kamui
Interior art by Satinka, Kamui and Ayame Emaya

BAD DOG BOOKS

TABLE OF CONTENTS

FOREWORD

This is a story about love, adventure, and what it means to be a hero.

A young hyena named Flint finds what he calls love in the arms of another male, an adventurer, and finds the world disagrees. Will he find a way to follow his knight in shining armor, or will he find that there is no place for him even in this world of magic?

The Hero was originally written for FANG, another fine publication of Bad Dog Books, and I was rather sad to see it rejected by its editor, Alex Vance.

As Alex put it, "This story is too long to publish in FANG Volume 3, and I regret to inform you that it has consequently been rejected. Of course, if you could increase the length by, say, double, it might be an excellent candidate for a novel."

I was thrilled, took up the challenge, and now you hold my first full length novel. I hope you enjoy it.

I would like to dedicate this book to my family, who always supported me in everything I wanted to do. They would be wise to put the book down though.

I also want to dedicate the story to Gary Gygax, and all the others who made Dungeons & Dragons possible. They sparked my imagination many years ago and started me down the path of fantasy fiction and to the furry fandom, and they have no one to blame but themselves for the crazy things I've done since.

Teiran

3

Ten of Swords

CHAPTER I

The necromancer moved through the darkness of the mine tunnel, dragging his captive behind him over the rough floor. The dark cleric was a tall Dalmatian named Bayon. The dog used a different name when visiting town of course, and had given a third name to the fox nobleman he had kidnapped. The fox struggled and whimpered as the dog pulled him over long forgotten rails and sharp rocks, but it was a futile effort. The fox's legs were bound and his paws tied behind his back.

Bayon had never learned what the fox's name was and he did not care. Nor did the Dalmatian care that the fox was crying in pain from the rough treatment. Bayon smiled in the darkness as he dragged the bound noble by the scruff of his neck. He liked inflicting pain. The fox had woken up when they reached the entrance to the mine and really began struggling once they crossed over the threshold of Bayon's temple, but the gag kept the vulpine's cries muffled. The Dalmatian dragged the fox through the temple's antechamber and toward the main chapel where everyone was waiting. The young noble struggled against the ropes binding his legs and paws, but it was no use. Bayon was very experienced at tying knots.

A cheer rose up from the acolytes as Bayon entered the underground chapel. The chamber was deep inside the earth, and so the dozen madmen who worshiped with Bayon could scream as loud as they wanted to without fear. Bayon paused in the doorway and basked in the adoration of his followers before making his way to the altar along the back wall. The Dalmatian smiled when his followers cursed and spat on the fox as they passed by, and the fox twisted and jerked in his bindings to avoid their kicks.

Bayon tightened his grip on the fox's neck, but it really didn't matter. The fox could not escape the ropes, and the acolytes would never allow him to run even if he did. The fox nobleman could not escape the fate that awaited him at the hands of the necromancer.

The acolytes began to chant as Bayon climbed the alter steps. One acolyte began to beat the ceremonial drum, and the steady pounding thundered off the stone walls of the temple like a heartbeat. Bayon stood before the altar of Mak'tchen and smiled, forcing his captive to bow before the altar. The Dalmatian thrust one paw in the air above his head, his fingers twisted into the clawed symbol of his deity, and the chanting and drumming rose to a deafening roar behind him.

Bayon closed his eyes and let the noise wash over him. It filled the Dalmatian with a dark joy that these craven men followed him so completely. The Dalmatian grabbed the struggling young noble's shirt and forced the fox to his feet. The fox yelped behind the gag as the dog grabbed his muzzle and forced him to look at the altar. Bayon smiled, watching as the fox's eyes grew wide in fear. Bayon was proud of the altar he had crafted for Mak'tchen and he loved the fear it inspired in his victims.

The altar was a grotesque carving of a beast's mouth. To an observer, like the quivering fox Bayon held now, the huge jaws seemed to be lunging out of the back wall of the temple, ready to swallow them whole. The jagged teeth were even covered in the blood of old sacrifices. The inside of the mouth was large enough to fit a full-grown horse, and the roof of the mouth was covered in carvings depicting the hellish afterlife of Mak'tchen, the Devourer of Souls.

Bayon had used dark magic to forge the altar mouth, and indeed the entire temple complex, from the living earth itself. An abandoned mine shaft had been the perfect hiding place for his cult, and over the past few months Bayon had scarified dozens of virgins from the surrounding villages to his dark god. Virgins like the struggling fox he was holding now.

Soon Bayon would use his magic again and bring the altar to life. The massive stone jaws would close down on the fox like an iron maiden, and the necromancer's spell would send the soul of his latest conquest, turned victim, to his dark god to fuel the Dalmatian's dark plans. Then Bayon would raise the fox's corpse as part of his growing zombie horde.

With a grunt the Dalmatian lifted the fox into the air by his throat, holding him just high enough off the ground that his hind-paws twisted in the air. With a flourish, he turned to his worshipers and presented the sacrificial fox to them, and the cultists responded with another bestial roar. The Dalmatian smiled and sniffed the air, enjoying the scent of fear that rolled off the fox in waves and the screams of his followers. This was his moment of triumph, and the Dalmatian was going to savor it as long

7

as he could. He drank in the moment, and then with a flourish of his robes Bayon flung the boy into the mouth of the altar.

The chanting and drumming stopped the moment Bayon released the fox, so that silence greeted the young noble's cry of pain as the dark god's teeth stabbed the fox in the back. It was a Mak'tchen tradition that everyone in the temple should hear the sacrifice's first cry of pain. The fox was left hanging there half in, half out of the dark god's mouth, like a morsel about to be swallowed whole. Bayon smiled as the fox struggled, blood dripping onto the floor. It looked like the mouth of his god was salivating blood in anticipation of a meal. The young fox's tearful sobs of pain filled the temple, amplified by the shape of the altar.

None of the true believers in the temple flinched or looked away from the frightening scene. Why would they? The fox was a sacrifice to their god. Some of the cultists, the ones who had spent too much time reading the unholy words of Mak'tchen, actually envied the boy's fate.

Bayon pulled his hood back, his white and black spotted face twisting into a huge grin as he leaned over the young fox. Bayon could see the fox's eyes darting back and forth as the noble got his first look at the inside of the altar mouth. Bayon relished the look of growing fear on his captive's face as the fox stared up at the hideously carvings inside the mouth of his god in terror. Images of torture and rape covered the inside of the altar and were coated in the dried blood of the previous sacrifices. They gave the young fox a very clear picture of what was about to happen to him and his soul. "Are you comfortable?" The Dalmatian sneered, and the fox gave a whimper of fear, begging for mercy as he stared at the dark carvings above him. The words came out as garbled nonsense because of the gag, but it was music to the dark priest's ears.

A shadow fell over the young fox's face as Bayon's second approached the altar and blocked out the meager torchlight. "Are you sure you've found a virgin sacrifice this time, Brother Bayon?" The badger named Ryul kept his voice low, so that the acolytes in the temple proper would not hear him over the renewed drumming.

The Dalmatian's eyes slanted and his ears flopped slightly as he jerked his head up and growled at Ryul. "Do not mock me," the dog snapped, "It is not my fault if you cannot tell when a girl has been deflowered." The Dalmatian smirked at his companion, flashing him the charming smile that the handsome Dalmatian used to seduce his victims, like the young fox on the altar right now. "Or have you forgotten my distaste of the fairer sex?"

The badger's lip twitched and his fingers spread out like fans, displaying his deformed claws. Ryul fought down the urge to claw the smirk right off of Bayon's muzzle. As much as Ryul would love to drive his enlarged claws into the spots on the face of his fellow priest, they were the reason Ryul could not do so. The arcane magic Ryul wielded was far more corrupting than the Dalmatian's divine prayers, and his twisted paws would expose him to the townsfolk of the nearby villages. "Fine," the badger spat, "but we do not have any more time for your theatrics. If we do not hurry, the stars will move out of alignment in a few days and we will lose this rare chance to find the..."

"Be silent," Bayon snapped, putting a bit of divine power behind the words. It was a simple spell, but Ryul's mouth snapped shut and his eyes burned as he was forced to obey the Dalmatian. Bayon flicked his tail back and forth, enjoying the moment of power over his fellow priest. "Good. Now if you are done proving why I lead this temple and not you, we can begin the ritual."

The Dalmatian turned back to the altar, and lewdly leaned over the squirming fox. Bayon put his head inside the stone jaws of Mak'tchen and almost lay down on top of the young male fox he had seduced, drugged, and kidnapped from the nearby town. The Dalmatian's weight pushed the fox down onto the jagged teeth, causing them to dig into the fox as the Dalmatian had one last moment of fun with his sacrifice. "See? My place is much cozier than yours would have been, isn't it? I would have enjoyed going to your place," the Dalmatian said mockingly as he licked the fox's muzzle slowly, relishing the disgust in the fox's eyes. "But I know Mak'tchen is so much happier you came here. He has grown hungry over the last fortnight since…"

Ryul turned away from the Dalmatian's taunting, gesturing at the acolytes who would prepare his scrying tools for the ritual. This would be the seventh time Ryul and Bayon had preformed the divination ceremony in the last two weeks, and still they had found nothing. The ceremony should have worked by now. It had never failed Ryul in the past. The badger crushed herbs and chanted under his breath, trying to ignore the Dalmatian's voice as he collected the virgin's blood.

Ryul's ear flicked back when the dog's words ended in a wet choking sound. The badger looked back as Bayon jerked, his paws clutched at the altar's lip, and his body stiffened. Ryul blinked in surprise as a red dot appeared in the white fur on the back of Bayon's neck, and the badger gaped in shock at the large knife-point that pushed out of the back of Bayon's neck.

Bayon toppled backward, clutching at the long knife lodged in his throat. The acolytes gasped in fear as a lithe, roguish jackal erupted out of the altar's mouth. He landed in a crouch over the Dalmatian priest. Ryul gave a hiss and jumped back, moving toward the safety of his followers as the jackal pulled a second long knife from his belt and drove it home in the thrashing Dalmatian's chest.

"You will die for this, infidel!" The badger spat, and he began to move his paws in a weaving fashion, blue light crackling between his elongated fingers as he cast a spell to strike the jackal down.

The crouching jackal merely withdrew his daggers from the corpse and pulled the fox off the altar's teeth, "I don't think so," the jackal said with a smirk and pulled the gag out of the fox's mouth.

Ryul backed away from the rogue and finished his spell, sending a dark bolt of energy at him. The black lightning should have struck the insolent canine dead, but the spell died before it even reached the rogue.

The young fox noble was smiling at Ryul, and the fear was gone from his features. A sparkle of magic faded from the fox's outstretched paw, and Ryul's stomach turned in fear. The fox was a mage as well.

The sound of steel being drawn from a scabbard behind him made the badger turn. Ryul looked behind him just in time to see one of the acolytes near the back rise up, cast off his black robes to reveal a wolf in shining armor, and cut the large bear who was guarding the door in half with one blow.

The badger's blood went cold as the wolf's blade left a trail of white, holy light in the air behind it. The wolf was a holy Knight. The bar holding the doors closed fell to the ground, cut in two by the same stroke that had felled the bear with ease. The badger could feel the holy energy rolling off the wolf as it began to disrupt the flow of the temple's dark magic. Ryul could not believe that a Knight of the Cross had sneaked into the temple undetected.

"Repent, necromancer," the Knight of the Cross called out as he turned to face the crowd of startled worshipers, the temple doors swinging open to reveal more adventures geared for battle, "For you will soon join your companion." The temple erupted into the chaos of battle, and Ryul hurled another spell in anger and fled.

With grunt of exertion, Ryul closed the stone door behind him. The noise of battle and the flash of magic vanished, leaving the badger in darkness and pain. With an equally dark curse, the young necromancer banished the shadows that filled the tunnel with a simple spell. A greenish flame sprang to life in his paw, and the badger's eyes darted back and forth as the magic flame lit the escape tunnel he had dived into during the pitched battle. The flame cast deep shadows on the walls around him, but nothing moved in the secret passage and no one banged against the stone door behind him. The would-be heroes had not noticed his escape.

Ryul could not suppress a cackle of glee as he leaned against the wall and started to limp down the corridor and away from the temple complex. His charismatic partner might be dead, and his followers would surely follow their leader's example, but he didn't care. Months of searching, plotting, sacrificing, and it was all for nothing. The stars would soon be out of alignment, and there would be no way for him to continue the search for the sacrifice Mak'tchen demanded. He had failed his god, and lost most of his possessions, but Ryul could still have his revenge. After all, he was a necromancer. Finding new followers would be an easy task. They were often just lying around.

The badger began to mumble to himself as he slid along the wall, cursing and spitting blood as his shuffled down the corridor, damning his most likely broken leg the whole way. He would have to find a way to heal himself and then he would extract his revenge on the adventures that had ruined his plans.

The little town of East Haven was quiet as the strangers rode in town with dusk on their heels. The village only had one real street, and that was actually the High Pass road, which ran the length of the kingdom across the northern mountains.

East Haven owed its existence to the High Pass road. It made a convenient stopping point for travelers going west across the Mistwood Mountains, and was about fifty miles to the west of the large city of Newcastle. The Green Briar Inn was the only building with a lantern out front, colored glass turning the light green, which meant it was the only establishment still open at this late hour. The only people who saw the strangers ride into town were the two bored coyote guards who made sure the street was safe at night and Flint, the inn's kitchen boy.

When Flint heard the sound of hooves trotting down the street, he stopped feeding the other horses in the stable and raced to open the outer door. The young hyena knew that the travelers would be stopping at the inn, because everyone traveling the High Pass road stopped when it was this late. Flint's round ears turned backward and he kept his black nose down as he peered out of the stable's doors. Flint watched the arrivals ride to the front of the inn and dismount.

Most of the shadowy figures went inside the inn's front door after tying their horses to the hitching posts. Only one of the travelers remained outside, leading a pair of the horses toward the stable doors. Flint threw his shoulder against the large wooden door and pushed it open, his paws sliding in the fresh straw as he heaved the large door open for the traveler. When Flint had the big door open, he scampered over to the other horses, trying to catch a glimpse of the person who had passed him by.

With his head turned back toward the stable Flint went for the nearest horse, but when he pulled on the reins to lead the horse to the stable, the hyena knew he had made a mistake. The horse was one of those large draft horses people bred for combat, and Flint was so short he was only eye level with its chin. The chestnut horse lowered it head and took one look at Flint before deciding that anyone who was that small could not possibly be in charge of him. The horse whinnied and flipped Flint over backward with a shake of its head.

The hyena yipped as he fell down, catching himself with his front paws so he did not get a noseful of dirt. The spotted hyena brushed his paws off as a hearty laugh came from the direction of the stables.

"Here boy, let me get that one for you," a gruff, but friendly canine voice said. "I'm sure my friend's noble-bred pony will be more agreeable than this old wild beast is." Flint's ears perked up as the traveler grabbed hold of the nickering horse's reins. The hyena turned to thank the stranger, and instead ended up falling into an embarrassed silence.

Flint flattened his ears and ducked his muzzle when he saw just who was standing beside him. The handsome wolf just smiled down at him before leading the big draft horse away. Flint tried to say something, but couldn't work up the nerve.

The wolf was a Knight of the Cross; he *had* to be. He was wearing a suit of silvery chain mail that seemed to glimmer even in the fading light, and it was the most intricate armor Flint had ever seen on a traveler. The Prophet's Cross, the symbol of the land's largest religion, had even been worked into the armor with gold-colored chain links. No man would wear armor like that unless he were a true Knight of the Cross.

Flint could barely contain his excitement. The hyena had never seen a real knight before. He had seen wizards, bandits, and noblemen as they passed through the village. Even a few traveling priests had stopped at the Green Briar Inn, but never a real Knight of the Cross.

The Knights of the Cross were the land's most fearsome warriors, holy men who swept evil from the dark places of the world and defended the innocent. Flint had heard all the stories about the Knights from the village boys. It had been a knight who foiled the plot to assassinate King Lawrence. A knight had slain the great dragon that had threatened the city of Feydowns with destruction. A knight had uncovered the murderous thieves' guild in the Port of Dawn and destroyed their leader, the High Priest of Shin-do, god of thieves. Whenever some danger faced the kingdom, it was a Prophet's greatest servants who rode to the rescue. Flint had listened to each of those stories with rapt attention, but meeting a knight for real was better than any story, and Flint had never imagined it would happen in a small town like East Haven.

An impatient snort and a tap on his shoulder broke Flint's daydream. The hyena felt his face grow hot as the short, svelte-looking pony beside him nickered in irritation and practically forced his reigns into Flint's paws. The hyena led the eager pony into the stable, got him some oats, and ducked his head in embarrassment as the knight walked past him a second time.

Once they had all the horses inside the stable, Flint stood beside the stable door with his paws nervously placed behind his back. He wanted to say something to the wolf and get his attention somehow, so he could tell the village boys he had actually talked to a real Knight of the Cross, but he didn't have any idea what to say to someone like this. Eventually, Flint said, "Um, so, are you really a Knight?" The wolf looked at him in confusion, and Flint's ears turned backward as he continued to talk. "It's just that with your armor, and your sword, and well, you look like a Knight of the Cross. You are, aren't you? I've just never met one before," the hyena trailed off uncertainly.

The wolf's muzzle broke into a slow smile as the short hyena's words tumbled over themselves. "Yes, I am a knight. Are you really a stable boy who is scared of horses?"

The knight stopped smiling when Flint's head went down almost instantly. "You're right sir, I'm so sorry." Flint flattened his ears back and tucked his tail between his legs as he grabbed hold of the stool he used to work around the horses. "These are my duties. You shouldn't be doing this."

The wolf gave Flint a slight smile and shook his head. "No please, I was just joking. I can handle things, thank you." Flint nodded at the knight as the wolf went about his business. Flint wasn't quite sure what he should do now. Most of the patrons who came to the Green Briar did not stay and care for their horses, but the wolf was checking each horse, removing their saddles, and making sure they were settled into their stalls.

Not that Flint minded the help. He hated taking off saddles more than anything else. He was too short to reach all the fastenings usually and the horses didn't cooperate much, but the wolf had been right. This was something he was supposed to be doing not the inn's customers. Just standing there as a knight did his job made the hyena feel more awkward than his fumbled attempt at conversation. Besides, Flint reasoned, this would probably be the closest he got to the wolf unless he was allowed to serve dinner. Instead of talking the short hyena climbed up on his wooden stool and went to tend to the horse in the stall next to the one the wolf was working in.

Flint could just see the wolf looking over the wall separating them as he climbed up beside the big, black horse in this stall. He reached over the horse's back to untie the only bag the horse was carrying. It was a small sack, probably filled with grain of kind, and it certainly looked light enough for Flint to carry.

When the wolf noticed what he was doing, he barked, "Not that one!" but it was too late. Flint had already untied the bag and pulled it into his arms. The little hyena's smile disappeared as he looked up at the wolf, and knew right away why the knight had tried to warn him.

The sack was heavy. Not just normally heavy, like it was filled with grain or gold coins, but so heavy that nothing but magic could make such a small bag weigh so much. The sack easily weighed more than Flint did, and the hyena tottered back and forth on the top of the wooden stool trying to keep his balance. The knight and boy looked at each other for a moment, as Flint huffed and panted, adjusted his grip and was just about to get the heavy bag under control, when the wooden stool he was standing on made a loud cracking sound. Then Flint disappeared from sight with a yip and a crash. The wolf folded his ears back and covered his eyes with a sigh.

The world was spinning slightly for Flint and he could not breath. The sack had come down on top of Flint's chest, forcing the air out of his lungs and pinning him to the ground. The hyena struggled to push it off him, but it was too heavy for him to move. It felt as if someone had crammed an anvil or two, inside the tiny bag somehow. Flint saw the knight rush around the horse, grab hold of the bag, and haul it off Flint with a grunt. Flint blinked in surprise as the wolf strained to lift the bag up, and over his shoulder.

"Careful there," the wolf said quietly as he offered the hyena a paw, "These magic bags can be tricky."

Tiny spots zoomed across Flint's vision like flies as the wolf hauled him to his feet. His face burned and his round ears were flat against his head. He'd never been so embarrassed in his life. He had been the butt of a hundred cruel pranks played by the village boys, but to be bested by a sack in front of a knight was beyond humiliating. Flint looked up at the taller knight, and he was far too worried about how he looked in front of someone most people would call a hero to notice that the wolf was blushing too.

Flint's stomach did flips as he brushed the straw and dirt from his fur. He tried to look away from the wolf, but standing this closely there was nowhere else for him too look. The wolf was standing so close to him that Flint actually caught his scent over the smell of horses, and that made Flint feel even worse. The knight smelled good, like the forest after a rainstorm. Flint probably smelled like unwashed horses. The hyena was just glad he had cleaned the stables the day before, or he would have fallen right into a pile of manure.

After a long awkward moment of trying not to look at each other, the knight backed away and they both continued tending to the horses in silence. This time, Flint let the wolf handle all the bags in case another one turned out to be magical. Flint shook his head as he fed the small pony. How rich did you have to be, to have a magical bag? Eventually the wolf left, carrying most of the gear inside the inn and leaving the rest of the work to Flint.

When he was done Flint hurried inside the back door of the inn and into the kitchen, still flushed with embarrassment.

~: :~

"Boy!" Tongish yelled as Flint got inside. "You'd better have that stew ready! I've got five hungry travelers out there." Tongish was the portly tiger that owned the Green Briar Inn, and Flint had been working for him for nine years now, ever since his parents died.

"I know that, I was just tending to their horses," the hyena said as he washed his paws and ladled the evening stew into big bowls, "and I'm not a boy anymore Tongish. I turned nineteen over three months ago."

Flint didn't even duck when the tiger cuffed him upside the head. The tiger's daughter, a young woman named Clara who was about Flint's age, snickered at the rough treatment Flint received. Flint glared at Clara and she just smiled back at him before pointedly laughing a little louder.

Tongish ignored his daughter and muttered. "Don't sass me, boy. Now get them a full supper and don't talk to them. Not a word, understand?" Tongish jabbed a finger at the hyena as he readied several mugs of ale and water for the travelers.

Clara smirked at Flint, her tail curling through the air as she leaned against the counter doing nothing. "Oh father, you know Flint only talks to the horses, after the other things he does for them," she purred. "Just look at the straw in his fur."

"I do not! Lots of people talk to me." Flint barked, brushing the last few pieces of straw off his pants with a nervous blush.

Flint barely ducked away from the second, halfhearted blow Tongish gave him. "Not a word, Flint." The tiger rumbled as he left the kitchen to bring the travelers their drinks. After a moment of smirking at him Clara followed after her father, leaving Flint to finish preparing the meals. Flint glared after the young tigress before turning his full attention to the task at hand.

The hyena stuck his tongue out of the side of his mouth and stood on the tips of his toes as he worked. Without his usual stool to help him, making dinner was much harder than normal. The counter was just too high for him to work on it effectively. It had been made for the tall tiger and his daughter, and it did not help that Flint was only four foot five. He could just get his elbows over the top of the high counter, and he had to work with his head poking over the side as he filled the bowls.

Flint tried to stretch the stew as far as he could so there would be some left over for him to eat, but five servings was just too much. The hyena had to add a little water to each bowl and stir it in just to make the thick stew stretch far enough for the travelers. A loaf of bread, some butter, and a block of warm cheese rounded out the meal. He carried the heavy tray of food into the common room with practiced skill as Tongish shooed his daughter away from the adventurers and back into the kitchen.

Flint smiled as the two tigers passed him by without taking the tray from him, and he got a good look at each of the adventurers as he passed out the food.

At one end of the table sat the knight. The gray wolf flicked his ears back and met Flint's eyes for just a moment before nodding in thanks for the food Flint handed him. The wolf flashed the hyena a big smile before bowing his head to pray. Flint just sort of smiled back and ducked his head in embarrassment. Everyone else probably thought the hyena was nodding in respect to a member of holiest order of knights in the land, but he was really trying to hide his blush at meeting the wolf's gaze.

Beside the wolf sat an elderly looking otter whose brown, thick fur had begun to gray around his short ears. He was dressed in the traditional vestments of a Priest of the Prophet, and the dark black cotton that made the white collar around his neck stand out even more. Flint looked at him with a little uncertainly as he set the bowl of stew in front of the cleric. Flint and every other boy in the village idolized the Prophet's knights, but Flint was wary of the Prophet's actual priests. Even though the Prophet was the only faith in East Haven, Flint was not very familiar with it and the stern glare on the local priest's face always made him uneasy.

The otter joined the wolf in prayer as the big grizzly bear sitting beside him tore into the loaf of bread Flint set down with almost wild abandon. Flint edged around the big bear carefully because the ursine had the look of a wild creature, not a civilized person. It did not help that the armor he was wearing was actually made out of tanned dear hides and was adorned with feathers.

The bear's image as an almost wild creature clashed rather sharply with the straight-laced fox in fancy clothes sitting on the other side of him. The fox had the bearing of a noble and was dressed in clothes finer than any Flint had seen before. Even the minor noble merchants who passed through East Haven did not wear clothing made out of satin and silk. Unlike the other adven-

tures, who all wore obvious weapons, the fox just had a strangely carved staff with him. The brilliant ruby at the tip of the staff and his embroidered robe made Flint suspect the fox was a wizard, but it was hard to tell. Flint had no idea what a real noble was supposed to dress like.

The last traveler was a powerful-looking jackal that seemed to take as much pride in his muscles as the fox did in his clothes. His fur was all black, and the dark short fur showed off his well-defined arms. He was dressed in form-fitting black leather that let him move easily as he sliced the cheese Flint set before him with a wicked-looking knife.

Flint knew the men were adventurers, and that was nothing new to him. Parties of adventurers came through East Haven often enough that he recognized them easily, but these men were different. He wanted to know more about them. Who were these people? Were they all holy men being lead by the Knight on some holy crusade? Were they missionaries returning from a holy pilgrimage? Maybe they were all bodyguards of the noble. Who was wealthy enough to command Knight of the Cross as a bodyguard? Perhaps the fox was royalty? They could all just friends coming home after a treasure hunt, loaded down with so much gold they had been forced to hide some of it along the trail somewhere. It would explain why their magical bag had weighed so much.

The possibilities raced through Flint's mind as he hung around the table listening in on their conversation. The five travelers looked so exotic, so powerful with their weapons and strange clothes. They stood out even by the standards of adventurers. Flint wanted to know all about them, because they were infinitely more interesting than the dreary townsfolk he saw day after day.

Flint watched them begin to eat, and as the knight and priest finished praying the jackal stood up and raised his mug above the heads of the others. He was a bit taller than the otter or fox, and about the same height as the wolf, which made him much taller than Flint. Everyone in the room was shorter than the bear. "All right, all right everybody before you all get too deep into that food I have something to say." The jackal pointed his mug at the otter; who seemed a bit surprised by the toast. "I'm sure that by now, Father Tully, you know that I didn't want you to come with us when we left Newcastle." The rest of the table laughed a little, but the otter merely clasped his paws together on the table and looked very serious.

"I would have never guessed that William," the otter said evenly, and the whole table laughed again. Flint wasn't sure why it was funny, but all of them were chuckling like the otter was telling their favorite joke. Even the priest now had a smile on his face.

The jackal even laughed, himself. "I fought with Aldain here," he said, gesturing to the knight, "for a long time about you joining us on this journey. I still don't know why he wanted you to come, but I was sure that an old priest like you would be nothing but a burden." The group laughed, and again Flint wasn't sure why. It seemed like a rather mean thing to say, but everyone had laughed at the jackal's words. The jackal raised his mug up and held it out toward the older otter, as did the rest of the table as the jackal continued his toast. "Normally I hate being proven wrong, but tonight I am happy to admit it. We would never have destroyed Mak'tchen and his priests without you, Father, and you certainly proved less finicky than the last priest Aldain brought along. If the Prophet had more priests like you in his service, then this world would be a far better place." The table cheered, and raised their glasses to the old priest. Father Tully flattened his small ears back into his slightly graying fur in embarrassment, and raised his glass as well.

"Well thank you William, those were very kind words." The otter arched an eyebrow before everyone took a drink. "Even coming from a hopeless heathen like you," he said and then he took a sip from his mug. The otter smacked his lips a bit, obviously not used to the taste of mead.

"Please Father Tully, call me Will," the jackal said as he sat down. "William was my father, and I'm not as old as you are yet." Everyone in the party laughed again and began to eat.

By now Flint felt really lost. Why had the priest called the jackal a heathen? Flint could not see any symbols on Will that he recognized as unholy ones. In fact, the only jewelry the jackal wore was a silver leaf brooch holding his cloak closed. Flint frowned, wishing he knew more about the faiths outside of East Haven. The only faith in the village was the Prophet's, and Flint had never been to the Sunday services at the local church. Sunday morning meant a changing of the bed sheets and a long day of hot laundry for the hyena, not religious services or family picnics.

Flint smiled as he stood beside the kitchen door waiting for an order. His ears twitched back and forth as he sought to catch every word of the adventure's conversation. The fox, it seemed, was an important noble because the otter kept referring to him as Lord Trenton. The bear was a barbarian named Tigh, and had only recently entered civilized life from the look and sound of things. Aldain and Will got into an argument about something, but it seemed really good-natured and in the end Father Tully settled it for them. It was the most interesting conversation Flint had been a part of in a long time, even though he had not said a word and understood less than half of what the adventures said to each other.

Back inside the kitchen, Clara crossed her arms in annoyance and flicked her tail back and forth as she watched Flint and the adventurers. "I don't see why you let him serve the guests, father. He has fleas," she muttered, "and sleeps with the horses. He smells awful and he probably has mange too. He's disgusting." The young tigress sniffed and turned her nose up, putting on her best sulk. "We should throw him out, not let him serve the most interesting guests we've had in weeks."

Tongish gave his daughter a sidelong glance as she stared out into the common room. While Flint was always a bit dusty in the fur, the hyena did not have fleas. Tongish would have thrown him out in a heartbeat if that were true. Whatever else the boy did, he always kept himself presentable for the guests. In fact, Tongish thought bitterly, Flint was often cleaner than was possible considering the chores he made the boy do. Cleaning out a stable all day should leave you smelling like horse manure, and no matter what his daughter claimed, Flint always smelled fine after he mucked out the stables.

That was probably the reason his daughter hated Flint so much. She could spend hours and hours preparing, but no matter what she did the patrons who came to the Green Briar inn saw her as a desperate, and rather plain, young tigress looking for a way out of her father's house. Flint, on the other hand, was always well-liked by the patrons.

The old tiger noticed his daughter's eyes lingering a bit too long on the wolf knight Flint was serving, and he knew his daughter was angrier about being unable to serve the handsome fellow than about being around the hyena. "We keep him because he works hard," Tongish muttered, "or do you want to clean the stables out after their horses leave?"

The tigress shot her father an evil glare. "Don't be funny," she sniffed again and stomped upstairs to her room.

"I wasn't," her father mumbled and went out to make sure Flint did not linger at the travelers' table too long and bothered them.

KNIGHT OF SWORDS

CHAPTER II

Flint spent the rest of the evening washing up the kitchen while Tongish brought the drinks and food to the travelers. The tiger had taken one look at the grin on the hyena's face when the travelers had called for more, and had forced the hyena to wash the dishes instead of serve. Flint glared at the sink that was full of dirty plates and cups. It had probably been Clara's idea.

By the time Flint had finished washing the dishes, his paws burned from the hot water and itched slightly from the soap Tongish made him use. Tongish made sure he always washed with hot water because it was the only way to get the thick stew the tiger made off the metal bowls, and it always left Flint's paws burned afterward. The soap was probably what kept his paws soft and smooth, but none of it really mattered to Flint at this point. The short hyena had become used to discomfort after years of working for Tongish. Besides, Tongish would do far worse than make his paws tender if young Flint didn't get all the dishes perfect on the first wash. Flint lazily flicked his tail back and forth as he swept the kitchen floor and Tongish lounged in a chair in the kitchen corner by the fire.

The tiger was smoking from a big pipe with his eyes closed when something banged against the wall outside. Flint perked his ears up and stared at the wall as the strange scraping sound continued, as if someone were clawing at the side of the inn. The tiger glared at the wall beside his head where the sound was coming from, and then looked at Flint with an annoyed glare. "Go see who that is, boy, and make them go away. We've got no more rooms, and I don't want our traveler guests to see any of the town strays." The tiger closed his eyes again and propped his feet up, taking a slow drag on his pipe.

Flint took off his apron and hung it on a hook by the back door. He lit the tiny lantern they kept by the back door and slipped out into the night. A rotting smell made the hyena's nose twitch, but he dismissed it. The butcher next door must have left something outside to rot by accident.

Flint stared into the darkness where the sound was coming from, his ears laid back flat on his head as his held the lantern up as high as he could. He could just make out the form of someone large leaning against the corner of the inn. They were too far away for the lamp's light to illuminate them clearly as their claws scraped on the wooden walls of the inn. "Hello?" the hyena called out nervously, and he saw the shape in the darkness turn toward him. The stranger's head was shaped like a bear's, but Flint could not tell who it was in the low light.

"I'm sorry but we don't have any more rooms…" the hyena trailed off as the bear began to slouch toward him in silence, moving slowly down the tiny alley between the inn and the butcher shop next door. A loud metallic scrapping sound made Flint tuck his tail firmly between his legs as an icy fear overtook

32

him. The air itself seemed to be getting colder somehow, and it made Flint's fur stand on end and his heart race. He took a small step backward. "You might try asking the bar down the street, they sometimes let people sleep in the common room!"

The lumbering figure emerged from the darkness and into the light of Flint's lamp, and the little hyena let out a yelp of fear. The bear wasn't a bear at all, at least not any more. Whoever this bear had been was long dead, and in their place was a gruesome zombie.

Flint's body froze in panic as the dead thing continued advancing toward him. The former bear was slouched over to one side because a huge chunk of flesh was missing from its left flank. Its once powerful jaw now hung by a thread of muscle, and it stared at Flint with empty, bloody eye sockets. Flint couldn't even tell what type of bear it had been before the grave claimed it, because the bear's fur was patchy and rotted away, like an old rug worn thin by the years. Flint trembled in fear as the dead thing lurched toward him. It dragged a heavy axe along the ground, the metal edge scraping with an ominous sound.

Flint wanted to run. He wanted to scream at the top of his lungs, but his heart raced so fast in fear that all he could manage was a desperate whine as his lantern clattered to the ground. It was a puppy-like sound that begged someone to help him. The hyena trembled, staring up at the vacant, eyeless stare of the bear as it loomed over him. The hyena's nose wrinkled as a ghastly, awful stench washed over his face and he looked up into the purple, bloated face of the thing that was going to be his death.

Flint stood frozen in fear as the thing lifted up its axe. The zombie's body tilted to the side as it lifted the bloody blade above his head. The little hyena whined again and closed his eyes as the

thing gurgled out a laugh, and Flint was sure that sound would be the last thing he ever heard.

Everything happened so fast after that. There was a loud crash from inside the inn, Tongish bellowed something, and then a howl filled the night as steel clashed on steel.

The little hyena opened his eyes and gasped in surprise. He was uninjured. Flint looked up at his rescuer. Clad in his shining armor and wielding a sword and shield, the wolf knight had thrust himself between the zombie bear and the little hyena. Somehow the wolf had taken on an unearthly beauty, his face twisted into a snarl as he held the bear's blow back with his shield. The wolf's body glowed as if the darkness of the night could not even touch his fur. That glow washed over Flint and made him feel safe, as if nothing bad could happen now that the knight was here.

The wolf howled in righteous fury and swung his blade at the zombie bear. The knight's sword flashed in a brilliant white stroke and carved a glittering arc through the bear, which fell in two huge pieces and ceased to move. Flint stared up in awe at the wolf that stood protectively over him.

The wolf looked down at Flint for only a moment, and his dark eyes met Flint's. The hyena stared up into those concerned eyes and felt a swell of heat in his face as he blushed. He couldn't explain it, but the way the wolf looked at him, the way he stood there protecting him, his presence made Flint feel so very small and yet so very safe. The wolf moved away from Flint as he jogged out into the main street, his tail waving in the air as he shouted for his friends to join him in battle.

Flint felt his legs unlock as the wolf moved away. He grabbed the lantern and scrambled after the wolf, wanting nothing more than to be close to the knight again. When he got to the end of the alley and stepped out into the main road, he regretted following the knight instantly. The hyena ducked back into the dark alley with a whine of fear and doused the lantern, hoping that the horde of walking dead out in the street had not seen him.

The lumbering band of the undead on the road was unlike anything Flint had ever seen. Even the young hyena's worst nightmares had never conjured up a scene like this. Dozens of foxes, wolves, deer, rabbits, and even a lion were there. Every species Flint had ever seen was represented in the ranks of the walking dead. He watched in horror as the dead men and women began to tear at the buildings of East Haven and attack the few townsfolk still out on the street. The screams of the villagers echoed through the night as the huge band of undead broke through windows and began to threaten the meager population of East Haven with total destruction.

In the middle of that hellish sight was a single spot of hope. The wolf knight was cutting a wide path through the walking dead, his sword hacking them in two or three pieces before they would stop moving. Now Flint could see for sure that the wolf was glowing. He shed a white light that seemed to burn the undead that got too close him, their dead flesh peeling away to dust as he fought against them.

Flint's ears perked up, and he turned his head toward the inn. There was a low rumbling sound coming from inside that built up steadily until the front door was thrown open from the inside. The fox mage appeared, and Flint's jaw dropped in awe. He had seen magic before, a few parlor tricks that the local midwife knew to dull pain and entertain children, but nothing like what the fox was summoning. A cloud of red light swirled around Lord Trenton's paws as they moved in a twisting, complex pattern. Flint was mesmerized completely by the sparkling as the fox brought his paws together, his wrists touching, fingers fanned out toward the undead crowded in the street. The red lights focused on the fox's paws, and a cone of flames leapt from them and into the street.

Flint half cheered as the fox's spell washed over a section of the undead army, their dry flesh bursting into ash under the onslaught of the fox's magic. The spell created a hole in the crowd of undead where the rest of the party could pour out into the street. Once in the street, the otter put his paw on the bear's shoulder, and a purple light flowed over the already large ursine. Flint watched in amazement as the bear began to grow to a truly massive size, his huge axe blade growing larger then Flint was tall. The jackal joined the wolf in a cry of battle and dove past the undead as if they weren't even there, to reach his wolf comrade.

The shrieks of the villagers turned to shouts for help as the adventurers joined the battle. Flint just perked up his ears and nearly bounced on his back paws as the party clashed with the undead. Flint watched without fear as the adventures cut their way through the undead horde.

The giant bear, Tigh, set upon the zombies with a roar and as he wielded his enlarged axe, the crescent shaped blade crackled with a deadly blue energy. Each blow the bear landed echoed with a sound like thunder. Tigh's attacks tore the zombies to pieces, and each swing gave the bear momentum. With each kill he attacked again in a charge that carried him right across the field of undead and down the street; his axe moving with a speed Flint did not think was possible. The bear's axe felled all the zombies that had survived the fox's spell and carved a path through across the square. The space the bear cut in the undead provided the otter and fox plenty of room to move unthreatened by the undead horde.

The otter left the inn's porch and in his best preacher's voice called out to the Prophet to smite the evil before him. In a flash of white light a group of the dead beasts threatening a family crumbled into piles of dust. The vulpine mage waved his hands in another complex pattern and traced a glowing rune in the air. A moment later, a group of the zombies were reduced to frozen chunks by a rush of frost that sprung from nowhere.

Creeping around the edges of the battle was the jackal. His daggers cut the legs off the zombies to prevent them from following the villagers, and he kept the zombies from threatening the bear from both sides as he raged across the battlefield.

In the middle of it all was the wolf, his glowing aura shining in the night. The knight's sword cut the dead in half and his shield kept them at bay. Flint watched in fascination as the wolf fought, his presence rallying the villagers and his companions as they clashed with the undead. The knight seemed to be moving in slow motion again, his shining armor protecting him from the blows of the dead. The bear and jackal seemed to be circling Aldain in wide arcs, using their faster movement to place foes between themselves and the knight, where they were ground into dust by the unrelenting attacks from the adventures. Flint stared at the wolf in a strange daze, unable to look away from that handsome male until his face grew hot and the inside of his ears turned red.

Flint stared out across the battlefield that had been his village home for so many years, his heart racing as a new kind of sound reached his ears. It was the sound of someone chanting a spell, but the words sounded harsh and vile to even the hyena's inexperienced ear. Flint looked at the fox and the otter, but neither was casting at the moment as they moved toward the rest of the party, regrouping for a push down the street.

Flint felt fear clutch at his heart again. There was someone else out there in the night casting a spell. Flint glanced back and forth, his eyes darting to all the familiar places the village boys used to hide and play tricks on him. Then he spotted the hooded figure standing behind the ranks of undead, on the other side of the main square in the shadows of building. His paws were glowing red with power as he traced a fiery sigil in the air.

Flint opened his mouth to shout a warning, to tell the adventures where the man was, but it was too late. The man's voice rose in pitch, and he raised his hands in front of him just like the fox had. The ball of fire that leapt from his paw drowned out Flint's shout as the street erupted into a storm of fire and brimstone. Screams of pain echoed through the night as the dead and the heroes alike were caught in the blast.

Flint gasped and shut his eyes as the brilliant explosion blinded him, and for a brief second wave of hot air washed over his face. It did not burn him, but he could hear the cries of the adventurers in the street as they were scorched. Flint opened his eyes and frantically tried to see what had happened to each one of them while still blinking away the bright spots in his vision.

The jackal had ducked behind a nearby barrel, and appeared to be unharmed by the blast. The fox must have caught only a glancing blow from a blast of the flame by diving back inside the inn, because he was on his feet peering out the doorway. The wolf, bear, and otter had not been so lucky.

All three of them had been enveloped in the fiery explosion, and they were the ones still screaming as their fur burned. Flint was about to run to their aid, but when the light from the fire began to grow brighter, not diminish, he looked up at the sky. The hyena's eyes jerked back and forth as he looked around the street at his hometown and a whine of fear escaped his throat. East Haven was burning.

Lord Trenton had been very careful with his spell. The fox had aimed away from his allies and the town's buildings, channeling most of his fiery spell into the ground so that it would only burn the zombies standing in the street. The opposing wizard had not been so kind. The hooded figure cackled in glee as the town began to burn around him, the thatched roofs catching on fire even through the magical explosion had subsided in moments.

Few of the people in the street fared any better than the buildings. The bear fell to the ground, bellowing in pain as he tried to put out his burning hide. Tigh's armor had actually caught fire, and was proving harder to put out than his fur. The otter priest did better with his thick oily fur and after he cast a spell to heal himself he seemed to be all right. Father Tully rushed to the bear's aid, emptying a waterskin on him to dampen the flames, but that meant he was busy dealing with Tigh instead of stopping the undead.

The dry, desiccated zombies themselves had suffered the worst. Any that had been caught in the blast fell to the ground in burning heaps, their unlife snuffed out by the flames. The fires that were beginning to consume East Haven were also put out to some degree, as Lord Trenton raised his staff and used it to dampen the flames on the houses and in his companions' fur. The fox moved his paws back and forth, smothering the flames as fast as he could. Everyone was busy dealing with the explosions effects, rather than its cause. Everyone except for the knight.

Aldain did not even seem to notice that the explosion had occurred. He dropped his shield and raced across the now empty main street with his fur still on fire, and struck the dark wizard with a savage two-handed blow of his sword. Flint watched as once again the wolf's sword trailed white sparks across the night sky and the blade cut deep into the hooded wizard's chest. Blood gushed from the wound, blackened by something, but the mage did not fall. He staggered backward, his hood falling back to reveal the face of a badger now covered in his own blood and scarred by countless cuts. He cackled again, a crazed sound in the now quieter street, and cast another spell at the wolf, his elongated claws clicking together as he chanted.

The spell sent a thunderclap echoing through the night as a bolt of lightning leapt from the badger's paws and across the street. The bolt passed through the wolf and flattened him to the ground before continuing on to strike the otter priest and the building behind him as well. Both men howled in pain as they fell and Flint's stomach leap into his throat as the wolf sagged to the ground. The hyena's scream was lost in the reverberating boom of thunder that rolled across the village. Flint ran to the wolf's side without thinking. He had to save the knight somehow, buy him the chance to run and get help. As Flint ran, he knew he would never make it to the wolf's side in time.

The badger loomed over the fallen knight, his paws crackling with a green and black energy, his robes billowing in the wind as he cast a final spell to finish the wolf off. The wolf struggled to raise his sword but the fire in his fur made his body betray him and he could not lift his blade to strike the necromancer as he cast the spell. Flint's eyes met the wizard's, and the badger seemed to take delight in the young hyena's presence. He wanted

Flint to watch the knight die.

That's when Flint caught sight of a shadow moving behind the mage, a reflection of light off something black and shiny in the night.

Flint faltered and stopped a few feet away from the knight as the badger's body stiffened and his eyes widened. His spell died on his lips, the gathered light vanishing as he gasped in pain and coughed up blood. The jackal appeared from behind the wizard, and Flint could just see Will's knife buried deep in the wizard's back.

Flint winced and looked away as the jackal finished the man, slitting the badger's throat from behind him in one smooth motion with his other dagger. The badger didn't even make a sound as he fell dead at the jackal's feet, the knife sliding out of his back, and landed next to Aldain. Blood dripped off the daggers as the remaining undead collapsed into heaps as well, the magic that had powered them now gone along with their creator.

"You all right Aldain?" The jackal shouted as he tried to put out the flames on the wolf's fur. The wolf rolled back and forth, and with the jackal's help the flames went out. The knight coughed roughly as he sat up, leaning heavily on the jackal for support.

"Yes, yes I'm fine," the wolf muttered, and Flint embarrassed himself by yipping with joy as the wolf rose to his feet unsteadily. "Oh that was foolish of me," Aldain said with a cough. "See to the others while I calm the village." Despite the pain in the wolf's voice, the jackal nodded and did as he was told. Flint stood a few feet away from the knight as the wolf dusted himself off. Flint's tail wagged back and forth and he looked up at the wolf in wonder. The knight was burned and cut and covered in blood, but his spirit had never wavered. He had never stopped fighting.

Flint caught the wolf's eye and the knight watched him for a few seconds before striding away to deal with the villagers who were now pouring out of their homes.

Flint felt weak in the knees and his face was hot like it had been after the explosion. The hyena had never seen anyone who was as brave or as strong as Aldain was.

∾: ∾

Flint paced back and forth in he kitchen of the Green Briar inn, not really sure what he was supposed to be doing now. He wanted to go see the wolf and thank him for saving his life, but Flint had no idea how to approach the knight. Just the thought of talking to the wolf made him sick to his stomach, as if he had eaten a jar full of butterflies. Flint fretted and ran his paw through his short mane, peeking out into the common room where the travelers were speaking to the townsfolk.

Flint knew he would not be allowed to go out and talk directly to them now. Tongish would be livid if he set foot in the common room with so many of the town's elders gathered there, and the hyena did not want to spend the night locked up in a closet. So he paced back and forth, trying to think of a way to see the wolf until the kitchen door opened and the fox mage poked his head inside.

The hyena blinked in surprise when the fox sniffed the air and wrinkled his nose a bit at the odor of the kitchen. Then he tilted his head to the side and smiled at Flint. "Hello lad. Have you got any more of that stew left?" he said looking down at Flint, who was actually a few inches smaller even than the fairly short fox.

Flint shook his head and tucked his tail between his legs. "No sir, I can make some though if you..."

"That's all right lad." The fox said with a shrug, "just bring me up some cheese and bread. I'm in the last room on the right, and I'll make it two silvers instead of one if you can bring me some cooked meat, you hear?" The fox left without even waiting for Flint's answer.

The hyena grinned ear to ear as he quickly got a plate of food ready. A silver piece was more money than he had ever been tipped before, and since Tongish didn't know about it he would be able to keep it all for himself.

As he set the plate down on the counter, Flint had an idea. If he was being paid for two meals, why not make two meals? He pulled another plate down and made a meal to bring up to the wolf.

~: :~

Flint carried the trays of food up to the second floor, and down the hallway to the fox's room. The wizard seemed quite pleased with the fried chicken from the night before, and paid the extra silver with a smile. Flint grinned and almost jumped for joy as he turned toward the knight's room.

Just as he was about to knock on the door it burst open and Clara rushed out of the knight's room in tears, her best dress trailing behind her as she ran. Flint pressed himself against the doorjamb, staring after the girl in shock. He had never seen Clara so dressed up around the inn before, and he had never seen her cry like that except in front of Tongish as a way to get him in trouble.

The wolf knight appeared at the threshold of his room and

looked down the hallway after her. With a shake of his head the wolf muttered, "Women," in an exhausted tone as Clara barricaded herself in her own room at the far end of the hallway. Then the knight noticed Flint. "Oh, hello." He said, blinking his eyes a couple times as the hyena smiled up at him. "What can I do for you?"

Flint shuffled his feet and held out the plate of food. "Umm, well, I brought you something to eat." Flint wagged his tail a little, forcing his ears up as he smiled at the knight. "I thought you might be hungry after all that fighting."

The wolf's muzzle curved up in a smile, the white fur under his chin shifting against the gray of the rest of his face. "How kind of you," the knight said and stepped back to let Flint inside his room. "Here, let me pay you for that," the wolf muttered. He sat down on the small bed and began rummaging through a small money-bag.

"Oh no, you don't have to pay, Sir." Flint said hastily, setting the plate of food down on the night-stand beside the bed. He put it down there instead of on the table closer to the door just so he could get a little closer to the wolf and catch a whiff of his scent again. The wolf's smell was a strange mix of pungent sweat, charcoal, and freshly fallen rain now. It made Flint's tail wag hard, and he tucked his tail between his legs to keep it still.

The wolf gave Flint a dubious look, "So, your master has suddenly become generous has he? I shall have to thank him tomorrow morning..." The wolf let the sentence trail off, and he had a knowing look in his eyes.

Flint flicked his rounded ears back and smiled sheepishly, his muzzle splitting into the toothy grin common among hyenas. The wolf would know if he lied. "Well, no, I paid for it."

"Then I should thank you for your generosity." The wolf said, and Flint squirmed, rubbing one paw against the floor.

"It was the least I could do." Flint rubbed his paws together and smiled at the wolf. "You saved my life."

The knight waved the comment away. "I was only doing my duty. No need to thank me." He pulled off the chain-mail shirt he was wearing. The action made Flint's heart flutter, because the thin cotton shirt the wolf wore underneath pulled up as well, revealing the wolf's muscular stomach for a moment. It also revealed several bad cuts and a nasty burn mark where the mage's lightning bolt had struck him. The wolf did not seem to notice any of that, and it only made him seem more exotic. The wolf shook his head and rubbed at one of his ears before running his fingers through his head-fur. When he smiled at the hyena it made Flint sigh.

An awkward silence fell over the small room, and the hyena searched for something to say. How was someone like Flint supposed to tell this handsome knight that just being around him made his knees weak? It sounded so silly in his head. Flint shifted uneasily as the wolf finished taking off his armor. His eyes fell on the wolf's shield, and the long scratch that marred the surface of it. "Did this happen tonight when you saved me?" Flint asked quietly as he ran his finger along the blemish in the wolf's otherwise perfect shield.

"Yes it did," the wolf said with a nod. "Don't worry about it though. I have an oil that will mend it." The wolf reached for a small jar on the bedside table, but the movement torn open one of the longer cuts on the wolf's arm, and he jerked his arm back with a snarl of pain as he began to bleed. Flint yipped and rushed to the wolf's side, trying to stop the bloodflow.

"Oh, oh, I'm so sorry." The hyena whimpered and tried to hold the wolf's wound closed to stop the bleeding. "I can get my sewing kit and stitch this for you. I used to do that when I cut myself with the knives down in the kitchen, and I've become good with a needle. I fix my clothes sometimes, and I even helped sew the sheets on your bed. I just..." Flint trailed off as the wolf gave a pained chuckle. Flint's ears flattened against his head as he realized how badly he was babbling.

The wolf gave him a slight smile and patted Flint's paw gently. "Don't worry," the wolf said, and a moment of confusion passed over his face. "What was your name?" he asked softly.

The hyena's ears twitched forward and then back again, and his spotted muzzle turned upward in a smile as the wolf held Flint's paw against his arm. The act of tending to the wolf's wound had suddenly become much more intimate. "Flint," he said softly, catching another whiff of the wolf's scent.

"Flint, I am Aldain. I'm a Knight of the Cross, as you so eloquently guessed back in the stables, and it is now well past the witching hour." The knight folded up his shirt with one hand and then patted the hyena's paw gently. "That means it is technically tomorrow, and I no longer require the skills of a tailor to heal myself. Only the Prophet." Aldain furrowed his brow and closed his eyes, as if concentrating hard on something. The wolf's chest tightened and his grip on Flint's paw grew as a white light surrounded his body.

Flint's eyes widened and his mouth made circle as the knight's wounds healed in a rush of holy magic. The wound underneath his paw closed up, the skin knitting back together before the fur grew back in matter of moments. Flint blushed softly as his fingers traced the wolf's arm, finding nothing but soft fur and strong muscle underneath. The cuts and bruises and even the burned patches of fur that had covered the wolf were now all gone without so much as a scar to show for them. The wolf's magic left nothing behind but a few wet patches of blood and dirt.

Flint's mouth moved, but no words came out. The wolf chuckled, and the hyena blushed before stuttering, "That, that's amazing. I've never seen anything like that..."

The knight patted Flint's paw again, "And how old are you?" he asked.

"Nineteen winters," Flint said breathlessly, his paws beginning to wander across the wolf's healed body, fingers touching his chest as he checked to see that all the wounds were indeed gone.

Aldain chuckled a little as the young man's paws touched him, and he smiled warmly. "Well, in my twenty four seasons I have seen far more spectacular things than a man who could heal himself. Of course, what I would really like to see is a hot bath. Do you think you could draw one up for me?" the wolf asked, and Flint laughed a little as the wolf leaned in close to him and bumped his black nose against the hyena's spotted cheek.

The hyena smiled and nodded vigorously as the knight squeezed his paw. Flint got up and practically raced himself to the kitchen, boiling water and filling the washtub down the hall with a spring in his step and a big wag in his tail.

When he had the bath ready, Flint returned to the knight's room and the wolf patted him on the head as he went to wash his fur. Flint grinned and watched the wolf walk down the hall, then turned back to the empty room. Flint rubbed his forearms as he stood in the knight's room, glancing around at all the strange things the wolf owned. Now that he was here, Flint didn't want to leave. It felt good being in a room that smelled of Aldain, surrounded by all of his things. Perhaps he would be able to stay if he made himself useful.

Aldain lay in the round wooden bathtub and sighed in contentment. He was completely naked and it felt marvelous to just relax in the water like this. The dirt and blood was gone from his fur, and he was beginning to feel like a person again instead something that had been scrapped off the cobblestones of a country road. In fact, the only thing that marked Aldain as the same bloody wolf who had climbed into the water in the first place was the gold medallion he wore around his neck.

The boy had done a very good job drawing up this bath, and the innkeeper obviously liked to take baths. There was a second tank of water so Aldain could wash himself with the fine bar of soap that Flint left and then drain the bath, refill the tub and soak in fresh warm water. There was even some sort of scent in the water that made the whole room smell good, like a field of flowers. The soap left no oil in the wolf's fur, and the hyena had left big fluffy towels for him to dry off with and a soft horse-hair brush to smooth his fur. Flint had even left two kettles of boiling hot water beside the tub to reheat the bath when it cooled.

Aldain smiled, humming softly to himself as he soaked in the warm water. He would have to thank that hyena boy later for such a fine bath. The wolf smiled at the thought of how eager the boy had seemed to touch him before. It was a shame that he had not thought to ask Flint to help him wash his back. Aldain sighed contentedly as he mused on that idea, which slowly aroused the knight. He chided himself for thinking about the boy this way, but the guilt of such sinful thoughts was quickly overshadowed by his growing arousal.

The wolf reached down and brushed his swelling sheath with one paw, causing his shaft to slide out into the warm water. The hyena would probably have said 'yes' without a thought as to why the wolf wanted him here.

The wolf's ears caught the sound of door opening, but Aldain only had time to open his eyes before the door was practically flung open.

Aldain jumped with a startled bark as the looming form of Father Tully strode into the bathroom. The wolf fell back into the water and quickly covered himself with his tail as the otter grimaced and looked away from the aroused wolf.

"You should learn to lock the door while bathing, knight." The otter covered his eyes with one paw and fumbled for the door handle. "It is a sin against the Prophet to expose oneself like that," the otter said as he closed the door behind him. "Especially to an old man!"

"Then you should learn to knock, old man!" the wolf shouted before collapsing back into the water with a sigh, his tail still firmly covering his crotch. Aldain shook his head when he heard Father Tully chuckle from outside, and he rolled his eyes at the old priest. That was the third time the otter had burst in on him like that during the trip. He seemed to have no concept of personal privacy. Aldain washed the last of the dirt from his fur and got out, the relaxation and arousal of the warm bath now gone.

~: :~

Aldain sighed happily as he left the bathing room and headed back to his room. The wolf had pulled on a pair of cotton shorts to make his way back to his room, and was wearing nothing else but his medallion. The family heirloom was made of gold pressed into the symbol of the Prophet's Cross and set with a brilliant emerald in the center. Aldain fingered the medal and enjoyed the freedom of his fur. It felt good to be out of his traveling clothes for once and into a comfortable pair of shorts, and it would feel even better to fall asleep in a real bed. Sleeping under the stars with his companions while wearing a shirt of metal was never as pleasant as sleeping in only your fur in a nice warm bed.

The wolf opened the door to his room without knocking, since no one was supposed to be in there, which made the young hyena inside jump in surprise. Aldain jumped a little too, surprised that the boy was still there. Flint was crouched on the floor beside the bed, his paws busily shining the wolf's shield.

~: :~

"You're still here, huh?" Aldain said, patting the hyena's head. It was cute how the hyena's ears swiveled back and he leaned into the touch. Aldain sat down on his bed with a sigh, the small room forcing him to sit right beside where the hyena was kneeling.

The boy blushed deeply and put his paws up on the bed, his ears still splayed out backward against his head. The young man's tail wagged back and forth as he asked, "Did you enjoy your bath, sir?"

"Yes I did, it was a very fine bath." Aldain smiled at Flint before looking over the crouching hyena's shoulder. "What have you been doing?"

The hyena's spotted muzzle broke into a smile, and he proudly showed off the work he had done on the wolf's shield. The long scratch was gone, rubbed away by the hyena's busy paws and the wolf's mending oil. "I wanted to fix this for you, Sir." Aldain smiled as the pup turned back to him, and one of the hyena's paw's came to rest on the wolf's knee.

"You don't have to call me sir, you know. I'm not your master," the wolf said, patting the boy's paw gently. "Again, that's very kind of you, but you did not have to do this for me."

The hyena blushed again, his eyes sparkling as he smiled up at the knight. "You saved my life. I have to repay you somehow." The hyena's voice trembled a little, and the wolf grinned a little at the cute way the hyena squirmed. Aldain could feel his heart flutter a little as he stared at the boy, and he felt Flint's gaze fan the flames of his attraction for the hyena.

It had been a long while since Aldain had last done anything about it, but the wolf's feelings for males never truly went away. The wolf had tried hard to follow the teachings of his faith, and view the things he felt as the whispers of demons in his ears. The church was quite clear about how wrong and vile lying with another male was, but right now Flint was making Aldain's loins stir in a way he had not felt in a long time.

The boy was being so obvious about his attraction to the wolf, but so shy at the same time. It was sweet in a way and very cute, and the hyena's bright green eyes looked up at him with such admiration and desire it made the older wolf forget about everything else.

For a moment they stared at each other, their muzzles just an inch apart. Aldain took the chance to examine the hyena's face and the patterns of his fur. At the end of Flint's muzzle was a patch of black fur, and little black spots the size of coins dotted his face and chest. The hyena's head-fur was cut short and was a rich brown color that turned into a short mane that ran down his neck into his rough cotton shirt. The rest of the hyena's fur was a rich cream color, mixed with a dirty brown of sorts that seemed to flow across his pelt. Aldain marveled at how clean and soft the fur looked. It was very strange for a peasant. Each of Flint's paws was covered in a stocking of black fur like a fox's paws, and the boy's eyes sparkled an emerald green color that seemed to draw Aldain in. Flint was even panting just a little, his pink tongue flashing in and out of his mouth as he knelt at the wolf's feet.

Aldain licked his lips a little as he reached one paw up to caress the side of Flint's face. The boy's rounded ears swiveled backward and Flint's cheeks turned red under his fur as he blushed again, but Flint's eyes never left the wolf's face. As Aldain stared into those happy, bright emerald eyes the wolf forgot about all his problems. The wolf just smiled and stared into that young man's eyes for a long time before shifting his paw and pulling Flint into a soft kiss.

Flint didn't know what to do when Aldain kissed him, but it made the hyena's heart flutter up into his throat. The hyena moaned softly and pressed forward into the kiss, letting the wolf's other arm slide around his back. It was a soft, tender embrace and they stayed that way for a long time with their lips pressed together. Flint marveled at how the kiss felt. The rough feeling of the wolf's lips pressed tenderly against his own. The way that the wolf's thick tongue tested his lips until Flint parted them, and then pressed against the hyena's tongue slowly. The firms caress of the wolf's paw on the back of his head made Flint whimper, and the strong arm wrapped around his shoulder made Flint's body tingle.

It was the most passionate moment in the hyena's life, and he blinked in surprise when the wolf finally broke the kiss. "Whoa," Flint muttered softly, his mouth working a bit. The way the wolf's tongue had moved against his own had been such a strange sensation. It had felt good, but now he was completely out of breath.

Aldain smiled at him, chuckling a little. "Your first kiss?" the wolf asked, his paw softly petting Flint's head-fur.

"Yes," Flint said breathlessly, smiling up at the wolf that was holding him. The way the wolf's fingers slid through his short head-fur made the hyena's tail wag.

"Let's fix that," the knight said softly and Flint found himself caught up in another, even more passionate kiss. This time the wolf turned his head to the side, and their muzzles meshed together as one. The wolf's tongue lashed into the space their muzzles now shared and pressed against Flint's tongue; curling around the hyena's smaller tongue as Aldain explored his muzzle fully. When Aldain breathed out through his mouth, the only thing Flint could do was breath in. Their muzzles stayed locked together as they kissed slowly and the wolf breathed for them both. The wolf's arms surrounded Flint's shoulders, and the knight embraced him with a strength the hyena had never felt before. It thrilled him to be in the power of such a male, to be at Aldain's gentle mercy. To feel this knight, *his* knight now, breathing in and out for Flint made the hyena want to faint from arousal.

Aldain was panting as well by the time he pulled back from the eager cub's muzzle. "You want to have another first?" he asked breathlessly, and the hyena nodded eagerly, his tail wagging back

55

and forth as he looked up at Aldain with complete trust. He had such a cute, young face, and Aldain could think of only one thing he wanted more at that moment than to kiss that pretty muzzle.

The wolf looked down at his crotch, where the fabric of his shorts was tented up by a barely contained erection. Flint's eyes widened a bit, and he looked up at the wolf in wonder as if he were asking permission just to touch the wolf. Aldain smiled softly at him as his paw caressed the young male's face gently. "If you want to," the wolf said simply, and it made Flint grin.

The wolf licked his lips as the hyena's small paws reached down and untied the cord holding his shorts closed. The boy was panting as he pulled the fabric back. Flint's eyes widened again as the wolf's cock sprang into view, bouncing a little as it was released. It was obvious the boy had never seen another male like this before, but he did not look even a little bit afraid.

A soft paw closed around Aldain's shaft, and the wolf sighed in pleasure as the pent-up desire was finally satisfied by the hyena's touch. Aldain smiled, licking the hyena's muzzle gently as Flint began to pet his shaft with his smooth paws. It was an awkward, halting process but it felt so good to the road-weary wolf. It had been ages since he had felt the caress of any paw but his own, and even that had become difficult under the watchful eye of Father Tully.

Aldain relaxed and he let Flint grow used to what he was doing before he coaxed the hyena further. "Go on, Flint," he whispered to the boy, his tongue flicking gently across the hyena's round ear. "Taste it." The hyena blushed so deeply his ears turned red on the inside and swiveled backward as he looked up into the knight's eyes, as if he didn't believe what he had heard. "Go on. You'll like it." Aldain said quietly, gently ruffling the boy's head-fur.

The wolf leaned back and propped himself up with one elbow to give the cub room. Flint looked down, gathered his nerves, and licked the wolf's cock. Aldain let out a low sigh as a wet ribbon swept across the head of his shaft and sent shivers up his spine. All it took was a gentle coaxing with one paw on the back of his head, and Flint was quickly licking and polishing the wolf's shaft with an eager smile. The boy's tongue was erratic and unskilled, and his teeth sometimes brushed across the wolf's shaft but he was so eager to please the knight it didn't matter.

Aldain let his head roll back and whispered encouragement to the hyena, "Oh yes. That's it, Flint. Now suck on it, yes that's it, right like that..." The wolf moaned loudly as the hyena's lips wrapped around his cock. Aldain smiled down at the cub as the inside of Flint's ears turned a crimson color. Flint sucked on the cock in his muzzle as best he could, his cheeks caving in as he sucked hard on the penis in his mouth. The young male slurped and lavished the knight's cock with everything he had, a big grin on his muzzle as it was filled with the wolf's throbbing dick.

Aldain sighed, his eyes fixed on the boy's happy face as he began to thrust his hips forward a little. The little hyena started to moan around the dick in his mouth, Flint's paws fumbling a bit as Aldain's hips began to move. It was a purely pleasurable sound, the moan of someone fulfilling his heart's desire. Aldain smiled at the sound, and if felt as if a weight had been lifted off his chest. A part of the knight had been worried the boy was just doing as he had been told to, but a happy moan like that meant Flint was enjoying this as much as he was.

The wolf watched as Flint's tail wagged back and forth, a furry broom thumping against the floor as he bobbed his muzzle up and down the wolf's shaft. His paw squeezed at the base of Aldain's shaft, right where the wolf's knot was beginning to form. The knight could feel himself getting closer and closer to the edge as his knot began to bulge, becoming so wide the hyena's paw did not fit around it any more. Flint put both paws on the wolf's knot, and Aldain couldn't stand it any longer. He leaned forward and put both paws on the sides of the boy's head, holding the hyena down by his flattened ears. The wolf began to thrust in earnest into the boy's mouth, breeding Flint's muzzle as fast as he could manage without choking the boy with his dick.

Aldain rubbed his muzzle against the top of Flint's head and groaned, his chest heaving as his cock throbbed in the hyena's mouth. Then he let out a strangled howl and hilted himself into the hyena's muzzle, his knot pushing past the boy's lips and forcing his muzzle open wide. Flint clutched at Aldain's thighs as the wolf shot his seed right into the young hyena's muzzle.

Flint gagged as the wolf pushed in deep and filled his mouth completely with wolf-dick. All he could see was the wolf's stomach, shaggy gray fur rubbing against his face and muzzle as the wolf's paws forced him all the way down on the hard shaft in his mouth. Flint could feel the head of the wolf's dick rubbing against the back of his throat, pulsing and jerking in his mouth as Aldain reached his climax inside Flint. The knight's howl rang in his ears and Flint gagged on Aldain, sputtering a little as the salty-sweet wolf-seed flooded his mouth and ran out the sides of his muzzle, treating the hyena to a taste he had never imagined before. Flint gasped for air, nostrils flaring as he dragged in the strong, sweaty smell of the wolf's crotch. The scent mixed with the smell of the wolf's semen in his mouth and invaded every thought Flint had. In that moment, Aldain's crotch became

Flint's world and the hyena moaned as the wolf took him. Flint sagged in the knight's grip, surrendering to the strong paws on the back of his head and the forceful dick inside his muzzle with a moan of pure pleasure.

Flint felt like he was floating, his senses overwhelmed by the wolf's orgasm inside his mouth, and he was panting hard by the time the wolf released him. Flint pulled back, licking at the salty taste in his mouth and the thick, creamy stuff that trailed from the wolf's cock tip to his lips. It tasted funny, but good at the same time. Flint had never thought of tasting his own seed when he played with himself, but now he wished that he had. Flint panted happily, looking up at the knight's face as the wolf's seed dripped from his lips.

The wolf's eyes were closed, and he was breathing heavily. The knight gasped and jerked forward when Flint began to lick the wolf's penis clean, and he squirmed a little as Flint licked up every drop of the knight's seed. Then Flint reached his paws up and pressed them against the wolf's chest, feeling the strong muscles there rise and fall as he breathed deeply. Flint hesitated for a moment, his lips quivering just a finger's width from the wolf's mouth. The knight seemed to be lost in another world as he gasped for air. Aldain opened his eyes and Flint smiled sheepishly. Suddenly they were kissing again, muzzles locked together as the wolf growled in desire.

Before Flint could get his bearings, the knight was roughly pulling Flint's tunic off his shoulders. The wolf's paws roamed across his back, finger's dragging through the hyena's short fur. Flint shuddered as blunt claw-tips raced across his back and his fur was pulled in one direction and then the next by the wolf's paws. The knight stood up suddenly, pulling Flint up by the scruff of his neck. The hyena gasped, panting as the movement broke their kiss. Flint didn't move as the wolf proceeded to strip him naked the rest the way. The wolf's muzzle stayed close to his, and Flint panted as the wolf's muzzle rubbed against his face. Then Aldain's thick tongue darted out to lick at the hyena's spots, lapping lovingly at his face in a way that made the hyena's knees weak.

Skilled paws undressed Flint until he stood naked in front of the knight, his tail tucked down between his legs. With a careful motion, the wolf lifted the necklace he was wearing from around his neck and set it on the dresser. Then the wolf kissed Flint again with so much passion Flint thought the knight might break him in two with the force of his hug.

Flint whimpered in submission as the wolf continued to kiss him and pet at his fur, each touch of his paws seeming to make the wolf more dominant. Flint could tell the wolf was fumbling with something on the night-stand, but he didn't care what. The wolf just kept kissing him, slowly turning them both around so the backs of Flint's knees were pressed against the bed. The hyena saw the small oil pot as the wolf set it back down on the table. The knight stroked his own cock, coating it in the slick oil. Flint was about to ask what he was doing when suddenly he was flat on his back with the soft bed underneath him and the wolf's strong body above. The wolf's lips hungrily pressed against his own as Aldain pushed Flint down onto the bed and kissed him with a deep growl.

The sound sent shivers down Flint's spine, but it wasn't a threatening sound. It was a husky growl of arousal from deep in the wolf's chest, and it made the hyena instinctively lift his muzzle up to expose his throat. Flint whined gently as he submitted to the knight completely, a big grin on his muzzle as he did so. The knight licked the underside of Flint's throat, and that made the smaller hyena squirm in pleasure and spread his legs reflexively. He yipped a little as the wolf's body descended into the valley between his legs and forced them open wide. The wolf made a low *woof* and his fur rubbed against Flint's erection as he held the boy down. On instinct alone Flint lifted his legs up into the air, his knees pressed against Aldain's sides, as the wolf kissed his throat again.

Flint's paws gripped the wolf's shoulders and his body tensed when he felt something firm and wet poking at his tail-hole. He whimpered a little, chewing on his lip as he realized what the wolf was about to do. It surprised Flint just how badly he wanted it to happen. The wolf's eyes met his own, and for a moment the knight was still. Aldain was pressed intimately against him in every way possible except for one. The knight was in complete control, but he had stopped nonetheless. Aldain looked into Flint's green eyes with a serious expression on his face. "This is going to hurt Flint. It will, because this is your first time. I will try my best to make it easy, but it might hurt badly if you can't relax yourself." The wolf's tongue slid across the hyena's left cheek in lupine kiss, making the young hyena shudder underneath him. His voice was full of concern, and he held the hyena tenderly in his arms. "Tell me to stop if it becomes too much." The wolf looked him in the eyes, his gaze full of concern for his young lover. "Understand?"

Flint nodded nervously, not trusting his voice as his paws shifted on the wolf's shoulders to get a better grip. The wolf smiled at him and they kissed again, their muzzles meshing, and the wolf's hips brought their bodies together as one.

A gasp of pain escaped Flint as the blunt head of the wolf's

shaft pressed against the ring of flesh that was his tail-hole. It was just a short, smooth thrust forward, but Flint was extremely aware that Aldain's penis was now inside of him. Flint shuddered and his tail-hole flexed in pain as the oiled shaft of the wolf's penis spread his virgin butt open. Flint tried to relax, tried to stay calm as the wolf took him, but it was just too much. A strangled whine of pain escaped his muzzle despite Flint's best efforts to keep silent. The wolf stopped pushing and in fact retracted a little, which made the pain dim somewhat. Flint panted, gasping for air as the wolf kissed him tenderly, holding himself just inside the hyena's entrance.

It was enough to make Flint cry. Not from the pain, that was fading away now and being replaced by a strange fullness he had never experienced. What made the hyena cry was the caring look in the wolf's eyes. The wolf looked right into Flint's eyes, a deep concern radiating out of the knight. Flint would not have stopped the knight from taking him roughly, but instead Aldain was being so careful. No one had ever shown that kind of compassion for him before.

This big, strong male was in complete control of Flint. Aldain could do anything to him. He was taking Flint as a female, but instead of just fulfilling his urges, the wolf was worried about hurting him. Flint pressed his muzzle against the knight's and licked his face gently as the hyena's tail grew accustomed to being taken open by another male.

It did not take long for the pain leave completely. Flint signaled this to his wolf by pulling on the knight's hips with his legs, coaxing the wolf to thrust into him. The knight did just that, burying himself deep inside the hyena with a soft moan of enjoyment. Then the wolf pulled back, only to lunge forward again. The sudden thrust and fullness made Flint cry out in pleasure, his legs hugging the knight's sides reflexively as the wolf filled him.

Aldain began mounting Flint with a slow, desperate passion that made the hyena's toes curl and his senses burn. It felt so good Flint could not think or move. Flint could only lie beneath the wolf and whimper in pleasure as he was taken like a female. The hyena's paws clutched at the wolf's strong shoulders and his body shook under the pounding of the wolf's hips. Aldain held Flint in his arms and thrust deep inside him, taking him completely.

Flint panted as the wolf's body moved back and forth on top of him, shifting the small bed they lay in. The hyena could feel the wolf's fur rubbing against his own, sliding across his erection as the knight filled Flint with his own hard cock. That feeling of being taken and filled up made the hyena's body tingle. Flint drew his legs up and locked his ankles behind the wolf's back, spreading his legs open wide so the wolf's body would rub more effectively against his shaft. The movement had other consequences as well.

The hyena gasped as the knight's next thrust plowed much deeper inside his body then the others had before. Aldain's cock pushed deep into Flint, pressing against something inside the hyena, some spot inside him that made Flint's body ache with pleasure. Flint had no idea what that spot inside his butt was, but the hyena moaned loudly about it as the wolf's cock battered the spot inside him with each thrust. The knight growled in pleasure as the change of position made it easier to thrust all the way in, and he began to roughly mate with the willing hyena.

Flint panted, marveling at the way Aldain touched him. The knight was nipping at Flint's throat and licking his face, one paw running back and forth through the hyena's head-fur in between kisses. The wolf's other arm was around his back, clutching Flint to Aldain's chest. The wolf's muzzle rubbed against the side of Flint's face as the wolf held him tenderly. Flint grinned and realized he could feel the knight's balls slapping against his rump. The wolf was thrusting all the way to the hilt inside him. Just the thought that the knight was completely inside him made Flint bite his own lip in ecstasy, and the feeling of the wolf's shaft inside him made the hyena cry out in pleasure.

Aldain's body began to shake as he fucked the hyena, his muscles tensed, and his hips thrusting erratically. Flint could feel the knot at the base of Aldain's shaft beginning to form again, and he knew the wolf was coming close to climaxing again. The hyena shuddered with desire at the idea that this time the knight would be spilling his seed deep inside him. Flint moaned as Aldain pushed his knot against the entrance of his tail-hole, the wolf's legs strained as Flint's newly deflowered passage resisted the thick knot. The wolf hunched his body forward and thrust hard, pushing past the tight ring of the hyena with a loud moan. Flint bit the wolf's shoulder to muffle his pained yelp as the wolf tied him.

Flint looked up into the eyes of his lover as Aldain's body began to jerk forward in short, rapid thrusts that went nowhere. The wolf's hips moved, but his penis just pulled at Flint's insides because the wolf's thick knot was trapped tight inside Flint now. It also meant that the head of Aldain's cock was now pressed hard against the spot inside Flint. That made the hyena's body ache with pleasure and his legs shook as he yipped in delight. Flint stared up into the wolf's eyes as Aldain humped him, and Flint knew he was in love.

Aldain was beautiful beyond words. The wolf's muzzle was slightly open as he began to howl, using Flint's shoulder to muffle the sound. Aldain's eyes were closed tightly, and the wolf's ears were laid back flat on his head, a look of deep concentration on the knight's handsome face as he came. His tail beat against the bed and Flint's feet, and the wolf's whole body shook as he pressed down into Flint and came. The hyena could feel the wolf's shaft as it throbbed inside him, pumping him full of another load of the knight's seed.

Flint trembled and gently hugged the knight's shoulders and head as the wolf held him down. Flint could feel the wolf's trapped knot pulling at his tail-hole, and he squeezed his tail-hole down hard to keep it inside him. It was already where Flint knew it belonged, and Flint was not letting it escape his tail now. The hyena shivered, his body singing in delight as his knight came inside him. Nothing had ever felt so good.

The hyena closed his eyes and pressed his face against the wolf's strong chest. Flint could not believe how wonderful this felt. Flint started to lick Aldain's face, grooming the wolf's face-fur gently as the knight panted. Flint belonged to this male now in every way possible. The hyena felt so safe lying beneath Aldain. It was a feeling of safety and belonging he had not felt since his parents had died. Flint was home.

Flint smiled as the wolf's weight lifted off him slowly. Aldain's chest heaved; he was panting so hard, and the knight stared into Flint's eyes. For a moment they kissed tenderly, just their lips touching. There was no need to deepen the kiss, the wolf was already tied inside him. They were one body now.

Flint tensed as one of the wolf's paws slipped between them and wrapped around his shaft. The wolf's other arm held the back of Flint's head, their muzzles pressed together as he began to jerk the boy off. Flint only lasted a few strokes before it was too much. Having the wolf's hard cock inside him made the touch of Aldain's paw a hundred times better. A few firm strokes on the hyena's aching dick and he was over the edge. The hyena's body tensed and his hips twitched, legs clutching at the wolf's as Flint's tail-hole burned with pleasure. The wolf's knot pulled at his insides and Flint moaned in ecstasy as the wolf's penis stretched him open and pressed firmly against the spot inside Flint that made his head swim with pleasure.

Flint cried out in a halting, gasping way, his paws pressed against the wolf's chest as he climaxed. The hyena's seed shot out of his dick in thick drops, the white cum coating his chest in small white spots to match the black spots of his fur. Flint's mouth hung open as he had the strongest orgasm of his short life. Aldain lay back down on top of Flint, his cock keeping them tied together.

They lay like that for a long time. The wolf's eyes were closed, and he panted slowly. Aldain's paws gripped Flint's shoulders gently, and he crouched over the hyena in a tender, shielding sort of way. Aldain seemed to be holding him as best he could, panting heavily as they both calmed down. Flint in turn curled up against the wolf, pressing his muzzle underneath the wolf's chin as he panted happily in the wolf's embrace, a huge smile on his face.

The wolf's knot stayed inside Flint for much longer than he expected it would, and the hyena became accustomed to the thick, full feeling the wolf's trapped penis gave him. Flint could feel the wolf's shaft throbbing inside him for a long time too, and he eventually realized that Aldain might still be cumming inside him. The knight had obviously spilled a much bigger load this time than before because Flint could feel it inside his tail-end. It was a squishy wet feeling in his guts, but Flint did not mind at all. In fact, he squeezed down on the knight's cock as hard he could, trying to keep Aldain hard for as long as he was able to. Flint did not want this blissful moment to end.

The wolf's shaft eventually grew soft and he slipped out. The wolf rolled off Flint's body and left the hyena panting for air. Aldain sat on the edge of the bed, panting heavily as well. Flint closed his legs with a soft whimper. There was an empty feeling in his tail-hole that had never been there before. Flint was surprised that his butt felt wrong somehow without the wolf inside him. Flint had to think about squeezing himself shut in an effort to keep the wolf's seed from leaking out of him and all over the bed. Flint sat up after the feeling passed and his tail felt normal again, and then he looked up at Aldain with a big dopey grin on his face.

Aldain was staring off into the dark room. The wolf's ears were drooped, and his tail was still. The knight's head hung low, so that his muzzle almost touched his chest. Flint crept over to the wolf and rested his head on Aldain's strong, broad shoulder. The hyena snuggled up against the wolf's side and closed his eyes after pressing his head against the wolf's chest. Flint smiled, the fur on his face pulled slightly to one side by the warm fur of the wolf's shoulder, the strong muscle under his cheek comforting him. In his haste to get close to the wolf again, Flint did not notice where the wolf was looking or that tears filled the knight's eyes.

Aldain stared across the room at his necklace that lay on the dresser. The Prophet's Cross glimmered in the soft moonlight and the emerald-studded medallion seemed to mock him from across the room. While Flint was filled with a happy joy by the act of sharing his body with the wolf, Aldain was drained by it. The wolf's heart ached, as his feelings for the boy warred with his faith. The hyena had sparked something inside Aldain, and the fire of his passion had burned brightly. Now the moment had passed, and the effect Flint had on him was fading in the face of Aldain's memories and beliefs. The wolf's joy was quickly consumed by the shame Aldain felt at committing such an awful sin, and he could almost hear his angry father denouncing him. Aldain hung his head, his ears pressed against his head.

"I'm sorry," the wolf said eventually, turning sad eyes to the boy's happy, smiling face.

"Huh?" Flint asked sleepily, opening his eyes to look up at the wolf. Flint's muzzle was split by a happy, boyish grin that made Aldain's heart flutter despite his sadness.

"I'm sorry. I should not have done this to you," he said quietly, his eyes looking away from the hyena's face. "I should not have forced you to sin as I do."

"Huh? Why are you sorry? It felt good," Flint muttered, rubbing his head against Aldain's shoulder. Flint's muzzle gently brushed against the wolf's chest, and he smiled into the wolf's fur. The wolf blinked in surprise as the little hyena actually slid into his lap. There was no hesitation, no reluctance in Flint's movements as he tucked himself into the arms of another man.

A slight smile crept across the wolf's face as he slipped his arms around the boy's waist. "You are such a sweet, innocent boy." The wolf whispered as his heart broke. *How could I have defiled such an innocent soul*, the wolf thought. The hyena smiled up at him with hooded eyes as Aldain began petting his head-fur gently. "I am so sorry I hurt you," the wolf whispered.

"I told you," the hyena said happily, "I've past my nineteenth winter. I'm a man now." Aldain chuckled just a little, shaking his head slightly as Flint ignored the apology and corrected him about his age again. Flint did not comprehend what the wolf was saying, and Aldain could tell it just by looking at him. To the hyena, nothing they had done was wrong, so the wolf's apologies made no sense. Flint actually had no concept of how wrong what they had done was.

"You are the kindest man I've ever met," Flint said before he kissed the wolf again slowly, his lips pressing tenderly against the knight's. "Besides, it didn't hurt much. Not really." The hyena's ear swiveled back and he blushed as he leaned against the wolf. "Well, just a bit at first, but that went away. It felt too good to hurt." Flint reached down and began to rub the knight's soft cock, hoping it would respond to his touch. A tremble ran down the wolf's spine, and Aldain sighed in pleasure as the young male's paw rubbed him and the hyena's muzzle pressed against his own.

"Will you... mate me again?" Flint asked hesitantly, his tail wagging a little at the thought as he pulled at the wolf's quickly growing erection.

Aldain cupped the boy's face in one paw again and stared into Flint's emerald green eyes. The boy was genuinely, utterly happy with this. There were no plots, no deceptions, and no games in the hyena's eyes. It was an innocent, simple desire to be touched again by the man he loved. Aldain could see the love in Flint's eyes.

For another moment, those emerald eyes made Aldain forgot his vows and oaths all over again. He forgot the world outside the tiny inn room, and saw only the excited young man who wanted to share his bed and his heart. Aldain laid Flint back on the bed and pressed close to the boy once more. "Yes, my little lover, I will," the knight whispered softly as his shaft slid back inside Flint's still-wet passage. Flint whimpered and moaned happily, squirming underneath the wolf as they mated again. The young hyena's legs wrapped around the wolf's waist again, hugging his hips as Aldain groaned into the tawny brown fur of Flint's neck. They began to mate slowly and tenderly. Aldain went slower this time, thrusting as deeply as he could into Flint, and so their love-making took much longer. Flint loved every moment of the mating, and he whimpered and moaned encouragements to the wolf through gritted teeth.

By the time Aldain's knot was fully formed again, the wolf was covered in sweat from head to toe and so was the hyena. With another howl and a tender mating bite Aldain hunched forward and tied the hyena a second time, causing the young hyena to climax with a happy bark that made the wolf blush.

The knight held himself deep inside Flint, staring into those emerald eyes as he came inside Flint again. The young hyena had a look of pure bliss on his face, and it made Aldain's heart sing just to look at him. Then the wolf collapsed on top of the hyena. Aldain was panting hard and unable or unwilling to move off the hyena this time. Flint got comfortable underneath the wolf, shifting himself a little as the wolf began to fall asleep on top of him. The knight stared into his eyes, and just before those big brown eyes closed for good he whispered, "I love you." into the hyena's ear. Flint fell asleep happier than he had ever been in his nineteen years of life.

Flint's ears twitched as someone knocked on the door to his room. He tried to get up, but found himself tangled up in Aldain's arms. The wolf instinctively clutched him back against his chest, and that made Flint's heart soar as the sleeping male held him. The hyena's whole body tingled with joy as the wolf hugged him protectively.

The knocking came again, and this time the wolf woke up with a start. The wolf blinked unsteadily, looking at Flint's smiling face in a haze for a moment. Then fear flashed in Aldain's eyes and he quickly got up. He almost fell out of bed, trying to untangle himself from Flint and the sheets. He got to the door just as it started to open. The wolf kept whoever it was from opening the door more than an inch, using the door to shield the room and his naked body from whomever it was outside.

Flint couldn't hear who was speaking to the wolf, but it was probably one of the knight's companions, come to wake him up. The hyena watched as the wolf closed the door and locked it. Then Aldain began to pack up his things, quickly collecting everything he had brought to the tiny inn room into a pair of saddlebags. The wolf ran a brush through his fur and used a scented powered to cover the smell of sex that clung to him. Aldain did not look at Flint even once while he packed. The knight seemed to be deliberately avoiding looking at the bed where the naked hyena lay. Flint stretched a little and yawned before pushing himself up so he was sitting on the edge of the bed. The hyena's paws swung just above the floor as he watched the wolf move back and forth.

The hyena rubbed the sleep from his eyes and pulled on his

shorts, saying nothing as the wolf dressed. It felt good just be in Aldain's presence, and anything he might say could destroy that. Flint felt safe being so close to the wolf that had saved him and taken him to bed. He knew should have been downstairs by now making breakfast for the other guests, but he wasn't going to leave this room now. Flint wanted to hold onto this feeling as long as he could, because he knew the knight was leaving.

Eventually Aldain was fully dressed and packed, his chain-mail shirt draped over the strong body that had held Flint so close during the night. The last thing Aldain put on was the small gold medallion from the bedside table, which he tucked inside his chain-mail so it rested against his fur. When he finally turned to face Flint, their eyes met and they stared at each other, unsure what to say. They were no longer lovers who had shared each other's bodies. Once again, Aldain was a stalwart Knight of the Cross and Flint was a peasant boy who cleaned the stables. It felt to Flint that an ocean separated them, even though he could still reach out and touch the wolf.

"You…" Flint's voice cracked, and he had to force back his tears to speak, "You won't stay, will you. Even if I ask you to?" Flint looked up at Aldain with tears in his eyes.

The wolf shook his head slowly. "No, I can't," he said, barely above a whisper. Flint could hear the sadness in the knight's voice, and tears were brimming in both their eyes.

"I could come with you." Flint got up and put his head against the wolf's chest, wrapping his arms tightly around the wolf's waist. Flint wanted to capture one more intimate moment with the wolf before he was gone forever. "I would follow you anywhere," the hyena whimpered softly, tears starting to run down his cheeks.

The wolf put one arm around the hyena's shoulders, but it brought Flint little comfort to be held this time. The wolf's embrace was cold, his chest covered in the ring mesh of armor instead of the warm fur Flint had become so accustomed to during their night together.

Flint looked up into the wolf's face as tears began to stream down his cheeks. Aldain's paw gently caressed his head, and for a moment Flint felt that tender spark again. It made his knees weak to feel the wolf's bare paw-pad against his face. The hyena breathed in the wolf's scent and smiled, his eyes half closed as he pressed his muzzle against the knight's paw. Their noses just touched.

Aldain stared at the hyena's face and his heart broke. Flint's face lit up with so much joy all because of something so simple as the touch of his paw. The whole world seemed to shine as Flint smiled. The sunlight streaming the window seemed brighter, and Aldain felt as if all the pieces of his life had fallen into place. For a moment, the wolf wanted to throw everything away just to keep Flint's smile for his own.

Aldain could leave the Order behind and build a house somewhere deep in the wilds. The wolf had the means to live with this sweet young man for the rest of his life in relative comfort. Aldain's heart ached for the happiness such a life would bring him, and he knew that he would be happy. Aldain could see it in the hyena's eyes. He would be happy with Flint, and he knew it was the sort of happiness that his life on the open road and his duties would never bring him.

The temptation pulled at him, and Aldain wavered. Then the knight hung his head, and brushed the hyena's tears away. No matter how wonderful it would be, he could not bring himself to betray his faith and abandon his oaths completely. Aldain had become a Knight of the Cross at his father's death-bed, a final promise as the old knight drew his last breath. He could not abandon that calling forever, even if his heart was tempted from time to time by a night of pleasure with another male. Not even if he loved Flint, and just looking into the hyena's eyes told Aldain that was true.

The wolf steeled his heart and he kissed Flint gently on the lips. "I'm sorry, Flint, but you know that can't happen. I have duties to uphold. I can't give you the life you deserve." The wolf took the hyena's hand and bowed his head in shame as the boy's smile faded away. "Here at least you can live peacefully and safely. You may not be a cub, but you are still young. You have too much life ahead of you to waste it on me." The wolf's words tasted bitter in his mouth, but he knew it was for the best. Flint had to stay here for both their sakes.

Flint nodded softly, tears still streaming down his cheeks. "I know. I just… Promise me you will come back one day." The hyena pressed his head against the wolf's chest. "I'll think about you every day and make a home here. So that you have something to come back to."

Aldain closed his eyes. How could he tell Flint he would never come back to this village? His vows were until death, but could he really shatter such an innocent person by denying him hope? Aldain sinned once more for the small boy who made his heart sing. "I will," the wolf lied, and kissed Flint on the forehead. "When my service is at an end I will come back to you."

The wolf reached into his shirt and removed the gold medallion from his neck. He draped the small golden necklace around Flint's head, and the hyena's ears twitched backward as the gold chain passed over them. The gold chain settled into the cream-colored fur at his neck, and the medallion made a gold spot surrounded by black ones. Aldain kissed away the tears from Flint's cheeks. "Keep this to remember me by," the knight whispered before turning away.

Flint sniffed a little as Aldain opened the door and stepped out of the room. Flint watched from the doorway, one paw holding the door-jamb as the other clutched the wolf's cross. Aldain went downstairs to the common room without looking back. Flint could hear the voices of the wolf and his companions as they talked, and the ominous sound of the inn's front door closing behind them as they left. Outside, the horses whinnied and Flint watched from the window as his knight in shining armor rode toward the west and out of his life.

Flint closed the door, tears streaming down his cheeks as he sobbed his heart out into the bed they had shared. The small room was cold without the wolf there to hold him.

Across the hallway from the knight's room, another door closed with a soft click. Behind that door, Clara seethed with rage at what she had seen.

PAGE OF CUPS

CHAPTER III

The day passed slowly, and Flint had to fight back tears as he went about his chores. Tongish did not care why Flint was upset. The tiger smacked the boy upside the head every time the hyena broke down in front of a guest, and by the time Flint had finished washing the dishes after supper his ears were ringing badly.

Flint sighed as he finished the last dish. His paws burned, his back was sore, and his heart ached in a way the hyena had not imagined was possible. All he wanted to do was go to his bed in the hay loft and collapse. The hyena sniffed a little, his paw touching his chest where the Prophet's Cross medallion hung around his neck. He glanced around and took the medallion out of his shirt. He held the small medal in his paw, his fingers running over the raised lines forming the prophet's cross. Over the course of the day, it had become a comforting gesture to the hyena, and the metal still smelled of Aldain. Flint knew that if he could curl up in the wolf's arms again than everything would be all right.

"Finding comfort in your sins, faggot?" Clara growled. "Or

have you stolen something from a guest?"

Flint nearly jumped out of his fur when the tigress hissed in his ear. He backed away from her, clutching the medal in his paw tightly so she could not see it. "What do you want, Clara?" Flint muttered, tucking the necklace back into his shirt, his paws falling to his sides.

"What do I want?" the young tigress hissed at him, her whiskers flaring out as she stalked toward him. "I want what should have been mine." She jabbed Flint in the chest, poking at the hidden medallion. "I can't believe you did this to me, a little degenerate like you. How could you possibly steal my knight in shining armor?" she hissed, her tail lashing back and forth.

Flint furrowed his brow and stepped back again, his tail dipping low as Clara growled at him. She was so mad that her fangs flashed as she talked. "I don't know what you're talking about." Flint muttered, dropping the last dish into the drying rack. He tried to ignore the angry tigress, but she leaned in close to his face.

"Yes you do. You slept with him, you little monster. You took that knight right up your tail when he should have been with me. I was going to leave this horrid little place with him, until you screwed everything up. I can't believe you'd actually stoop that low." Clara's nostrils flared as she stared right in Flint's face, but the hyena did not look away.

"What are you talking about?" Flint said quietly, and the tigress laughed in his face.

"What am I talking about? You, you perverted little tail-raiser." The tigress grinned ear to ear, her perfectly cared-for fangs glistening at Flint. "You're the worst kind of sinner. A dirty and disgusting sinner, and you don't even know it, do you?" Flint didn't even blink as she snickered at him. "Well, you had better do everything I say from now on. Because if anyone finds out about what you did with your dishonorable knight, Flint, you're *dead*." Flint panted as she spoke, and the way she talked about him and Aldain made the hyena want to hit her.

Then Clara ran her claw-tips across Flint's muzzle, and the hyena gasped when she scratched him hard enough to almost break the skin on his nose. Then her paw grabbed at the chain of Aldain's necklace and pulled the medallion out of the hyena's shirt. Flint barked "Hey!" and grabbed the emerald-studded medal away from her.

"You better give that jewel to me right now, you dirty little tail-raiser. Maybe I'll be able to sell it for enough to leave this rotten little town. Once I get to Newcastle, boys like Aldain will be flocking all around me anyway." Clara shrugged her shoulders and held out her paw expectantly.

Flint stared at Clara in shock slid the medallion back into his shirt. "I don't care what you want," the hyena muttered quietly, and the tigress' eyes narrowed. She bristled, but for once Flint was going to take Clara's bullying. "He loves *me*, not you," Flint said as he slid past the taller feline. His paws trembled as he grabbed the big washtub of water off the counter, and he stood his ground when she rounded on him. The tigress eyed the large tub of hot, dirty water between them as Flint said, "And when he comes back, he's going to take *me* with him. Not you." The hyena took a cautious step toward the innkeeper's daughter, who backed away slowly. "Now leave me alone." Flint muttered angrily, the water sloshing slightly in the heavy tub.

For a tense moment they stared at each other, neither one moving. Flint let out a sigh of relief when Clara turned and stormed out of the kitchen, cursing under her breath.

Flint's paws were trembling so badly he nearly dropped the tub when he poured the wash water outside the back door. Flint set the tub down beside the counter to dry and closed the back door of the inn with a heavy sigh. Flint couldn't believe what had come over him. He had never talked to Clara like that before, but the things she had said... Flint's tail bristled a little bit, and he rubbed a paw through his head-fur.

They were just lies. She was just mad that Aldain didn't like her more. Flint silently wished that when he went up to the small room over the stables there would be someone special waiting for him.

The hyena was about to take out the medal again, and so he jumped badly when the kitchen door flew open and Tongish stomped into the kitchen with a growl.

The big tiger looked madder than Flint had ever seen him before. The innkeeper's tail was puffed out like a bottlebrush and it lashed back and forth as he loomed over Flint, an accusing finger pointing down at the much shorter hyena.

"Boy! Tell me she's lying. Tell me now!" he roared and bared his teeth in anger.

Flint whimpered and ducked away from the tiger. "What, what are you talking about?" Flint stammered, scarcely avoiding the tiger's big fist as Tongish lashed out at him. The tiger's blow just barely connected with his shoulder but it sent Flint tumbling to the floor all the same. Flint blinked in surprise and clutched his shoulder. It had been a real punch, not just a disciplinary swat. Tongish had never hit him like that before. The tiger would probably have knocked him out cold if he had connected.

Tongish snarled down at Flint. "The knight, you rutting little tail-raiser! Tell me Clara did not see you come out of his room this morning." Tongish pointed at his daughter, who was standing smugly in the doorway with her arms crossed. Flint's eyes widened and his ears flicked backward. His mouth hung open a little as he stared in shock at Clara's triumphant, evil grin. Flint looked back at Tongish, and the tiger was staring at the medallion around Flint's neck that had been knocked out of his shirt by the tiger's punch.

"You were, weren't you?" The tiger's voice was cold and deadly, and Flint looked up into Tongish's eyes. The tiger was studying his face carefully, and Flint knew there was no way he had concealed his reactions well enough to lie now. He just whimpered softly, "Please, I don't understand what's wrong!"

Tongish grabbed him by the scruff of his neck and dragged him to his feet. The hyena struggled and stumbled, his arms flailing uselessly as the tiger opened the back door and hurled him out into the street.

Flint yelped in pain as he rolled to a stop against the side of the butcher's store. He staggered to his feet as the inn's door closed, and the hyena's paws thudded against the wooden door as Tongish barred it from the inside.

Flint panted, staring at the closed door in shock. "Tongish?" he called out. Only silence answered him. "Tongish! Open the door, please!" The hyena's voice took on a higher pitch, and he flattened his ears as he whined. Flint raced around the inn to the front door. His shoulder throbbed after he banged into the door and found it solidly barred from the inside. "Tongish!" Flint cried out, a loud whine that echoed in the quiet night. No one answered, and a few people in the street turned to stare at Flint as he crumpled against the inn door.

The hyena sniffed, sobs overtaking him. Flint's claws dug at the wood of the door uselessly, and the hyena threw back his head and howled pitifully as cold night began to fall.

After a minute, an upstairs window opened up, and Tongish leaned outside. The tiger's angry stare bored holes in Flint. "Shut it boy, you hear me? If I ever see around here again, I'll get my sword."

Flint's heart sank as he looked up at the tiger's angry glare. Tongish was deadly serious. The hyena searched for anything to say but there was nothing. He just swallowed nervously and stayed silent as the tiger closed the window.

Flint looked around the small main street of East Haven. A few people had pulled back their curtains, but none of them seemed willing to come over and see what was wrong. Only one of the town's two guards seemed the least bit interested, but the coyote had not even stood up from the low wall he usually sat on.

Flint slumped against the side of the inn in despair. Tongish had thrown him out. Nearly ten years serving the tiger after his parents died, and just like that he had no home. Flint glared at the ground and kicked a rock away. Not that the inn had been a good home, but it was a place to be. It was a life. Now he had nothing.

The setting sun reflected off the golden Prophet's Cross that hung around his neck, and the little hyena felt a smile creep across his muzzle. *You have a life here.* That was what Aldain had said, wasn't it? Now there was nothing keeping him here. He could follow Aldain as far as he wanted too now.

Flint raced down the street and stopped in front of the bored coyote that sat on the wall at the edge of town, guarding against intruders. "Where was the knight's party going?" he asked, breathless and with a big grin.

The coyote shifted and stared at him for a second. "Newcastle."

"Where's that?" Flint asked, his tail beginning to wag back and forth as he looked up at the coyote.

"It's fifty leagues west of here down the High Road." The guard pointed down the road, and Flint nearly jumped for joy as he dashed off down the path.

"Hey!' The coyote called after him, and Flint skidded to a stop. The guard grunted as he dropped down from the wall, digging into his pockets. "If you're going to run off like damn fool, boy, you had better take this." Flint held out his paws and the guard dropped several coins into them. Flint stared at the coins, and realized he was holding more money than he had ever seen in his life.

The coyote shook a finger at Flint. "And you had better buy food with it, you hear me?" The coyote growled roughly at him. "It's nearly a two-week walk to Newcastle. Be sure to take the right fork when the road splits, or you'll never make it there, understand?" Flint grinned up at the coyote and yipped in agreement. The guard looked sternly down at him, until a slight grin pulled at the coyote's muzzle. Flint laughed and then rushed back into town to buy food.

The guard shook his head and went back to his post.

~: :~

Flint jogged down the path, his paws sliding across wet stones as the rain beat down on him. The hyena was soaked to the bone,

85

his fur now merely a soggy wet mass that clung to him and slowed him down. Lightning flashed, and Flint ducked under a nearby tree in fright. He stood beside the tree, shivering as he tried to wipe the worst of the water out of his fur. Then, the sound of some great old tree crashing to the forest floor made Flint jump again. The small hyena gripped the shoulder-strap slung over his shoulder with both paws, nervously looking around the green forest.

Flint wanted to stop and let the storm pass, but it had been raining for several hours now and showed no signs of relenting. The rain was so cold, Flint was afraid that if he stopped running he'd freeze to death. Flint panted as he let himself rest against a tree as long as he dared, eating a chunk of bread from his bag. The rain almost made it soft enough to chew.

It had been six days since Flint had left East Haven, and he was beginning to wonder if he would ever make it to Newcastle at this rate. He had been doing pretty well so far even if the going seemed slow. He had lots of food; so much it slowed him down. Flint was just glad the bag he bought was strong enough to prevent thorns from tearing the leather. He had a good canteen and a strong knife with a sharp point. Flint felt pretty good about the things he'd purchased with his money. He even had a few coins left over, just a few silvers, in case he had to continue on past Newcastle in his search for Aldain.

Flint's muzzle broke into a wide grin as he took the last bite of his bread. *Aldain.* Just the thought of the wolf warmed the young hyena, and he started off down the road again.

As Flint jogged around a bend in the road, he found where that tree had fallen down. A massive redwood lay across the road, completely blocking it. Flint walked up to the fallen tree, and when he reached a paw up he knew for sure he'd never be able to climb over it. He was just too short to manage it, so the hyena padded around one side of the tree, his paws squishing in the mud as he reached the bottom end of the tree.

What he found confused the small hyena. The tree had not been struck by lightning or felled by the wind. Some woodcutter with a very big axe had chopped it down. Flint didn't think the woodcutter had planned very well; anyone coming down the road would be pretty upset by the fallen tree across the road. The hyena stared at the tree for a moment before turning to move on.

The sound of twigs breaking and a low chuckle caused Flint's ear to perk up. He turned toward the woods, and his round ears flattened against his head when he saw the large, mean-looking ram holding that axe. The heavy-set sheep tapped the axe against one paw, his big curved horns seeming to match the large curved blade of the axe he held. "Well, look at this... a pup out wandering where he shouldn't be," the ram muttered.

"What do you mean?" Flint said, his head tilting a bit to the side in an unconscious show of confusion. "I'm just following the road to Newcastle."

The ram turned his head to the side, looking at Flint closer with one eye, and then the other. The way the ram snorted and laughed at Flint made his tail droop. "You don't get it, do you?"

Flint blinked, shifting his bag from one shoulder to the other as the ram continued to creep closer. "Get what?" Flint said meekly, smiling a little at the taller ram.

The ram chuckled softly, his breath billowing in the cold rain. "I'm a bandit, pup." Flint's eyes widened as the ram dragged a thick fingernail across his axe blade. "And you are about the dumbest mark I've ever seen." Flint yipped and turned to run as the ram laughed so loudly that it sounded like thunder to the scared hyena.

Flint's paws splashed in the puddles formed by the rain, and his fear would have allowed him to outrun the hulking ram if the bandit had been alone. Instead Flint only got about five feet before a whirling bola came flying out of the trees and tangled his feet together, sending him sprawling in the mud.

Flint hit the ground hard, his front paws sliding in the mud as he landed muzzle-first in a puddle. Flint spluttered and pushed himself out of the water, gasping in shock. He tried to scramble to his feet, to free his legs, but someone grabbed him by the collar and threw him on his back hard. It was a ferret, a nasty-looking man who stuck a thin sword in Flint's face. "Stop struggling," the ferret muttered and Flint froze, staring up at the blade in fear as he lay on the ground in the mud. The rain made Flint blink and his ears twitched as the ram tromped up to them both. "Good shot, Carl," the ram said as he put a hoof on Flint's chest to hold the hyena down.

"Thanks, Boris, but you're right. This one was pretty easy to catch," the ferret said as he reached for Flint's bag. The hyena struggled for a second, trying to keep the ferret's paws away from his supplies before the ram stepped on him harder.

"You struggle and Boris here will crush your chest, pup," the ferret muttered absently, pulling the bag from Flint's paws. Flint yelped in pain as the hoof dug into his chest, and he started to cry as the ferret took his paws and bound them with a short length of rope. The hyena's tears of pain mixed with the rain in his fur as the ram forced him to his feet and off the road, marching him like a prisoner in front of him.

Flint trudged in rain to the bandits' campsite, hidden from the road in deep brush. The hyena whimpered when the ram shoved him to the wet ground near a tree, and he struggled against the rope holding his paws together for a few seconds before the ram waved his axe at Flint menacingly. That made the small hyena curl up in a ball, tears running down his face as the ferret sat down with his bag.

"Food, food, food," the ferret muttered, transferring bundle after bundle of Flint's food from the bag to a large wooden chest they had in a shelter from the rain. "Damn, this one's got nothing but food. It's getting harder and harder to make a dishonest living like this Boris. We need to find a better road to live off. Ah, here we go. Shiny coins."

Flint watched as the ferret pulled the last few silver coins he had out of his bag and spun them in the air. "No," Flint whimpered as the ferret pocketed them.

"Yes, oh yes, pup" the ferret sniggered as he walked over to Flint. Flint flinched away from the ferret's mean smile as Carl knelt down beside him, his short sword stuck point-down in the ground by Flint's legs. The ferret Carl leaned in close to Flint, and the hyena could smell his awful breath.

"You're just a little poor traveler aren't yah? A peasant. That makes you a much poorer catch than we wanted." The ferret's smile took on a sinister, almost lewd twist to it as he dipped his nose down and stared at Flint, who squirmed and tried to look away from the ferret. "It took Boris there a long time to cut that tree down, and we can't have you running off to tell someone about our camp."

The ferret grabbed hold of Flint's knee, twisting his leg to force the hyena to look at him. "Now Boris and me, we like killing people as much as the next bandit does. Boris does a lot more, the most in fact, but I'm willing to talk him out of it for a price."

The ram let out a chuckle at that, and he eyed the ferret with a mean grin, "You're despicable, Carl."

"Shut up, Boris," the ferret snapped, looking over his shoulder much farther than most people could turn their heads. Flint felt queasy just looking at the way the ferret's neck twisted, but it got worse when Carl's head snapped back to look at Flint with an evil glint in his eye. "You want to live, don't ya?" Flint nodded and whimpered, trying not to look the ferret in the eyes. "Well then," Carl smirked, "You got something to make it worth my while pup? Any family jewels perhaps?" the ferret finished with a low snicker.

Flint gasped when the ferret's paw grabbed his inner thigh right beside his crotch. He kicked at the ferret, struggling hard against the ropes holding his paws together, *anything* to keep the bandit's paw away from him. Despite the cold rain, the fear of dying, and the adrenaline rush of being captured, that touch made Flint so sick to his stomach he almost threw up.

The ram snorted loudly when he saw the ferret feeling the hyena up, his breath curling up in front of his horns. "Leave him alone, Carl, he's just a kid."

"So?" The ferret looked back at his companion with a smirk. "It's cold, and it's been weeks since we snagged a good looking boy alive, especially one with a pelt this soft. Besides, you can have him after I'm done. You know I prefer someone with," the ferret's eyes lit up as he spotted a hint of gold around Flint's neck, "family jewels."

Flint turned his muzzle away from the ferret's paw as it moved to his neck, and he whimpered loudly when the ferret pulled at the gold chain around his neck. "Whoa… Boris, check this out… A mighty fine necklace don't you think?" Flint snapped at the ferret's paw, trying to bite him as hard as he could as the thief lifted Aldain's medallion off his neck. Flint struggled, about to shout at the bandits to leave his medallion alone, but Carl grabbed his muzzle. The ferret held the hyena's mouth shut as he stared at the emerald in the center of the medal.

"Just look at the gem Boris, that's more than we'll find on this road in a week. Hell, that's worth more than we've made all month." The ram whistled softly when the ferret held the medallion up for him to see. Boris was standing really close to them now, and Flint could see the way his britches bulged in the front. Despite the ram's halfhearted attempt to stop the ferret from touching Flint, the ram was obviously looking forward to his chance at Flint. That bulge gave the hyena an idea. The idea turned his stomach, but Flint realized this was his only chance to escape while they were both distracted by the medallion.

"Damn, this is a good piece of work!" Boris muttered. "Where'd a kid like you get a thing like—*hurk!*" The ram didn't finish his thought because Flint balled his paws together into fists and hit the ram as hard as he could on the bulge in his crotch. Boris dropped the medallion and fell backward, clutching his deflating erection and bleating in pain.

Carl's head turned toward Flint and in that moment of surprise he grabbed for his sword. Only, the ferret had made the mistake of holding Flint's muzzle shut with his sword arm and that meant he let go of Flint's muzzle first. This time when Flint snapped at the ferret's paw his teeth caught fur and fingers. Even Flint's small hyena jaws proved strong enough to crack bone.

The ferret was screaming in pain and clutching his broken

paw as Flint scrambled to his feet, grabbed Aldain's medallion off the ground, and ran as fast as he could.

Boris snorted loudly and rolled over onto all fours. The ram pulled a small hatchet from his belt and heaved it at the fleeing hyena, but Flint slipped in the mud and the axe whirled over his head. As he stood up the hyena grabbed his bag, and then he ran from the camp.

Flint was tumbling and sliding through the wood, thorns and branches tearing his clothes and cutting him as he squeezed through the underbrush. The hyena panted, gasping for air as the rain falling on him washed away the sickening taste of blood from his mouth. As he ran he could hear the rampaging anger of the ram behind him growing farther and farther away, and eventually Flint saw Boris turn back at the sound of Carl shouting for help.

Flint spit the last of the ferret's blood from his mouth. He bit through the rope at his wrists, wiped his muzzle with the soaking wet fur on his arm, set Aldain's medallion back around his neck and started off in the direction he hoped the road was in.

~: :~

Some time later, after dusk had fallen and the rain had stopped, Flint found the road again. He trudged down it as far as he could force himself to go, unwilling to stop for fear that the bandits would come looking for him after Carl set his broken fingers. Flint was trembling tired, soaking wet, and on the verge of tears when he stopped for the night.

The short hyena collapsed against a small tree with a bush growing beside it, his head-fur plastered to his face as he curled up in the small hollow the two plants formed. Flint laid the bag across his lap and checked to see what was left, but his paw went right through the bag. Somehow, in the fight, or the flight afterward, a hole had formed in the bottom of the bag and most of its contents had spilled out. Only the hyena's metal canteen remained, tucked securely in a smaller inside pocket, and even that was now dented. Flint collapsed on the wet ground and began to cry, his paw curling around the only real possession he had left, Aldain's gold medallion.

~: :~

Flint wearily put one paw in front of the other, staggering slightly as the sun beat down on him through the trees. Traveling to Newcastle and finding Aldain had sounded like such a wonderful idea two weeks ago, back in East Haven. After the bandits had attacked him however, Flint discovered why most people never left their tiny hometowns. Walking through the Mistwind Mountains was not easy going, even on a well-traveled road like the High Pass.

Doing it without food was something Flint now considered akin to madness. The little hyena shook his head and laughed at himself. It probably was a good thing he had nothing and no one to go back to, otherwise he would have turned back after being robbed.

During the morning, everything in the mountains was covered in the dense fog that gave them their name. Without the road to follow Flint would have been hopelessly lost ages ago.

By midday the sun burned off the fog and turned the rocky road into an unbearably hot strip of dirt. The heat often forced

Flint to find refuge in the trees along the roadside. That meant getting bristles in his fur, tangled up in vines, and stuck by the sharp thorns that seemed to be everywhere. Still, it was better than trudging on the rocky path in the heat.

Sometimes, it rained in the afternoon and soaked Flint to the skin, his fur unable to hold back the torrents of cold water that came crashing out of the sky or the mud that clung to his hind-paws. Those days were the worst, and he often had to find shelter and hide from the rain, afraid that more bandits would be waiting for him around the next bend.

Flint lifted the canteen slung around his neck to his mouth, and when nothing came out he snaked his tongue up the opening to get the last drops of water before forcing himself to move forward again. At least when it rained he had water to drink. If he kept walking, he might find another stream where he could drink his fill and restore his canteen to a heavy fullness.

The small sack he had been carrying food in was long gone now, discarded as useless with the gaping hole in its bottom. Flint groaned slightly as his stomach reminded him of another gaping hole that should be filled. Flint would not be hungry of it weren't for those two horrible bandits. The meager coins the coyote had given him had bought more than enough food for two weeks, especially for someone used to not eating much each day and working hard. At least the food had lasted as long as it did. Flint seriously doubted he would have been able to make it this far without being able to eat that first week on the trail. He had not found many plants he recognized as edible along the way.

Flint crested a rather large foothill and was pleased to find that it formed the edge of the Mistwood forest. He stopped to lean against a tree, and the hyena's spirits brightened when he looked out over the rolling green fields toward the city of Newcastle. The High Road snaked down the valley, past many farms and fallow fields and right into the city. It was a real city too, not the tiny rest stop that East Haven had been. The city had a high wall around it, and an honest-to-goodness castle built alongside the river. Flint had never seen a place that looked so incredible. Flint rushed down the valley, scrambling over rocks and fallen trees until he hit the flat road between the farmlands.

The farmers of the valley were out in the spring air, sewing their fields with heavy, ox-drawn plows. Some of them even looked up in curiosity at the small hyena running past their farms, panting loudly enough for some of them to wonder where the fire was. Flint did not stop, however; he ran all the way to the city gates with his tail wagging back and forth the whole way.

The guards at the city gates were far more attentive than the guards he was used to at home. They were dressed in real armor made of metal plates, not the dirty leather armor the coyote brothers had made themselves. The guards even prevented him from entering the city at first, demanding to know who he was and why he was running so fast. They seemed really threatening to the short hyena, just by holding their spears across his path.

At least, they were until Flint told them he was looking for a knight. At that point, one of them saw the gold medallion around his neck and let him pass without further question. Flint kissed the little Prophet's cross and grinned, racing through the streets in search of his knight.

Flint was quickly lost inside the city. Everyone he asked told him that the castle was the place to look for a knight. The Church of the Prophet had built the castle that was the town's namesake as their main chapel in the region, and they would know where to find one of their knights. Finding the castle, however, proved far more difficult than Flint thought it would be.

Sure, he could see the main tower from anywhere in the city. The keep rose up several stories above even the largest town-house, but the streets between him and the castle were a maze of buildings, alleyways, and tiny markets. Carts did not stop for anyone underpaw and no one wanted to help him look for Aldain, so the hyena had to dodge and duck his way through the streets. It seemed like forever before he reached the castle gates. The guards did not look eager to let him in either, and refused to even talk with him in some cases. Flint was about to despair when he heard laughter that made his heart jump. It was Aldain's voice.

Flint spun around and yipped for joy when he spotted the wolf. Coming down the street was Aldain, followed by the jackal Will, Lord Trenton, and even Father Tully. They were all walking as group, and Aldain was laughing at something the jackal had said. It was a big hearty laugh that made Flint smile. Flint felt like his fur was standing on end and he almost danced in the street. The wolf was really here. He had found him! Flint raced toward Aldain; shouting the wolf's name.

~: ~

Aldain was laughing so hard that his stomach hurt when he heard someone call his name. He turned around toward the voice just in time to catch whoever it was right in the chest as they barreled into his arms. The wolf yelped in surprised as someone short threw his arms around his neck and clung to him, nearly knocking Aldain over backward. The wolf's arms instinctively

closed around the person to keep them from falling, but he quickly let go once he realized who it was hugging him.

"Flint!" Aldain barked in surprise as the hyena's grip around his neck pulled him forward, making him stoop slightly. "What in the hells are you doing here?" The wolf gaped in shock at the young man. The rest of the party stood around them, mouths open as the smiling hyena started to talk.

"I found you! I can't believe I found you! I know you told me to stay but I walked all the way here because Tongish threw me out of the inn. He threw me out with nothing at all. I guess he was mad that you chose me over Clara, but I still don't understand why he would be mad about you not sleeping with her, because he was always mad when someone did that, but it doesn't matter now, because now I can follow you anywhere. I'm so happy!" The hyena's words tumbled out all in one quick breath as he nearly bounced in place with joy. When he finally ran out of breath he kissed Aldain right on the lips.

Flint's joyous reunion ended in one quick shove. The hyena felt like he had been stabbed in the heart as Aldain pushed Flint off him and then backpedaled away so fast he ran right into a wall. The wolf's eyes were as big as plates, and he stared at Flint in utter disbelief. There was a collective gasp from the wolf's companions, and Flint was just as surprised that Aldain had pushed him away.

The fox mage put his paws up to his muzzle and with a girlish laugh said, "Oh my god." The jackal sneered a bit and glared at the wolf, but he laughed a little too. The otter, however, did not laugh. In fact, Father Tully was so angry that he was shaking all over, and he stared at Flint with a fire in his eyes the likes of which the hyena had never seen before.

"What did you say, boy?" the priest shouted, his staff banging heavily on the ground as he stomped up to the hyena. "Is what you just said true? Did you follow us here from that inn in East Haven? You were with Aldain the night we were there?" The otter roared, his words carrying a good distance as he shouted in Flint's face.

Flint turned his head to the side, his round ears twitching backward as he stared up at the angry otter's face in confusion and fear. Flint had no idea how to react, so he just sort of shrunk in place. Aldain had shoved him away, and now the otter was yelling at him. The little hyena's mind barely worked as the otter shouted his questions. "Yes," Flint whispered, and the otter rounded on Aldain like a whip.

"Nothing happened, did it? 'Must have been another wolf in the village', huh? Do not lie to me again knight. Did you sleep with this boy?" The otter pointed at Flint, and everyone seemed to blush this time. The jackal looked away, the fox had a sympathetic look on his face and Aldain looked like he was about to die as the otter's staff thumped him in the chest.

Aldain blinked once in shock as he pressed back against the wall, his eyes fixed on Flint's face. Time seemed to be caught in this one horrible moment for him. Everyone was waiting for him to answer. The short hyena looked up at him with such an innocent face, his big green eyes filling with tears at the sudden rejection. Aldain looked into those eyes again, and the wolf knew he couldn't lie about what they had done. Not in front of Flint. It would break the boy's heart and Aldain could not bear to do that.

"Yes…" he said, and the admission made Flint's face light up. The hyena began to move forward again, trying to hug Aldain a second time, but the otter priest swung his staff hard and dealt Flint a painful blow to the head. The hyena cried out like a wounded pup and collapsed to the ground, which made several of the onlookers wince.

"You perverted scum, stay away from him." Father Tully swore under his breath, and the otter clutched his staff like it was a mace. Flint whined in pain and rolled away from the priest, and found the jackal Will was suddenly crouched over him protectively. Flint blinked unsteadily, the black face and muzzle seeming to swim in the air above him as the jackal checked his head. Father Tully meanwhile got right up in Aldain's face again.

"I knew you were breaking your vows. Why do you think I insisted I come with you, knight? Did you think you could hide this from us forever?" The otter hissed angrily, waving a paw at the rest of the group. "These heathens have affected your mind, and now you consort with this, this... tail-raiser like a filthy pervert? What did it bring you, knight? Was that moment of pleasure worth your damnation?" Aldain winced, and looked away from the angry priest's face, a low whine escaping his throat.

"You disgust me," the otter muttered and turned to the guards that had come running because of the commotion. "You there," the otter commanded, "bring the boy and the knight. We'll see how you like being tail-raisers in jail. Maybe we can starve the sin out of you both till you stand trial."

The crowd that had gathered gave a collective gasp, which was echoed by Lord Trenton. "Father Tully, that's not fair..." the fox started to say, but the otter rounded on him as well.

"Do you wish to join them, Lord Trenton? I have my suspicions about the status of your tail as well, and I can produce more than enough proof to ruin you." The otter's tone left nothing to doubt that the proof would be found, real or not.

The fox's big blue eyes narrowed, and he glared daggers at the priest. "Do not threaten me, holy man. You know there is nothing you can do to a true noble." The fox twitched his tail back and forth in anger, and his paws took on a fiery blue glow. "And if you try to take that boy with you, then I will stop you."

"You would dare attack me?" The otter's paws began to glow as well, but his were wreathed in a violent red light.

On the ground, Flint let out a whimper as the jackal touched his forehead gently. The hyena looked up at Aldain for help, but the wolf seemed frozen. Flint reached his paw out and struggled to touch him, his vision beginning to blur badly. "Help me…" Flint whined, his paw reaching out for the wolf's cloak as the jackal did something he could not see. The wolf's eyes locked with Flint's, and they seemed to harden for a moment.

Aldain was about to move when Will shouted, "If anyone so much as moves, then this priest sings soprano come Sunday morning."

Flint looked back at the jackal who was crouched over him, and he was shocked to see that Will had drawn his knife and placed it rather discreetly between the otter's legs, right up under Father Tully's thick tail. Father Tully was standing very, *very* still, and the guards had stopped their advance on the fox mage. Will held the dagger in place as he stood up, putting his other arm around the priest's neck, where the jackal's second dagger pricked at the old otter's throat. "And if you say one more word of that spell, holy man, you will never sing in church again. Understand?" The jackal's voice was a growl in the otter's ear that Will made sure everyone could hear.

Everyone seemed to freeze as Will held Father Tully at knife-point. "Here's how this is going to work," the jackal said quietly, addressing the guards and the crowd in general. "You lot will leave, and the boy will stay with us. You go quietly, and nobody gets hurt. If anyone makes trouble for us after today, then the old man here misses his next sermon. Got it?" the jackal hissed, and pressed the knife closer to the old priest's throat.

"You can't do this." The otter muttered angrily, but the glow was leaving his paws and the guards were backing a safe distance away.

"Sure I can. Now beat it." The jackal shoved Father Tully away from the group, and the priest stumbled a little before finding his feet. Father Tully rubbed at his throat, and glared at the jackal.

"I will not forget this." The otter said coldly.

"You had better. I'm good at scaling castle walls, and I bet you'd make an excellent choirboy. Understand?" the jackal said with a sneer, and followed the threat up with a rather rude gesture with his knife. The otter turned his back on the party and stomped away in a huff.

A few seconds passed and Flint sat up unsteadily. Father Tully was a few feet away when he turned back toward them, his eyes still filled with a fire. "Knight! What do you think you are doing just standing there? Follow me!" Aldain blinked in surprise and looked up from Flint's face at the retreating priest. "Now," the otter barked angrily, "Or you will find yourself cast out of the Order of the Cross before you can take another breath."

Flint looked up at Aldain, and the knight's eyes met his. Aldain began to smile just a little bit, his shoulders relaxing until the otter's next words cut through the air like knives. "Your family, of course, will be disgraced by the news."

Flint watched Aldain's face as the wolf's muzzle twisted into

102

a mournful expression. Flint's vision was growing blurry, but he could see the knight's heart and his faith fighting for control, and the hyena bit his lip in fear. The wolf's tail drooped low, and he flattened his ears in shame. The wolf's eyes met Flint's for just a moment, and he whispered, "I'm sorry," before slowly turning toward Father Tully and the castle.

"No!" Flint shouted. He got to his feet and tried to run after Aldain, but he stumbled almost immediately. The jackal caught him and held him back by the scruff of his neck. Aldain turned to look back at Flint, and his face was a mask of shame and sorrow. "No," Flint whined loudly, but the wolf did not move toward him.

"I'm so sorry Flint..." Aldain's voice sounded dead and all the emotion was drained from his face. Just looking at him broke Flint's heart. The knight's once shining face looked like the corpse he had first saved Flint from.

Aldain looked up at his former companions to say goodbye, but the jackal cut him off with a shake of his head. "You've made your choice Aldain." The jackal said angrily as he held the struggling hyena back. "You can't apologize now. I'll make sure he stays safe, you coward."

Aldain nodded once, and then looked at the fox. "Trenton," he said simply, and the fox just hung his head in sadness as the wolf turned away. Aldain's eyes lingered on Flint, and his jaw trembled as he took another step away from the hyena.

Flint shouted and tried to follow Aldain, but the jackal held him firmly in place. Flint's vision began to blur again, and it suddenly felt like he was falling as the wolf moved farther and farther down the street. It felt like he was outside his body, and the hyena could only barely hear himself shouting as Aldain followed Father Tully around that last corner and into the castle. When the castle gates closed behind him, Flint's world collapsed into darkness.

PAGE OF SWORDS

CHAPTER IV

When Flint was conscious again, all he could feel was pain throbbing from the side of his head. It hurt so badly it overwhelmed all his thoughts. The hyena tried to clutch at his forehead, but he could not move his arms or legs. He struggled to open his eyes but the world swam across his vision as if he was underwater and the world was melting. A face formed out of the colored swirls drew close to Flint's face. He tried to pull away from it, but he couldn't, and then a heavy paw came to rest on his forehead. Flint cried out in pain at the touch, but then the pain began to recede almost immediately. The face cleared, and the face of the coyote holding his forehead came into view. He had a strange green robe on, with a large hood that draped over his face. Flint met his gaze for just a moment before he lost consciousness again.

～ ∶ ～

Flint opened his eyes slowly. His head no longer hurt, but he was unsure of exactly what had happened. It seemed like a dream, but he could not be sure. He pushed himself up onto all fours unsteadily and shook his head a bit, trying to clear his thoughts.

"Welcome back to the land of the living, little one." Flint turned his ears towards the sound, and then looked over at the jackal that was sitting across the room at a small writing desk. It was Will, and his black fur seemed to glimmer in the lamplight. He was dressed in a white shirt and brown shorts, and those colors seemed to leap out on him because of the deep black color of his fur. The jackal was holding a thick iron bar in one paw, which he raised and lowered in smooth motions. He seemed to be swapping the heavy round bar back and forth between both paws, and Flint numbly realized that this must be how Will kept his body so well defined. "You feeling better?"

The hyena worked his mouth, trying to get the taste of sleep out of his mouth. "No," he whispered softly, surprised that talking hurt his throat a little, "Where am I?" the hyena muttered uncertainly, looking around the small room. The jackal smiled as Flint rubbed a paw across his muzzle, trying to get the fur on his face to return to normal instead of the matted mess it was.

"One of the finest flop houses of Newcastle. No questions asked of the patrons, no answers give to the guards. Trenton and I brought you here after you passed out in the street." The jackal set the heavy bar down and began to stretch out his legs, shaking them a bit. "Father Tully got you pretty good, cracked your skull I think. I'm surprised you woke up so soon after being healed from something like that. I thought you would be out all night."

Flint flattened his ears a bit, as the jackal's words sorted what had happened from his dreams. "Oh." he said quietly, sitting up on the edge of the bed. He numbly realized his shirt was missing and that it was night outside. He had actually been unconscious all day. Flint rubbed the side of his head where Father Tully's staff had caught him. It did not hurt any more, so the coyote in his dreams must have been real, just like everything that had happened with Aldain. Flint rubbed a paw through the short fur on his chest and was about to ask Will another question when the jackal did something completely unexpected.

Will got up from the chair, but instead of just standing up the jackal placed both of his front paws on the floor and did a hand stand out of the chair. Flint stared, blinked his eyes, and stared again as the bulky jackal's legs went right over his head and up into the air. The jackal moved his front paws, walking on his hands for a moment before doing the splits with his long legs. Flint's mouth dropped open as the jackal began to do a whole routine of stretches and strange poses, twisting his muscled, but obviously lithe body into many positions Flint did not even think were possible.

When he thought he could say something without making Will fall over, Flint asked, "What… what are you doing?"

The jackal twisted his head to look at Flint, "Stretching." Flint blinked and shook his head. Will had one foot and one hand on the floor, but his other leg was stretched up towards the ceiling so that his back was curled in an odd way, his other arm stretched out to the wall for balance. Flint could not believe the jackal had not fallen over. It was hard to watch Will move from one strange position to another without feeling like he was watching a baker make pretzels. Slinky, black pretzels made entirely out of muscle, but pretzels.

"Why?" the hyena asked, his voice filled with curiosity.

Will went back to standing normally. "Because I'm a thief," the jackal said with a slight shrug.

Flint tilted his head to the side. No one who was a thief would just admit that right? Sure, those bandits had, but they were bandits. It was obvious what they were. Flint felt his face grow hot. At least it should have been obvious.

Will sighed a little bit when he saw the look of confusion on the hyena's face. "I break into tombs, Flint, not houses. The old kingdoms buried a lot of things. Treasures, secrets, magic. They also left traps, locks, and puzzles behind to guard those things. And I," the hyena's eyes followed the jackal's head as he did a small flip back flip, landing almost in the exact spot he started from, "can get past all that."

"Oh." Flint said quietly as the jackal sat down beside him on the bed. Will was panting slightly now, and he took a large drink of water from a canteen. He handed it to Flint, and the hyena drank deeply. When he had finished the water, Flint held the metal container in both paws, turning it over and over nervously. The sheer oddity of the jackal's behavior had calmed him down, but he could feel the sadness creeping back into his chest now that they were just sitting together. The jackal was digging through a large sack, which appeared to be the only gear he had. The sack looked vaguely familiar.

"Will?" Flint said quietly, and the jackal glanced up at him.

"Yes?" he said simply, and Flint was struck by how odd the jackal's muzzle was. Flint had not looked at it up close before, but Will's muzzle was narrow and the way his cheekbones were set made the jackal look like he was always smirking.

"What did I do wrong?" The hyena said quietly, his ears drooping a bit.

"What did Aldain do wrong, you mean?" the jackal said. Will

looked up at Flint, and he was struck by the sheer despair on the boy's face.

"No. What did I do wrong? I don't understand what happened. Why everyone got so mad." Tears began to well up in those big green eyes, and the hyena seemed to be searching the jackal's face for an answer. "Why did Father Tully hit me? What did I do to make Aldain push me away like that?" The hyena began to stumble over his words and he began to cry openly. "Why would he leave me? He said…" Flint's sobs got so loud that he choked slightly, a yip escaping his throat as his cheeks turned into rivers. "He said he loved me."

Will stared at the boy beside him in shock. He was blaming himself for the wolf's rejection. How could Flint believe that, when the wolf was so obviously the one at fault? The jackal watched the boy for a moment, big tears flowing out of his emerald eyes. Then Will realized what Aldain had seen in Flint, what had made the wolf lay with him. Flint was an innocent.

The hyena simply didn't understand what was wrong about his feelings. Flint just wanted the man he loved to hold him, and then everything would be okay. The sincerity in his desire was so simple it pulled at even Will's heart. Flint cared for the wolf so completely that he didn't understand anything else, and wanted nothing more than to undo whatever it was he had done wrong.

That kind of unconditional love was something Will had never seen except in a mother, and it made him angry that it had been thrown away so carelessly. Aldain was a fool to give Flint up. Will moved closer to Flint, putting his arms around the small hyena. "Come here, cub, come here," He whispered softly.

Flint's sobs turned back into words for just a few seconds. "I… I'm not a cub. I'm nineteen…" the last word was more of a moan than anything else, and Flint buried his head into the jackal's lap and just cried. Will held him gently, rocking the crying young hyena back and forth without saying anything.

The truth was Will didn't know what to do. Everything about this young man seemed out of place. He'd walked two weeks through the mountains to find Aldain, and yet his fur was clean and soft as if he had just bathed. The hyena's emotions were so raw and powerful. Will had never encountered someone like Flint before. The jackal had never even seen a male cry before, and no female Will been with had ever been so open about her feelings.

After all, Will was the bad boy. He was the one girls went out with when they wanted a thrill. Not the marrying sort of man, as one girl had put it. When they wanted to cry like this, they went back to their boyfriends. The jackal closed his eyes and sighed, hugging the sobbing hyena. If Will ever found someone who loved him like this young man loved Aldain, Will would never have let go of them.

Will tried to think of something to say, but he just couldn't think of a way to explain what had happened. The boy just had no concept of what was wrong with being a tail raiser.

Will put one black paw on Flint's head and began to pet the small mane of dark fur that formed his head fur and ran just down his back. The jackal was surprised again by how soft and smooth the fur was. "Flint, you need to understand some things about the world before you can understand what happened today. Okay?"

Flint turned his head a bit, his big green eyes looking up at the jackal. They caught Will by surprise, the intensity of their gaze making the jackal jump. "Like what?" he sniffed softly, his nose pressed against the jackal's belly.

The jackal suppressed a sigh and tried to force the words out. The boy looked much too cute and vulnerable for Will to be cruel about this, even with tears streaked down Flint's face. "You didn't do anything wrong Flint. This isn't your fault, okay?" Will drug his claws through the boy's head fur, trying to comfort him.

The boy's chest rumbled just a bit, and he stopped crying. "How is it not my fault?" Flint turned over slowly to lie on his back. Will bit his lip as the hyena's shoulder's rested in his lap, and Flint pressed his muzzle against Will's stomach. It brought the young male much closer to parts of the jackal Will did not want to think about right now. "I… I followed him. Aldain told me to stay in Easthaven, but I had to follow him. Is that what Aldain is mad about?" Flint's ears lifted up, and he looked up hopefully at the jackal. "That I don't have a way to support myself any more? I can get a job here, there must be an inn that needs help…"

The jackal flattened his ears and sighed, his paw coming to rest on Flint's chest. The hyena rested back against the bigger male's lap, his ears drooping a bit. "No Flint, that's not it." The jackal sighed, and cursed his one-time friend. He would make Aldain pay for this. Breaking this poor boy's heart was not something he had signed up for. "Flint, have you ever known a tail raiser before Aldain?"

Flint shook his head a bit, his tears stopping for the time being. "No, is that some type of knight?"

The jackal laughed a bit, his ears twisting forward as he looked up at the ceiling. This time he cursed the Goddess, because this had to be some kind of trick she was playing on him. Will leaned back a bit, just to get some distance between his muzzle and the hyena's. "No, not usually. A tail raiser is a male who lays with another male, like you did with Aldain."

Flint's ears swiveled backwards, and he squirmed a little as he blushed and looked away from Will. Will tried hard not to find the genuine reaction as cute, but the young man seemed to brim with youthful attractiveness. "Oh, umm… Okay." Flint muttered and put his paws on his chest as he lay on Will's lap, Flint's tail actually curling up between his legs to cover his crotch even though he was wearing pants. It was perhaps the cutest thing Will had ever seen, and it made him grit his teeth so he wouldn't become aroused.

Will shook his head and smiled, petting the hyena's head fur softly with one paw. Flint's head fur was fine and smooth, and the jackal could run his fingers through it easily. It was nice just petting the boy. "You don't know much about the Church of the Prophet, do you Flint?"

The boy shook his head, "No, I never went to service on Sundays. I always had to do the washing."

Will sighed softly, rubbing his face with one paw. "The Church believes that tail raisers are abominations. Their Prophet hunted them down in the old days. He believed them to be devils in disguise. It's all nonsense of course, but they've convinced the King it's true. After they saved his life, he owed them a lot, and so the King has outlawed being a tail raiser. That was why Father Tully attacked you like that, and why Aldain told you to stay in East Haven. Aldain did not want his tryst with you to become public knowledge."

Flint blinked a bit, and Will wasn't sure the boy fully understood. "So, he was trying to protect me?" Will scowled as the boy searched for a way to digest this without shattering the image he had constructed of Aldain.

"Aldain was protecting himself. He didn't want to lose his knighthood." The jackal corrected the hyena, a bit of anger creeping into his voice. "He should never have been with you in the first place. When you and Aldain spent the night together, he broke almost every vow he took as a Knight of the Cross."

Flint began to sniffle again, and his chest trembled slightly with repressed sobs. "But... But Aldain wanted me to be safe. He was going to come back after he had finished his duties. He just wanted me to be safe until then." The boy's words were becoming desperate, and he sat up to look the jackal in the eyes. The boy's tail was suddenly out and wagging as he perked up his ears. The hyena put his paws on Will's chest as he crouched beside the jackal on the bed, literally in the begging position, "Aldain did this because he didn't want me to get hurt." The hyena's eyes pleaded desperately with the jackal. "Right?"

The jackal petted Flint's head softly, and he looked right into the boy's eyes. "He was never coming back, Flint. A knight serves the Prophet until he dies." William Jacks felt like the most horrible, cruel, jackal in the world as he watched Flint's heart break.

Flint's jaw began to tremble, and his small black nose twitched like he was about to sneeze. The hyena's small round ears turned backwards, and the boy's eyes filled up with tears again. The boy's chest heaved and his paws clenched and unclenched, gripping the jackal's shirt tightly. Flint tucked his tail so far between his legs it wrapped around the front, concealing his crotch again as the boy fought back the tears. Will put his arms around the young man, cuddling him gently. The hyena's muzzle pressed against Will's neck and the jackal sighed softly, hating himself and Aldain completely. Then it was like the levees broke and all of Flint's emotions came tumbling out. Will closed his eyes as the boy howled into his shoulder, and he hugged Flint tight as the boy broke.

"Hush, hush... It's going to be okay." The jackal whispered and Flint slid his arms around Will's neck. Will gasped a little at the force of the boy's hug, and he hugged Flint back just as tightly. "It'll be all right," the jackal muttered, and they held each other as Flint cried for a long time. The jackal's ears pressed against his head, and he rubbed his muzzle against the boy's face.

It hurt just hearing Flint cry. It was the most soulful, true emotion the jackal had ever heard but Will was sure telling him was the right thing to do. Aldain was not coming back for him, especially not now. The boy needed to get over him, but that did not make the jackal feel any better about what he had done.

It was so strange. Will had not felt this bad about hurting someone in a long time. Will had stolen things all his life. He'd lied to more people than he could possibly remember, and even killed them when he had to. Sometimes more than he had too. Will's life had always been hard. He was not a noble like Trenton or a knight living some grand crusade. The jackal was a thief because he needed to eat, and in the process he had stolen, lied, and cheated his way across half the continent to make it to this tiny inn. He'd destroyed people's lives because it was easier than doing real work.

Yet somehow holding this crying young male made him feel more guilt than anything else he'd ever done. It made his heart ache to hear Flint sob into the fur on his shoulder. Maybe it was because the cub was so naïve. Maybe it was the hyena's eyes. Will had no idea what rock the boy had been living under, but he was so innocent. It shocked the jackal because he had never met someone truly innocent before. Will narrowed his eyes, his paw

116

petting the hyena's short mane. Maybe if he could make Flint smile again then things would be okay.

Flint sniffled, rubbing a paw across his muzzle as Will pushed him back a little bit. "Come on now," the jackal said evenly. "There's no reason for all this. You can always find someone else who loves you…"

"No, no I can't," Flint sniffed, rubbing the end of his nose with the back of his paw. "How could anyone love me, after what I did to Aldain? He was so kind to me, so gentle, and I ruined his life!" The hyena's eyes pleaded with the jackal, and Will did the only thing he could think of doing. He kissed the boy.

It was a short and awkward kiss, with a little too much tongue on the jackal's part, but it got the point across. "Stop it." The jackal growled as he stared into the suddenly quiet boy's eyes. "Just stop it. You cannot be with him, but you can still make a life for yourself. Okay?" The jackal rubbed Flint's face, holding one ear between his dexterous fingers.

Flint blinked, shocked that the jackal had kissed him and even more surprised by the intense, determined look on Will's face. "Okay." The hyena breathed slowly, and all the nervous despair seemed to melt away.

Will leaned forward and rubbed his muzzle against the hyena's face gently. "You did nothing wrong Flint, Aldain did. You're going to be okay. You can start a new life somewhere else. I promise Trenton and I will help you. Okay?" the jackal said with a slight smile.

Flint nodded slightly, and thought about it. The jackal was right of course. He could start over. Even if he never saw Aldain again, as much as that would hurt, finding a new life had to be better than what he had back in East Haven with Tongish and his spoiled daughter.

Besides, Will was being really kind. The jackal had saved him from Father Tully after all, and maybe there was still hope of Aldain changing his mind. Flint felt the corners of his muzzle creeping up into a smile at that thought. If he tried hard enough he might be able to change how things had turned out. The hyena clung to that thread of hope like a lifeline. "Okay…" Flint said quietly, smiling slightly at the jackal. For the first time since waking up in this strange room he didn't feel like crying.

"Okay then." The jackal ran a paw through Flint's head fur and stood up. "Now, you need to eat. I'll get you some food and we can sleep. The bed's big enough for two, and I have an extra blanket you can use." The jackal's paw inspected the lump on Flint's head, and the spot still felt tender to the hyena. "If your head is still hurting in the morning then I'll take you to a healer again, all right?" Flint nodded as Will went down stairs to get some food.

The hyena sat on the edge of the bed, his paws swinging back and forth in the air as he looked out the window. He could see the castle lights from here, and he knew somewhere inside was his knight. Despite what Will had said, Flint would have given anything to be with him at that moment.

~: :~

Aldain would have also given anything to be in that little inn room with Flint. Instead the wolf was kneeling in the massive council chamber at the castle, the inner most sanctum of the Prophet's church in Newcastle. The wolf's tail twitched, and he felt more nervous than he had in a long time. Not since his final initiation ceremony had so many stern-looking priests surrounded him, and they all wore dark expressions tonight.

Father Tully was so enraged by what had happened that he had sought to convene the council immediately. The problem was, most of the local high priests lived outside the castle in what Aldain considered rather lavish villas or the their own personal temples in the surrounding cities. The Prophet's laws dictated the way a Knight could stand trial, and so Tully and Aldain were forced to wait for enough senior priests to gather. Aldain had spent most of the day kneeling in the center of the temple's main prayer circle, as Father Tully waited along side him.

The otter had been pacing back and forth around the edge of the circle for hours now, alternating between lecturing Aldain and stalking in silence. The sound of the priest's sandals slapping against his webbed feet and the stone floor had become maddening as the sunlight diminished and the number of attending priests grew steadily. It was like the otter had become a vulture, circling some dying beast. In a way, Aldain supposed he was.

Aldain sighed a little, wishing he could at least stand for this part of the trial. Underneath him, the floor was a tiled mosaic of the Prophet's Cross. It had always impressed the wolf when he came to the council chambers before, but now all it did was hurt his knees.

As he knelt before the gathering council, Aldain wondered what he was going to say in his defense. There was no way the wolf could argue his way out of this. He had admitted the truth right in front of the otter, in front of entire crowd. It was possible Tully had even been using his magic to read him at the time, which meant the otter knew it was the truth for sure. Aldain knew certain priests of the Prophet had the gift of true sight and could tell when someone is lying to them. It was not nearly as reliable as a Knight's ability to sense the presence of evil, but it was worth more than gold in the council's eyes. Father Tully might have sensed his sins as clearly as Aldain had sensed the walking dead back in East Haven.

Aldain could not help smiling at that horrible irony. If he had not become a knight when his father died, then there would have been no one to stop him from staying with Flint. They would have to leave the kingdom to be truly safe, but it would have worked. Aldain could have been happy with the small hyena. He would not be here now, facing charges for following his own instincts. He would be in bed with Flint instead, making love to the young hyena as much as he wanted too.

Yet if he had never become a Knight of the Cross then Flint would have died in that little back alleyway. Instead of being saved at the last moment, the hyena would have been tore apart by the evil Aldain had sworn to destroy. The wolf hung his head, as the council listened to Father Tully's testimony. It was a sad joke for the world to play on him, that what kept them apart now was what had kept Flint alive then.

Aldain was so lost in though by this point, he almost missed the sound of hooves echoing across the tile floor. The wolf's ears perked up just as the chair in the center of the table was pulled back, and the sixth priest, who would serve as the judge, joined the council. The noble looking horse looked right at Aldain, and the wolf felt a chill run down his spine as he met the gaze of Argo Steadfast.

Aldain had known Argo his entire life and took no comfort in having the horse decide his fate. The horse had been one of his father's closest friends and adventuring companions. Argo was a Knight of the Cross as well as an ordained priest, one of the few who held both positions in the Church. He had not always been a follower of the Prophet, but a convert of Aldain's father. Argo was hard and strict, and Aldain's father had treated him like an adopted son. Aldain did not fondly remember the times the horse had wintered at the family estate.

The horse had become worse after Aldain's father had passed away. Argo had inherited the old wolf's sword, and Aldain knew the horse was trying to honor the legacy of Aldain's father even more then he was. In the last five years, Argo had risen quickly to command the Order as the Cardinal of Steel, the highest rank a Knight could possibly achieve. If Argo was here, then something was going on that Aldain did not yet understand, but there was no way the horse's presence could be a good sign.

As he stared at Argo, Father Tully passed in between them on his circuit around the prayer circle surrounding Aldain. As the otter passed by, Aldain's eyes caught sight of a small pin on the priest's neck. Aldain's chest tightened in fear as he recognized the symbol of the Inquisitors pinned to Tully's collar. It had never been there before.

Unfortunately, Aldain had little time to ponder the significance of that because the last priest had arrived, and Aldain could not help smiling a little bit when he saw who it was.

With the clatter of something falling down outside, a dark brown tabby cat named Father Thomas swept his way into the room. He wore a dirty brown robe tided closed with a simple rope cord, and he looked as if he had been running a good distance not long ago. "I'm terribly sorry for the delay," the disheveled tabby muttered as he straightened his robe and draped his sash of office that marked him as a priest around his shoulders. Aldain suspected the tabby cat had been forced to search for it before leaving his tiny parish on the outskirts of the city.

Thomas was a soft-spoken tabby cat who Aldain knew well. In fact, until he had been promoted a few months ago, the cat had traveled with Aldain on the occasions when the party felt having a full priest with them would be an asset. Thomas's promotion to full priest had prevented him from going this time, and as Father Tully sat down at the table, Aldain wondered just how much of a coincidence that was.

The cat continued to excuse himself as he made his way to his seat as several of the other priests rolled their eyes. "I was marrying a couple all the way out in Asheville when the runner came for me. I'm sorry if I delayed us, oh!" The tabby jumped a little when he looked up from his seat at the council table and saw Aldain kneeling there. "Well hello Aldain, I did not realize you had returned already. Did your journey go well?" The tabby's voice was as bright and cheerful as Aldain remembered it to be, but it did not brighten the mood of the priests around him.

"No, it did not." Father Tully snapped. The otter did not look at all pleased by Father Thomas's appearance. The otter took one more look at the slightly shabbily dressed tabby and snorted through his thick whiskers. He carefully averted his eyes to the book in front of him, as if he were casually searching for a passage of text as he said, "And it would do you well not to remember not to speak on such familiar terms with a prisoner in future proceedings Father Thomas. I know you are new to this process, but a level of distance must be maintained," the otter muttered as he sat down.

Aldain felt a pang of sadness as Father Thomas's tail fluffed out and he stared at him. "Prisoner?" the tabby muttered in disbelief, "What in the world could you mean Tully? Argo, Aldain is one of your finest knights."

"Was," the horse sitting in the middle of the table muttered darkly, "He was a fine knight. It is the purpose of this council to see if his still maintains that position." Argo said the words as if they were entirely normal, but Aldain could sense something dark clouded the horse's mood.

Thomas looked like he was about to stutter some sort of retort, but the older priest who was sitting beside him shook his head in warning to the cat and Thomas fell silent. Aldain was silently glad the priest had shushed his friend. Now was not the time to defend him. There were protocols to follow in such a trial like this, and with Argo leading the council tonight Aldain hoped that Thomas would follow them.

"Now that a suitable council has been gathered," Argo said in a clipped tone of voice, "I call upon Father Tully to address the council as to why we are brought here tonight."

Tully stood up at his chair, nodded once to the horse, and said in loud voice, "I have called this council to discuss a grave situation. I have come to council to call for the excommunication and death of the knight know as Aldain Sine'Dane for crimes against the Prophet."

Aldain had not known true fear in a long time, but as the otter said those words it clutched at the wolf's heart like a vise. Death was not the punishment for sodomy, certainly not the first offence. Something was terribly, terribly wrong. He would have protested had someone else not beaten him to it.

"What?" Father Thomas yelped as he jumped to his feet. The poor cat was so startled the word came out as a yowl. "You must be joking Father Tully! This man, this man is an Knight of the Cross!" The tabby was panting as he stared across the council table at Tully, and Aldain noticed the cat's claws had dug into the tabletop.

"Be quiet, Father Thomas," Argo said in a hushed tone. "If you wish to defend the accused you will be allowed to in due course." The horse looked back at Tully, who nodded slightly in respect to the horse, "Continue."

"As I was saying." Father Tully stepped away from his chair and clasped his paws behind his back. It was the classic pose of a priest about to make a sermon, and the ease with which Father Tully spoke frightened Aldain.

"Some of you are aware of my personal feelings about the Order of the Cross. I have expressed them repeatedly in council chambers, but I know some of you," the otter glanced at Thomas and Aldain a moment longer than the other priests, "are not familiar with my teachings on this matter. So I shall instruct you in what I believe is a growing problem in the church. A tarnishing of the Prophet's name that must be wiped clean before it becomes a permanent stain."

The otter began to pace around the prayer circle, using his staff and sandals to heighten the effect of his words, the footfalls and loud cracks setting a jarring counter point to his soft words. "It is my belief that the most faithful of our flock are allowed to much leeway in their dealings with outsiders. They have become susceptible to outside influences, and thus corrupted." The otter turned to face Aldain, staring at the wolf from his right side. "I believe that men like Aldain are too great an asset to our church. They should not be allowed to roam unprotected in a world filled with so many corruptive influences."

Father Thomas practically laughed as the otter delivered his speech like he was giving a Sunday morning sermon full of fire and brimstone. "You must be joking, Father. The Knights of the Cross are the people most equipped to deal with temptation. They are the most resistant to it. How can you possibly be calling for the death sentence to be applied to one of our most pious servants?"

"I have called for death because it is the moral thing to do, as laid out by the Prophet in the old days." The otter's face showed no signs of compassion. "The High Priest has called an Inquisition to rid the land of evil, and I do not feel that the Knights are incorruptible. I feel that the Knights of the Cross are just as susceptible as everyone else is to the darker urges of life. They are allowed too much freedom of movement and association, and it makes them more likely to be corrupted." The otter turned to face Argo, tactfully avoiding Aldain and Thomas's gaze. "Tonight I bring you proof of that. The knight Aldain proves my claims to be true. He has become corrupted in his dealings with lay people and the unfaithful, and I demand you act to correct the problems in your Order."

Aldain listened to Father Tully's words with a deep sense of dread. The wolf had been tricked somehow. The otter was using him to further his own goals within the church. It was a power play of some kind. Aldain's stomach turned to ice. Father Tully was on a mission from the cardinal of the Inquisitor against the Order. It was a month long journey to Newcastle from the High Citadel where Argo lived, the only way he could be here tonight was if Tully sent for him before they even left to destroy the Mak'tchen temple. That was the only reason why Argo would have come here to Newcastle. Now the wolf was facing a sentence far more severe than he had expected too, and his actions might damage the Order in a way he had never imagined.

The knight looked around the council chamber slowly. Aldain kept his head bowed low and his ears folded back in shame as he carefully eyed the various high priests. Most of them were nodding slowly, and several of them had the pins marking them as inquisitors. Only Father Thomas seemed upset by the otter's words.

The tabby cat struggled a bit as he stood up to speak. Aldain looked his old friend up and down for a moment, and he knew he was going to lose his case. The cat's mouth opened, closed, and opened again in exasperation. "I cannot believe what I am hearing."

"Perhaps," the Argo said quietly, "you would believe if you attended council more regularly, Father Thomas."

"Yes," the cat said quietly, "It seems I have been tending to the wrong flock. I had taken my advancement with a bit of reluctance, and remained at my parish out of a desire to help my followers. It seems I could have been doing them a much greater service here."

"I do not see how," Father Tully snapped, "when you so obviously missed the epidemic when it was under your nose for so long." The otter stamped across the room to Father Thomas, "Tell me, how did you miss Aldain's tendencies? How did you miss the signs that he was a sodomite? A tail raiser unfit to wear the cross around his neck, much less wield a sword in service of the Prophet?"

"A sodomite?" the tabby blinked in surprised and glanced at Aldain. "That is the charge?" Father Thomas met Aldain's eyes for a moment, and the wolf looked at his old friend reluctantly before casting his eyes to the ground in admission of shame. The cat's brow furrowed, the brown and black lines creasing across his slender muzzle. "Oh Aldain," Father Thomas whispered, and Aldain felt truly sorry for his friend. The wolf hung his head as the tabby slumped into his chair, completely disheartened.

"Yes, Aldain." The otter turned on the wolf having put down the only opposition he was facing. "Tell us what happened since I came to travel with your merry band of heathens and infidels. Let everyone know what I have only alluded to until now. I would not want your former friend to think you went to the gallows without cause." Father Thomas flinched slightly, and Aldain glared at the otter with contempt.

"Very well." The wolf growled. He stood up slowly, his knees aching slightly. "As you know, at the beginning of the year the Knight's council gave me the task of defending the area around Newcastle. The Order is mighty, but few, and so we have long depending on our ability to rally people to the Prophet's cause. To find people who can help us in our goals."

"People like the Goddess worshiper and admitted thief William?" Father Tully spat dramatically, "Or that savage of a bear Tigh. Perhaps we can talk about you tail-raising noble friend? What was his name?" The otter's voice rose slightly at the end of his interruption, mocking the knight. Aldain narrowed his eyes, and he felt his hackles rising. The otter was baiting him at this point, trying to get him to explode in anger and prove his point. The wolf was not going to give the otter the satisfaction.

"Yes, like Lord Trenton, who is not a tail-raiser. He is a wizard, and that makes him extremely helpful in combating the Prophet's foes such as the Mak'tchen cultists we faced." The wolf straightened his back, letting his hackles settle. "And Will is not a thief any longer. I have reformed him, and given time he could be persuaded to become a faithful follower of the Prophet instead of a Goddess worshiper. That is the reason knight's journey with heathen masses," the wolf said evenly, his eyes meeting Argo's, "The Order behaves in this fashion to save souls. My presence has often prevented my fellow adventures from turning to the easy and corrupting paths that exist in their lifestyles. I have brought them to the path that the Prophet wills for us to travel, just as my father once did."

"But you have turned to those corrupting paths yourself, haven't you?" Tully shot back. "You have become a tail-raiser, and it is well known to the faithful that adventurers are more likely to be sodomites."

"That is not true." Aldain snapped, and he regretted the anger in his voice when he saw the otter raise an eyebrow.

"Oh really? Is it not true that one week ago you bedded the stable boy of the inn we stayed at?" Tully said triumphantly, "That you consorted with him, in the most disgustingly carnal ways possible? Or perhaps you lied today when you practically shouted that to a crowed street?" The otter's words dripped with sarcasm, and Aldain knew there was no way out of this.

Aldain could feel every eye in the room on him. This was the moment of truth, and it did not matter if he confessed or lied now, he was signing his death warrant.

"That is true." Aldain whispered quietly.

"Then you have your answer your Grace." Father Tully turned to the horse leading the council, and Aldain lowered his eyes when he saw the disgust on the horse's face. "I have brought you proof of the Order's corruption."

Argo's voice wavered, "Thank you, Father Tully. You have been most helpful, and that will be noted in my reports." The horse looked down at the huge, intricately tiled prayer circle Aldain stood in. For a moment he seemed to be in prayer, asking the Prophet for guidance. The horse's voice was strong now, and filled with determination. "If there is no further business, I call for a judgment on the matter at hand, and..."

"Wait, wait!" Father Thomas shouted, and the horse stopped. Several of the priests in the room raised an eyebrow in annoyance at the tabby cat, but Argo seemed almost relieved to be interrupted. Father Thomas leapt to his feet again, and Aldain recognized the wild look in his eyes from his days of adventuring with the old tabby cat. It meant the cat had an idea, and it was probably completely crazy. This was going to get interesting. Thomas jabbed a finger at Aldain, and almost laughed with glee as he said, "You were fighting against a Mak'tchen cult, weren't you Aldain?"

The wolf looked over at his old friend, and the tabby cat's eyes were wide as saucers. "Yes, we were." He said evenly, and he knew several of the other priests were reading his words for lies.

"I don't see how that makes any difference," Father Tully muttered, "It does not change what he did."

"Yes, yes it does!" Thomas almost screeched at the otter, and his muzzle broke into a fierce grin as he came around the table to face Argo. The tabby's tail lashed back and forth, like he was stalking something. "Your grace, I have traveled with Aldain and his party for a much longer time than Father Tully. What the good knight says is true. He has been a good influence on his fellows and they have not influenced him in return."

"I know he is your friend," Father Tully said, "but you should not defend an admitted..."

The cat drew himself up to his full height, which did not

amount to much, but it made him eye level with the short otter. "I have never seen even a hint of corruption in Aldain, and never suspected for a moment that he might raise his tail to a man." Several of the priests sneered at the way the tabby described that, but Aldain knew Father Thomas was much more in tune with the common people than any of the other high priests in the room.

"Your confidence in him is admirable, Father," Argo said quietly, "but it does not change the crimes he has admitted to."

Aldain wondered what was going on inside the tabby's head as he continued to smile happily. "Yes, he admitted to sinning after he battled the Mak'tchen." The tabby glanced back and forth at the assembled priests, who did not seem to understand. "Don't you see? They must have enchanted him during the combat, and caused him to become a tail raiser."

Father Tully and several of the other priests scoffed loudly. "You cannot seriously want us to believe this nonsense," the otter muttered, turning his back on the tabby.

"It is not nonsense Tully. I have seen it with my own eyes. That is how they gather worshipers and spread dissent in a community. A Mak'tchen cultist can corrupt even the staunchest defender of justice." The tabby cat stared at the cardinal in front of him, letting the horse easily read his words for lies. "I have seen a mother eat her own children and a father slay his whole farm, family and livestock, in a single night. One Mak'tchen priest even convinced a mayor near Feydowns to poison a well."

Father Thomas turned to the assembled priests in turned as he spoke, and the tabby's words seemed to have some effect. "Every time, the corruption was subtle at first and grew over time until they could no longer be concealed. Their actions were unconscionable, yes, but they had been enchanted. That must be what happened here, we have simply discovered it early." Thomas turned to Argo, and looked the horse in the eye. "The church does not condemn those who have been unwittingly corrupted to death." Several of the other priests looked at Thomas with open anger, but the horse seemed to weigh his words carefully.

"This is true." Argo muttered quietly, "We do not condemn a man to die for sins other make him do."

Father Tully banged his staff on the floor, and the graying otter's anger was nearly boiling over. "You cannot believe this rubbish your Grace. Aldain must stand as accused, as a sodomite, or there will be no way to even bring charges against the boy."

Aldain felt a chill run up his spine. "Please my lord," the wolf said quickly, "The boy was not at fault, I was. He wanted nothing to do with me."

"Then why did the boy follow you?" the otter countered.

"You said it yourself, he is a boy. A cub that does not know any better." Father Thomas said evenly. "If a Knight of the Cross told him it was acceptable, he would believe it. Especially if he was one of the faithful." Aldain met Father Thomas's gaze for a moment, and he knew that the tabby was covering for him. Thomas did not believe that Aldain had been corrupted; he knew that Aldain had done this of his own free will. He just did not want to see the wolf die.

"I agree. The young are much more easily influenced than others." Cardinal Argo said loudly, signally the end of the debate. "You have not proven your claims Father Tully, but I am glad you have brought this situation to my attention." The otter cursed and turned his back on the horse, stalking to his seat without another word.

Argo continued, "We must be sure that Aldain is not going to continue his spiral into darkness because of what the Mak'tchen priests have done." The horse's gaze shifted to Aldain, and he watched the wolf carefully. "Will you submit to a cleansing by the priesthood to prove your innocence in this matter?"

The wolf drew in a slow breath as every eye turned towards him. Aldain knew what such a cleansing would mean, what it would do to him, but he did not see any other alternative. The Inquisition was using him against the Order of the Cross. His friends would be hunted down and killed if he refused. Aldain's heart ached as he thought about Flint being chased down by his own church. The wolf would do anything to prevent that from happening.

Aldain looked up at the council with no regrets. "Yes my Lord, I will."

~: :~

Flint lay in the bed beside Will, staring silently at the wall. It was so dark he could barely see the wood grain, even though he was so close to the wall that he could smell the ancient wood clearly. Flint sighed a little, trying to force his mind into silence and then sleep, but he could not stop thinking.

Everything was just too similar to his night with Aldain, and yet the differences nagged and pulled at Flint's thoughts. His belly was full of the same kind of meaty, thick stew Tongish always served. Flint had happily eaten every bite of the bowl Will had brought him. The food had settled his stomach after his long trek with no food, and calmed him down considerably. It was nothing like the night the hyena had spent with Aldain, when he had eaten nothing at all, and been so nervous he probably would not have been able to eat anything.

Flint shifted his legs a bit, careful not to brush against Will's long legs. He was sleeping beside a male again, in a real bed for the first time since he had slept beside Aldain. Yet the jackal was under a different blanket, not hugging him tenderly as Aldain had done. The way the bed curved under Will's weight and the heat from his body reminded Flint of the wolf's embrace, but the hyena suspected Will would not touch him, even accidentally, during the night.

The desire to be touched, even just once, pulled at Flint's heart until his chest ached. Aldain had made him feel so special, and Flint wanted to feel that way again so badly it hurt Flint just to think about it. Try as he might he could not help crying just a little. The hyena hid his head under the pillow Will had given him, hoping his tears would not wake the jackal up.

Will opened his eyes when his sharp ears detected Flint's muffled sobs. The boy was trying hard to conceal them, but to someone like Will they echoed in the night. The jackal reached a paw out, crossing from under his blanket to Flint's. The hyena choked a bit and jumped slightly as Will touched his shoulder gently. The boy pulled his head out from under the pillow and looked back at Will. Flint's eyes gleamed in the low moonlight, and Will rubbed his paw across Flint's shoulder. Flint moved backward towards the jackal, and Will slid had his arm under Flint's head like a pillow. "What's wrong?" the jackal whispered as he held the hyena gently.

Flint gave a soft sigh once Will's arms were around him. "Nothing…" Flint, muttered, his tears drying up much quicker this time than they had before. They lay together like that for a while, and Will noticed how nice it was holding Flint like this. It made Will feel strangely content to cradle the hyena's muzzle in one arm while the jackal's other encircled his chest. The jackal frowned a little as the young man shifted his lower body, bringing the hyena's rump up against Will's midsection. The jackal licked his lips a bit, as the comfortable feeling fled and was replaced by a nervous tension. Will could feel the hyena's bushy tail rubbing against the inside of his leg, and it made the jackal's arms tremble. Will tried to shift his hips back away from the young man, but Flint's body followed, and before Will knew what was happening, he was spooning the young hyena under a single blanket.

The jackal started to panic just a little as the hyena's tail wagged a little and began to brush against his crotch. Flint's rump was pressed right up against his crotch, and Will could feel the hyena's trapped tail rubbing against the fabric covering his sheath. The jackal bit his lip and tried not to think about the wagging tail and what lay beneath it, but his body quickly betrayed him. When Flint turned to look back at him, Will had to suppress a whine as the tip of the jackal's erection began to press under Flint's tail.

"Will?" Flint whispered silently. That softly spoken word was an almost desperate request. The jackal knew what the boy wanted, and it sacred Will that he wanted it too. Almost on instinct, the jackal's hips moved slightly and pressed forward against the hyena. The jackal let out a soft whine, but he could tell Flint was already moving in response to his unspoken answer. The hyena's body shifted slightly in his arms as the hyena fumbled to remove his pants. Will shuddered, the warm blanket surrounding them suddenly not enough as he felt the hyena's leather britches slide down his legs and off his body. Will felt the soft, almost downy fur of the hyena's bare butt rubbing against his pants as the hyena pulled off his shirt. Will held his breath, trying not to pant as the hyena's naked body came to rest against him. The only thing left on Flint was the gold medallion around his neck, and only the jackal's thin clothing separated them as Will hugged Flint tightly. A soft moan of desire slipped out of Will's muzzle as he clutched the naked young male to his chest. Flint looked back at him again with eager green eyes and a slight smile. "Please?" the hyena whispered, and the jackal could not resist.

The jackal's black paws, usually dexterous and steady, fumbled with the drawstring of his shorts. Will pushed his pants down around his knees and then kicked them away, panting as he tore off his shirt. The jackal rubbed his paws across the hyena's bare back; his fingers sliding through the short soft fur and pressing at the black spots of the hyena's coat. Will brushed his muzzle against Flint's neck as he lay on his side behind Flint, the jackal's naked body rubbing slowly against the hyena's backside. Without a sound, Flint's tail flicked to the side and Will's erection slide up between the young male's cheeks, the tip pressing eagerly against the hyena's waiting tail hole.

Will whined gently again as he came so close to mounting the hyena it almost hurt. Flint smiled slightly as he exposed himself to the jackal's probing shaft, and the hyena made the cutest murring sound as Will nibbled on the back of his neck possessively. Will was panting hard now, his paws clutching the boy's body desperately. He wanted nothing more then to push inside the hyena right to the hilt, but Will knew the boy would need some sort of lubrication. Will rolled away for a moment, and leaned over to grab a jar of oil from his bag. The jackal usually used it grease squeaky hinges, which made entering a house in the dead of night much easier, and he suspected it would make entering the hyena much easier too.

Will fumbled with the jar as he applied the oil to his shaft. Flint lay very still beside the jackal, his ears turned back towards Will as he stared at the wall. The jackal moved behind the young male again, and Will's slick shaft pressed against the hyena's back door. The jackal slide his arms around Flint from behind, and the hyena's leg lifted up, opening himself up to the jackal. Will's paw took hold of Flint's, and he pressed up close to the hyena.

Flint's body tensed as the jackal's penis entered him and the hyena's fingers laced with Will's, squeezing the jackal's paw tightly as their bodies joined. Once he was all the way in, Will took the hyena's other paw in his own and rolled on top of Flint. The blanket slid to the floor, and the males lay joined on the bed together, the jackal's front pressed against the hyena's back, and Will's crotch pressed firmly against Flint's backside. Flint was whimpering softly, a slightly pained sound as the jackal's shaft entered him completely, but he was smiling too. The taller jackal smiled back at him, Will's muzzle over the hyena's shoulder so it was even with Flint's as he began to mate the young male.

Flint began to whimper and moan as Will thrust inside him, his paws clutching at the bed sheets as they mated. Will tried to think about what he was doing, but he could not focus as he mounted Flint. Their bodies pressed together as Will's hips moved, the jackal's shaft sliding in and out of the hyena's snug rear. Will moaned into the fur of Flint's neck, his eyes closing as the pleasure began to build. Breeding the young male was turning out to be very different than the women he had been with in the past. Flint's butt was only a little tighter than most girls he had taken before, and that snugness felt good, but it hardly

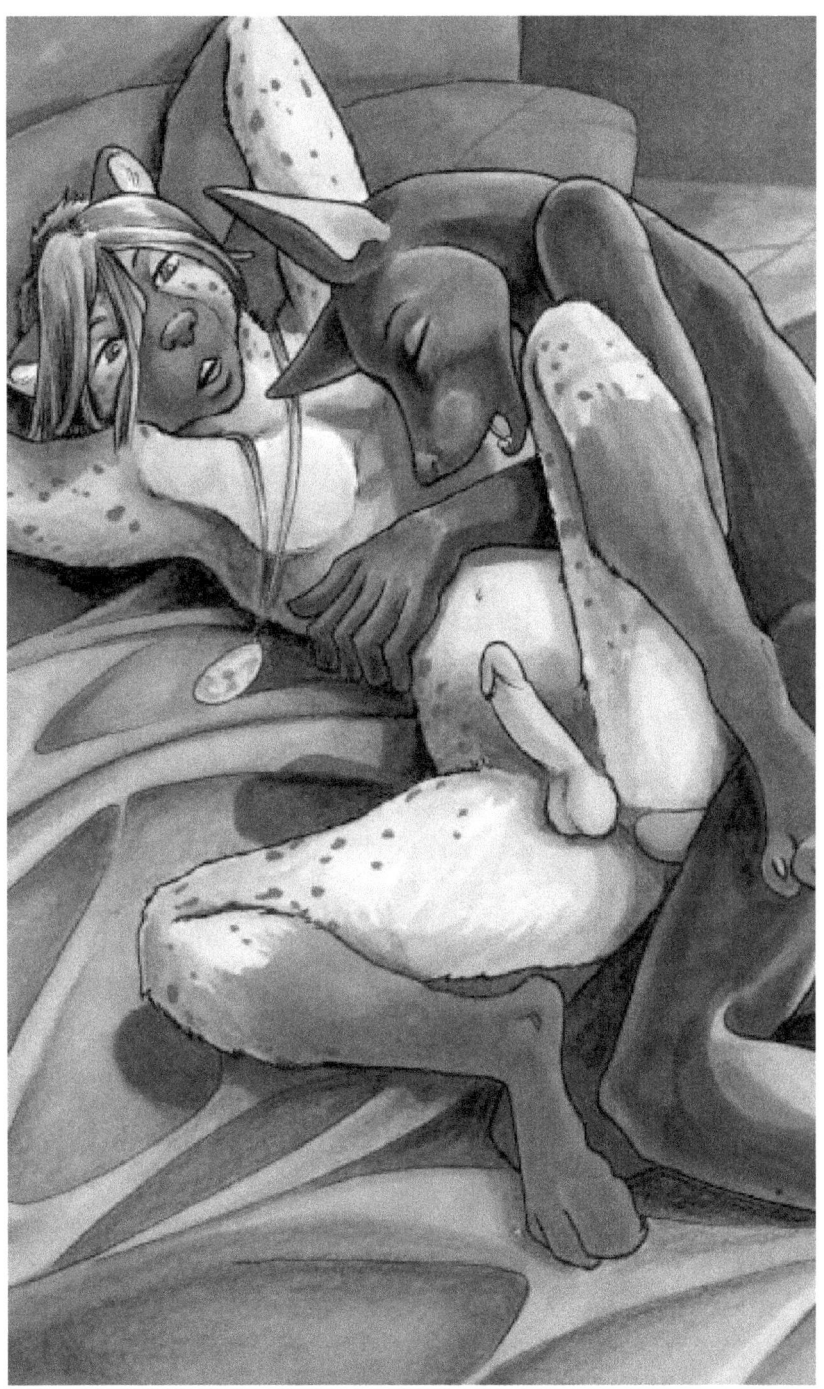

explained the difference Will felt.

It had to be the way Flint reacted to being fucked. The young hyena yipped and squirmed underneath Will. Flint's body was shaking as he pushed himself back against Will's thrusts in a way no woman had ever done. Most of the girls Will had been with in the past had merely laid there without participating much at all as he thrust into them. With Flint it was very different. Each thrust of the jackal's hips made the boy's body jump and shake. The hyena's soft paws clutched at the jackal's paw as his rump wiggled and pressed back against the jackal's hips, and the sounds Flint was making only made the jackal want more.

It was easy to tell how much Flint wanted this. Flint wanted the jackal's cock so badly he was practically impaling himself on Will. That made Will's hips move a faster, and the jackal moaned in pleasure as he took the hyena's tight rear. The jackal pressed his muzzle against Flint's, his body shaking and tensing as he thrust down into Flint. It was so strange breeding the young male. Will had thought it would feel wrong and disgusting. Instead, pushing inside Flint felt so right the jackal could not imagine sex being any other way.

Will slipped his arms around Flint's chest and hugged him tightly as he held the small hyena down. Will was shaking all over now. It felt like his body was on fire as the ecstasy coursed through the jackal. Will clutched Flint's paws, their fingers laced tightly together as Will bred the hyena from behind.

The jackal could feel his knot growing, bumping against the hyena's tail hole as he got closer and closer. Will whined softly and bit the back of Flint's neck gently, his teeth catching the gold chain around Flint's neck as the jackal's knot swelled and tried to push past Flint's tight ring. Will wanted to tie with they hyena so badly. The jackal's body ached as he made love to Flint desperate to join their bodies together. Will pulled Flint's rear up a little bit and thrust hard, pushing as deeply as he could into the hyena, battering the young male's butt until his knot slipped, agonizingly slowly, into the hyena's tightly clenched tail hole. The warmth of Flint's body wrapped around Will's knot and squeezed, making spots dance across Will's vision. Will let out a low howl as the warmth of the hyena's body wrapped around his knot and squeezed, pulling at the jackal's most sensitive spot. The jackal hugged the young male with all his might, and he could feel Flint's tail doing the same thing to his knot. Will's body trembled with pleasure, his mind reeling from the pleasure as he filled Flint's butt with cum.

Flint gasped right along with Will as the jackal tied him, and not just because the jackal's hug had forced all the air from his lungs. The hyena closed his eyes and smiled, his body tingling as a male joined his body with Flint's once more. The strange, wonderful fullness of being taken returned to Flint, and the hyena basked in that feeling as the jackal on top of him huffed and yipped in pleasure. Will was still making halfhearted thrusts that went nowhere for several minutes, but Flint didn't care. William was inside him, tied with him, and once more a male's shaft was battering the spot inside Flint's butt that made the hyena moan in pleasure. The jackal's thrusts were going nowhere fast, and Flint loved it. Flint began to buck his hips, rubbing his own cock against the bed sheets underneath him. Will was holding his paws so tightly the jackal might never let go, but Flint wanted, needed release while the jackal was still inside him.

Flint had to know if it would be as good as when Aldain had taken him.

Flint grunted and shifted his body underneath Will's. The jackal's weight held him down firmly, pressing him into the bed. That pressed Flint's cock against the sheets, and the hyena barked and whined as he ground himself against the rough cotton. Flint shuddered and his body jerked as the jackal's thick knot pulled at his insides, and Flint could feel the long shaft of the jackal's dick inside him, hard as a rock as it pushed against his insides and battered his pleasure spot. Flint closed his eyes and squeezed down on that shaft, his body shaking as he humped the bed until Flint came with a high pitched bark and low moan.

The two males lay together for a long time in silence, the dead stillness of night enveloping them like the jackal's black body enveloped Flint. Will held Flint tightly, his arms wrapped around the hyena, his fingers laced with Flint's so that the hyena's arms were crossed over his chest underneath Will's arms. Will held Flint like that for a long, long time, straddling his body as they both came down from their climaxes. Eventually, Will stopped panting long enough to force out an exasperated, "Why?"

Flint opened his eyes, and stared back at the jackal. Will stared into those green eyes, and he knew he could never let the hyena go now. Flint's emerald eyes trapped the jackal's heart, and Will never wanted to escape. "Because I needed to know." Flint whispered, his voice sounding far away and his eyes taking on a distant quality.

Will just nodded slightly and he collapsed to the side, pulling Flint's body to the side with him. They ended up in the same spooning position they had started off in, and Will pulled a single blanket over both of them. Flint nestled his head back against Will's shoulder, resting his muzzle in the crook of the jackal's elbow and closing his eyes. Will stared at the young man in his arms, a male he had his cock buried balls-deep inside. Will watched as Flint drifted to sleep, and the jackal wondered what exactly had just happened between them.

Will could not sleep. While Flint's eyes closed and his breathing slowed, the jackal's heart beat a mile a minute and his mind raced. How stupid could he be, to bed the hyena so quickly? What had made him say yes? Will's chest tightened as his shaft grew soft and slipped out of Flint. Part of the jackal wanted nothing more then to get hard again and tie himself inside the boy once more. It would feel wonderful. He knew it would. It would be right. This was where Will belonged. Will blinked, shaking the feeling away.

The thief had to use all his skill to slip his arm out from under Flint's head without waking him. Carefully the jackal slipped out of the room, a silent shadow in the night. Will felt a real pang of guilt about leaving the sleeping hyena by himself, but he had to get away from the charming young man at least for a little while. It felt like his head was filled with cotton when he looked at Flint, and he needed to think clearly for a while.

Will made his way down to the common room, and he was not surprised to find the bull barkeep was still awake. A place like this often stayed open all night long. Will blinked, rubbing the side of his head as his thoughts cleared. The jackal caught a whiff of the sex lingering on his paw, and he realized what he had just done. Screw thinking clearly. Will sat down at the bar, bought a bottle of the strongest booze the bovine had, and began to drink.

～ ：～

By the time someone else sat down beside Will, he was half-way though the second bottle of liquor. The jackal's head was flat on the counter, his eyes were closed, and Will was well on his way to a bad hangover. Will's ears swiveled towards the person, and when he caught the familiar, musky scent of fox Will opened his eyes. Trenton looked down at the wasted jackal with a big grin, his muzzle resting on a paw that was propped up on the counter top.

"Having a little celebratory drink are we?" Will could just see the fox's tail as it flicked back and forth behind him. Trenton sat there looking smug in his fancy clothes, and the fox's smile was all the proof the jackal needed to be sure that Trenton knew he and Flint had been together.

The jackal pushed himself back up into a sitting position with frown. "Don't start Trenton. I'm not in the mood tonight for your games."

"Oh come now, don't be that way. You have to tell me. Was he any good?" The fox took a small sniff of the liquor bottle and wrinkled his nose before poking the jackal's muzzle playfully. "It's not often you bed a male."

The jackal snapped his jaws at the fox's fingertips and Trenton yipped in fright, but the fox pulled his paw back unharmed because Will missed on purpose. "I do not want to talk about it." The jackal said in a deep growl, and the fox gave him an angry glare. Will poured another glass of liquor, but Trenton grabbed the glass away from the jackal before he could drink it.

"Well too bad Will, because you're going to have to talk about it soon. Flint is going to wake up with the sun. Country folk always do, even after a roll in the hay. You're going to have to be there for him." The jackal sighed in frustration as the fox took the bottle away, sniffing the strong liquor with distaste, "And you had better be sober too."

The jackal growled a bit, but his tail drooped at the fox's words and his ears swiveled backwards. "You think I don't know that? Damn it," the jackal slammed his fist onto the bar, "how could I be so foolish?" The noise woke up a couple of the sleeping drunks and the force of the jackal's blow sent a few mugs clattering to the floor. The bartender did not even flinch; he just picked up the fallen mugs and went back to wiping the bar down. This was not the sort of bar that had breakable mugs.

"Really Trenton, what the hell was I thinking?" The jackal muttered as the fox motioned to the bartender and ordered a much weaker set of drinks for them both. "The boy is crying his eyes out one minute because Aldain is an idiot, and then I go and do the same damn thing he did."

Trenton frowned a bit as Will hunkered down close to the bar again and pressed his ears flat against his head. He had never seen will react this way before. The jackal stared intently at the glass holding his new drink. "Yes well, you didn't mean to bed Flint did you?" Trenton asked.

"No," the jackal muttered, his fingers drumming against the glass in his paws, "Yes. I don't know Trenton. I wanted it pretty badly, but I could have picked a better night to try out your particular sin for the first time."

Trenton's smile widened and the fox's tail flicked back and forth, "You're first time huh?" The fox chuckled a bit, drinking the fruity wine he had ordered. "And I'll agree you could have chosen a better time, but I wouldn't put you in the same class of foolish as Aldain."

The jackal chuckled just a bit, "Yeah, he really screwed that boy up bad."

Trenton's smile diminished a bit, and the red fox's paw rubbed Will's shoulder. Their black fur mingling slightly as the fox scritched the jackal's back fur gently, "He's a Knight of the Cross, Will. They do everything big. Especially screw up." The fox gave a great sigh, and his shoulders sagging as he finished his drink. His previously cheerful voice dropped down low, and he stared into his drink as he muttered. "I can't blame him though. He has never really controlled that part of himself very well."

The jackal snorted slightly. "What is that supposed to mean?"

"Just that," the fox said with a slight shrug, his fancy clothes shifting a little as he adjusted his position on the uncomfortable stool, which was not made for someone to sit properly in. "Aldain has never been able to resist a male who was interested in him. He certainly never turned me down when I put my mind to it." The fox said the words with a smirk, but it was all for show. Will could tell Trenton felt genuinely sorry for the wolf.

"You're joking," Will sat up again with a look of disbelief on his face, "He didn't."

Lord Trenton chuckled. "Oh he most certainly did, and we spent more than just one night together."

The jackal shook his head in disbelief; having never suspected his two friends might be sleeping together. "When?"

"When haven't we? That first trip he was with us coming out of Aberdeen? Aldain nearly fell over from lack of blood when I swished my tail at him that first night."

The fox laughed a little with Will, who was so surprised his mouth was hanging open. "You're kidding? You did it on the first night?" Will muttered, keeping his voice low so no one else would hear.

"The second night, thank you." Trenton said with a grin, "I'm not that easy. Then there was the week we all spent trapped in Irena, put up in the fancy hotel by my father? Oh, and I will never forget the river Isis thanks to him." The fox had a dreamy, far away look on his face as he recounted the times he and Aldain had spent together. They were obviously some of the fox's favorite memories.

The jackal just laughed at how ridiculous it was. Will had never even suspected the wolf and fox had been together. Will had always known about Trenton being a tail raiser, the fox practically shouted the position of his tail from the rooftops. Trenton had actually done so on at least one boisterous evening the jackal could remember, but Aldain being a tail raiser really surprised the jackal. "So what, you two have been doing it for the last three years now?" Trenton nodded slightly, smiling just a bit. "How did you two keep this quiet for so long?"

"I guess we didn't." the fox shrugged, "Father Tully suspected something didn't he? I'm sure Tigh knows. He walked in on us once." The fox chuckled a bit, his muzzle tilting upward as he smiled. "He was not happy about that. I never took him for the possessive type, but that bear was really mad I was sleeping with someone else."

Will almost spit the sweet wine he was drinking out. "Wait, what? You and Tigh?" the jackal cursed a little and grinned at his friend, "Now you're joking with me. Right?"

The fox shook his head, the black tips of his ears flipping back and forth before perking up again as he continued to grin at the jackal. "Oh no, Tigh and I had a thing for nearly a year. He was just quiet about it is all."

"So what, am I the only one you haven't raised that bushy tail for?" The jackal punched Trenton lightly on the shoulder, and the fox just laughed at him.

"Oh please Will. I've flaunted it for you more times than I can remember." The fox pushed the jackal away playfully, his wrist hanging limply as he pointed at Will's chest. "If you had been the least bit interested, you could have had me years ago. Don't blame me just because you missed your chance to catch my fox tail." The fox smirked, sipping his drink and swishing his tail dramatically. "Besides, I heard your first time through this fine establishment's paper thin walls. Sounds like you enjoyed yourself just fine."

Trenton could only tell from the way Will's ears swiveled backwards and his tail drooped a bit, but the jackal was obviously blushing. "Oh Goddess, don't remind me. I can't believe I did that. He just…" the jackal trailed off, staring into his drink in embarrassment.

"He just what?" Trenton prompted, leaning in close to his friend with a mischievous smile that Will returned.

"Flint asked me to," the jackal muttered, spreading his paws helplessly, trying to understand why he had given himself to the hyena so quickly. "He looked me in the eyes and said 'please', and all I could do was say yes," Will muttered in shame.

"Well, that's not all you did." The fox whispered with a smirk, and the jackal rolled his eyes.

"You are a horrible fox, you now that?" Will said angrily, but this time the slight grin on his muzzle genuine.

"Yes well, this horrible fox is going to bed and so should you." Trenton finished his drink and stood up, his paw resting on Will's shoulder. "Flint is going to wake up, and somebody has to be there for him. I cannot bear to hear him sobbing anymore."

The jackal sighed softly, "Well then you had better go back to my room, not yours. I can't go back up there, not yet. Tomorrow is a day of remembrance, and for once I could really use guidance from the Goddess."

The fox sighed is exasperation. "Oh please, that's not what this is about. You want to run off to see your druid friends and ask if being happy with another man is fine with your precious deity."

The jackal shot the fox an angry glare, his eye darting around the room to make sure no one had heard the fox use his deity's name. "And what if I do? Just because you don't believe…"

Trenton waved him silent with one paw. "Yes, yes I know all that." The fox tossed his cloak around his shoulder, fastening the brooch with his family crest closed. "But you'll excuse me if I have a low opinion of the various faiths right now. This will make you the second man to run out on that boy today because of their religion."

"At least I'm actually coming back and not just saying I will," Will snapped, glaring daggers at the fox.

"That's true." Trenton sighed, looking down into his drink. "So shall I meet you at the temple then? I'll get Flint some equipment tomorrow and we can leave town from there?"

"What about Tigh?" Will asked as he got up and made his way towards the door. "Where's he gone off to?"

Trenton hopped off the bar stool and followed the jackal to the door. "Oh I almost forgot. That's why I came looking for you in the first place. I did not expect to find you drowning your sorrows down here. I was almost hoping to interrupt some festivities upstairs." The fox flashed Will a grin, and his tail flicked back and forth as they reached the door. "Tigh won't be coming with us this time. I think he found somebody here in Newcastle he wants to stay with for a while."

"You think?" the jackal raised his eyebrows and crossed his arms over his chest, "And what do you mean stay with?"

Lord Trenton's slim red muzzle broke into a huge grin. "Well, he had fresh whip marks, a pair of manacles on his front paws, and the biggest grin I've ever seen on a bear before. So I think going to be busy for a while."

Will held up his paws and said, "Right, I don't want to know. I think I've found out more about the position of everyone's tails tonight than I ever wanted to know. Just," the jackal hesitated, and looked serious for a moment, "Just tell Flint I'll be back soon okay? I want him to understand that I'm not leaving him." The jackal's words had a hard, determined quality to them that made Trenton frown slightly.

Trenton nodded, and Will slipped out of the bar and into the night. The fox sighed and watched him go, closing the inn's front door and making his way upstairs.

~: :~

The lantern overhead cast an eerie yellow glow across the alleyway as Father Tully waited. The otter tapped the end of his tail against the cobblestone impatiently. The evening had not gone quite as he had planned it, but there was no reason to think he could not salvage the situation to his advantage. With the right leverage, Aldain could be convinced to recant his explanation of the Mak'tchen influences and admit to the fullness of his crimes. All Tully needed to do was find the right way to get the wolf to cooperate with him and the other Inquisitors. The otter looked up as someone large and stocky rounded the corner, their hoofed feet clopping against the stone street.

"It is about time you arrived." The otter muttered as he watched the ram approach him. "I was about to leave and find someone else."

"Ah come now," a slimy voice said behind the priest. "We're here on time. No reason to get tetchy." Tully raised an eyebrow as a part of the shadows behind him moved, and a ferret slunk into the light beside his ram companion. "Aren't we on time Boris?" The ferret said easily, looking up at the tall ram, "I thought you said a turn past the witching hour, and that's what time it is." The ferret's limber body allowed him to bend his neck back so far it made Father Tully cringe slightly. "We wouldn't be late to our own appointment for the healing forgiveness of the Prophet now would we?" The ferret held up his paw, which had several fingers bandaged in a crude splint.

"I suppose," The otter muttered, "But if you complete this task for me it doesn't really matter does it?" Father Tully muttered a quick incantation and his paws were surrounded in a bright blue aura. The ferret held out his paw, and gasped in pain when the otter grabbed the broken fingers roughly. Carl sighed in relief though as the otter's magic healed the broken fingers. The ferret nodded as Boris, who seemed to relax a bit.

"All right holy man, what's the job?" Boris snorted, ignoring the happy chirring of his partner as the ferret tested out his mended fingers.

The otter shifted a bit and wiped his paw on his robes. "I need to you to retrieve someone for me so they can stand trial. A young hyena boy has just come to the city from a town called East Haven. He goes by the name of Flint. Have you seen him?"

The gleam in Carl's eyes was deadly as he flexed his mended paw into a fist. "Oh yes, we've seen him, holy man."

MAGICIAN

CHAPTER V

Flint felt something touch the tip of his ear ever so gently. It brushed against only the small tuft of fur that extended past his actual ear, and the movement of his fur tickled the skin underneath. The hyena's head was cradled gently in someone's lap, and the sound of their singing mixed with the sound of birds in a beautiful melody that Flint's mother had once sung him to sleep with.

The hyena opened his eyes slowly and stared up into the pale blue sky at the bright sun. The sunlight seemed to wash over Flint and he felt warm and safe. Flint could feel the grass he was laying on through his naked fur, the slim blades of glass pushing up through his short fur to caress his skin like fingertips. Flint sighed happily, his claws digging into the soft, thick grass. Flint smiled as gray paws covered his eyes and blocked out the bright sun. The big, strong paws pressed lightly against the hyena's face, one paw over each eye. The hyena smiled slightly as the familiar scent of a wolf, the scent of earth after a storm, mixed with the smell of grass, and the wolf's song mingled with the wind as it whistled through the grass and Flint's bare fur.

The paws slide away from his face, fingers trailing back across his muzzle, over his closed eyes and across his forehead. Flint smiled up at Aldain as the wolf looked down at him, his head blocking out the sun so that all Flint could see was the outline of his face, the strong muzzle and triangular ears surrounded by a halo of yellow light as the wolf sang to him. When he finished the song, the wolf fell silent, and they stared at each other for a long time.

"Hey there little one." The wolf said quietly, his paws resting on Flint's shoulders. Flint could tell the wolf was smiling, even though he could not see it. The light, happy sound in his voice told the hyena every thing he needed to know.

"Hey." Flint muttered, his eyes filling up with tears of joy. He reached a paw up, feebly touching the wolf's cheek. The wolf touched Flint's face gently in return, and Aldain's brushed away the tear forming on Flint's cheek as he sang quietly.

"Why are you so sad Flint?" The wolf asked the question in such an even, simple way that Flint could not think of a response. Aldain had not even paused his song to ask the question, they simply happened at the same time. The wolf's paw brushed a second tear away from the hyena's cheek, "Is it because I'm gone, or because you were with Will?"

The hyena's paw felt heavy, and he let it slip away from Aldain's cheek and fall to his chest, the wolf's song lulling him back into sleep. "Because you are gone." Flint whispered, and he felt like his heart would finally break as he admitted it. The wolf's face drew close to Flint's as Aldain kissed away a tear from Flint's cheek.

"Then perhaps you should go find me." The wolf whispered, and his face moved to the side. The sun burned away Flint's world in a warm, yellow ocean that took away all his pain, and he followed the wolf's song as it danced on the wind, leading him home.

~: :~

Flint rolled over slowly, his ears following the sound of the song. Aldain's words died away, and a softer voice took their place. Flint opened his eyes a bit and found himself in the bed he and Will had shared for the night. The jackal's scent was strong, and Flint could feel someone else sitting beside him on the bed. Flint could feel the blankets and soft sheets rub against every inch of his fur, and his tail ached slightly as if it were empty. The hyena sighed slowly, and rolled over to face Will.

It was not Will in bed with him, not even another jackal, but a red fox. Trenton was fully dressed in green and purple silk, his tunic and pants a far cry from anything Flint had ever worn. The fox had one leg crossed over the other, with a massive leather bound book open across his lap. It had hundreds of pages, several bookmarks dangling between the pages, and was wider than the fox was. Trenton's ears twitched back and forth, and his muzzle followed his finger as he traced the strange symbols in the book with a claw and sang under his breath.

Flint sat up slowly, and one of the fox's ears twitched backwards towards him. Then the fox glanced back at Flint. "Hey there little one," Trenton said tenderly as he closed the book and turned towards Flint. The fox reached his paw out and scratched the hyena's short brown fur that formed his mane. Flint smiled as the fox's black paw rubbed between his ears. It felt good to be touched.

"Hey Trenton," Flint muttered. The hyena blinked slowly, rubbing the sleep from his eyes as he yawned, his muzzle opening wide and white teeth glinting in the sunlight pouring in the window. His dream lingered in his thoughts, and disoriented Flint slightly as Trenton's claw tips gently scratched between his ears. The hyena let out a soft murr as the fox's paw gently rubbing in small circles across his forehead and down his neck. The gentle scratching felt good, so the hyena leaned into the paw.

"You enjoy your night with Will?" The fox asked casually, his paw moving from the hyena's shoulder to the front of his chest.

The hyena's ears swiveled backwards and Flint's face grew hot as he dipped his muzzle in embarrassment. The fox obviously knew what had happened. "Yes," Flint muttered quietly, unable to look the fox in the eyes. Suddenly, the blanket wrapped around his waist did not seem like enough cover for the hyena, but he could not pull the blanket out from under Trenton.

"It wasn't the same, was it?" Flint looked up at Trenton, and the fox had a look of genuine sadness on his face. Trenton's ears drooped just a bit, and his blue eyes told the hyena that he knew exactly why Flint had slept with the jackal.

Flint shook his muzzle a bit. "No, it wasn't." He took a deep breath as his heart fluttered. "It was nice," the hyena said slowly. Flint sniffed, trying to calm himself down so he would not cry. "It just wasn't Aldain." The hyena finished, all the desperation he felt coming out in those words.

Trenton's arm slipped around the hyena's shoulder, "Oh sweetie I'm sorry." The fox muttered before kissing Flint on his folded down ear. That made the hyena's ears rise up, and he leaned into the fox's hug a little.

The hug was gentle; just one arm draped around the hyena's shoulders followed by a soft squeeze from the thin fox, but it

154

comforted Flint a great deal. This was a hug from someone who really understood how he felt, and it calmed the hyena greatly. "I know what it's like when the first man you love rejects you." The fox said quietly as he slipped his other paw into Flint's. "I want you to know that it gets better, okay?"

Flint rubbed his free paw across his eyes, wiping away the tears that had not yet fallen from his eyes as he squeezed Trenton's paw. "I don't think it will. I, I tried to be happy. I tried to start over with Will, tried to feel happy again but I can't. It wasn't the same. I wanted to enjoy being with Will," the hyena dipped his muzzle and smiled a little, the insides of his ears turning red as Trenton hugged him softly. "I did enjoy it."

The fox's muzzle rubbed gently against Flint's cheek, and the fox hugged him softly. "But it wasn't the same." Trenton said, finishing the hyena's thought.

Flint closed his eyes, his paw gripping the fox's tightly. "No," Flint said quietly, fighting his tears back as hard as he could, "I mean, it was. It was nice, but I don't love him." The fox's paw squeezed back, and Trenton pulled Flint closer to let the young hyena's muzzle rest on his shoulder.

"Don't worry sweetie, things will be okay. Will's not leaving; he seems quite determined to see you happy in fact. He had to take care of some things, but Will is coming back and then the three of us will find some place you can be happy. Okay?" Trenton tried his best to make the words sound happy and cheer the hyena up, but Flint's downcast gaze did not change a bit.

"I... I can't. There's just this hole inside me. It's always been there and Aldain made it go away." The hyena banged his fist against Trenton's chest, and the fox was surprised by how gentle even the hyena's angry outburst was. "Aldain made me happy for the first time in so long, and I can't go back there without him."

"Then you need to try to get him back." Trenton said softly, and Flint looked up at the fox with surprise in his eyes.

"What?" The hyena said quietly, a little surprised the fox was not trying to talk him out of it like Will had.

The fox's smile was sad, and he shrugged his shoulders slightly. "You have to try to get him back. If you don't, you'll regret it forever honey."

Flint rubbed his eyes, sniffling a little bit as he sat beside the fox. "But Will said that Aldain would never come back, that the Order…" Trenton stopped the hyena with a paw over the end of his muzzle.

"Aldain probably won't come back sweetie." The fox's words had a strange, sad finality to them. Trenton believed them completely, and it made Flint's growing excitement deflate again. "That's not why you're going to try," the fox said as he slid his arm from around Flint's shoulder and patted his knee softly. "You're doing this because if you don't, you'll spend the rest of your life wondering if things could have worked out differently somehow." The fox's long tail twitching so it rested against Flint's thinner, scraggly tail. "You don't want that kind of regret hanging over your life Flint, trust me."

Flint watched the way the fox's eyes shifted to the side, and he stared off into the distance. "That happened to you?" the hyena asked quietly, and Trenton nodded slightly.

"Yes," was all the fox said before his eyes came back to Flint's face. The fox smiled as he looked into Flint's big green eyes.

Fear clutched at Flint's heart, and he was almost too afraid to ask, "Was it, was it with Aldain?"

The fox's muzzle split into a smile and he chuckled softly, a lighthearted, happy sound. "Oh no sweetie. No, Aldain was not my first. I may have been his, but he was definitely not mine." Trenton's smile returned, and he cocked his head to the side a bit. The noble fox's face was handsome when he perked his ears up and smiled.

"Oh," Flint mumbled as he blushed a little bit. "But you have been with him. This, wasn't just a one-time thing for him then? What he did with me?" The hyena rubbed his paw together, as he nervously realized just how little he knew about his knight in shining armor. What other secrets were hiding in Aldain's past? The hyena's muzzle dipped low again, and he sagged in defeat. "I guess Will was right. He never really loved me." Flint whispered, and he was heartbroken to admit it.

The fox's eyes narrowed a bit and he cupped the chest fallen hyena's muzzle in one paw. "You might not be the first boy to catch his eye, but he did love you Flint. He must have. Aldain gave you this." Trenton reached out and touched Flint's chest, where the golden cross Aldain had given rested against his fur. The warm metal pressed against Flint's skin, and the hyena's eyes came to rest on the green jewel set in the center.

"This is a Knight's Medallion Flint. It marks the wearer as a devoted servant of the Prophet, and each one is unique. This one used to belong to Aldain's father. A man Aldain's father saved forged it for him as a gift," Trenton said holding the medallion gently, a finger tracing over the golden cross relief. "Aldain once told me that his father wore it every day, and that the old wolf had given it to him on his deathbed. Right after Aldain took his Oath of Service and became a knight like his father had been. The only time I have ever seen Aldain take it off was when we were intimate together." The fox let go of the medallion, and it came to rest among the hyena's spots, shining softly in the sun like a golden spot in his fur. "Whatever happens, never doubt that he loved you Flint. Even if it was just for one night."

Flint looked up into Trenton's eyes and he could feel his lower jaw quiver as he tried to say something, but he just couldn't. The feelings of joy and sorrow that had washed over Flint made talking impossible, and the hyena felt like his heart would burst he was so happy and yet so heart broken at the same time. The fox just smiled awkwardly at Flint, his red fur shifting slightly as he opened his arms for a hug. The hyena just threw himself into the fox's arms and let the emotions go. Flint's eyes watered as Trenton held him gently. The fox's paws rubbed at Flint's short mane, and he let the hyena cry quietly.

After a long while, Trenton patted the hyena's back and pulled away from him. "Now get dressed, we have a big day ahead of us." The fox picked up his book and started walking towards the door.

"What are we doing?" Flint asked as his head tilted slightly to the side. The fox turned around with a slight swish in his hips and tail, and flashed the hyena a big grin that made Flint blush slightly.

"We're going to get your knight back, and to do so I will have to buy you a lot of things just to get you close to him again. So get dressed, and I'll take care of the rest."

Flint blinked in surprise, and he grinned like an idiot. "Thank you!" he shouted and he sprung up to hug the fox happily. "Oh thank you Trenton, I'll never forget this." The hyena pressed his face into the fox's silk shirt and hugged him with all his might.

Trenton laughed, and rubbed his muzzle against the hyena's forehead. "My pleasure sweetie. Aldain was my friend a long time

158

before he became your lover." The fox pushed the hyena back just enough so that they were nose to nose. "Just promise me that this time, if he turns you down I get to be the one to comfort you at night, okay?" Flint blushed deeply, his muzzle ducking a little as Trenton chuckled at him. "I would love to see more of the fine view you just gave me." Flint blinked in confusion, and then blushed deeply when he realized he was still naked. Flint scrambled back to the bed and covered himself with a sheet, smiling nervously as Trenton left the room with a laugh. Then Flint rushed to get dressed as fast as he could.

~: :~

Flint stayed close to Trenton as they made their way through the city. The bustle and noise of so many people made the hyena uneasy, and it was hard to keep up with the fox in the crowd.

Their first stop was a blacksmith. The gruff old bull running the place gave Flint a stern looking over before selling him a slim sword and a small round shield. Trenton promised that Will would show Flint how to use them properly, but the hyena felt awkward just carrying them around. He doubted he could ever actually use the blade to hurt someone.

Next there was a general store of some kind, where Trenton bought food and traveling gear for the hyena. Flint couldn't believe how many little things the fox bought, or how much the fox seemed willing to spend to equip him properly.

Their final stop was a tailor's shop. Colorful bolts of silk, cotton, and leather were draped across the shop. Flint looked around the strange shop with trepidation, and he yipped in surprise when a brightly dressed husky poked his head around a divider. The dog had a bounce in his step and a huge grin on his muzzle. "Trenton! My favorite customer, what are you doing back so soon?" The husky hugged Trenton, his curled tail bouncing up and down as the fox greeted him in return. "You know I won't have that vest you ordered ready for a week."

"I know Charles, but I had to bring Flint here by," the fox as he patted the hyena on the shoulder, "He needs a few sets of traveling clothes before we can leave tomorrow, and maybe some of your better leather armor? He needs something nice to wear as well."

Flint lifted his ears up with an embarrassed smile as the dog turned and looked him over. "Oh my," the husky said, raising his eyebrows at the fox, "He is a cutie. New friend you found on your the last adventure?" the husky muttered as he walked around the hyena.

The fox smiled slightly as the husky finished his inspection, "A friend of Aldain's. Will and I are going to take care of him from now on." Flint glanced between the two effeminate males as they shared a knowing look.

"Ah." Charles said quietly as he turned back to Flint, "Well lets see what you can do for you then shall we?" The husky's smile returned full force, and Flint blushed as the husky knelt down and began to take his measurements.

Trenton wandered around the store while the husky made Flint blush with compliments about his legs and soft fur. Flint had never been fitted for clothing before, and the way Charles touched and smiled at the hyena certainly didn't help. After trying on several pants and shirts changing behind a thin silk screen, the hyena was so aroused and nervous his paws were shaking too hard to work the small buttons.

160

"Why don't we take a break huh?" the husky said when Flint failed to work the same button for the third time. "If you head out the back door and down the alley, there's a little bakery where you can get something as sweet as you are." Flint blushed again, moving away from the smiling husky as the tailor turned and looked at Trenton "I need to talk with your fox friend a bit," The husky's smile widened as he looked over at the fox. "I have a few questions to ask him about our mutual friend Tigh." Flint blinked at the mention of the bear, which made the husky's tail wag like crazy.

"Oh, so you're the one huh?" Trenton broke into a big grin as he held up a bolt of black silk, "I was wondering why that collar looked so familiar." Flint blushed, not sure what the two were talking about as he ducked out the side door of the shop.

The hyena sighed, breathing in the fresh air reluctantly. Flint finished buttoning his new shirt up, calm now that he was away from the smiling husky. The way Charles looked at him, and touched him as he fitted Flint for clothes made the hyena so nervous. The husky was always staring at his eyes and smiling. Flint wandered down the short alleyway between the buildings to the bakers. He bought a small pasty with the coins Trenton had given him earlier in the day, and ate it slowly as he walked back to the shop. Flint was almost at the door to the tailor's when a shadow passed over him as someone stepped in front of him and blocked out the sun.

"Well look at this," Boris the ram muttered as he loomed over Flint, "A cub out wandering where he shouldn't be."

Flint dropped his half eaten pastry and turned to run, but Carl grabbed him before the sweet dessert even touched the ground. The ferret grabbed Flint's arms and pushed him into

Boris, who clamped down hard on the hyena's shoulders with his big hands.

"Help! Somebody help!" Flint yelped, his feet kicking at the ferret. Carl snickered and drew a dagger, and Flint stopped struggling when the ferret held the blade against his throat.

"I wouldn't be so loud, if I were you. I'm just looking for a way to pay you back for that broken paw, and the old priest didn't say anything about you being healthy when we brought you back."

"Priest?" Flint blinked in surprise, "What are you talking about? Where are you taking me?" The hyena grunted as Carl forced a gag in his mouth. The hyena tried to bite the wadded up cotton, but it tasted foul, like someone's feet. Flint whimpered as Boris picked him up and started to carry him away towards a wagon waiting out in the street. The hyena's paws kicked uselessly. Boris was just too strong for him to get away.

"Don't worry cub, I'm sure the old man won't do anything as bad to you as I plan to. After all, I don't think he'll mind if we deliver you a little late."

"But I think he'll mind if you never show up." Carl didn't get a chance to respond to Trenton's flippant comment. The ferret turned around just in time to spot the fox standing in the back door to the shop, paw outstretched. One of the rings on Trenton's fingers gave off a flash of bright white light. The ferret yelped as the fox closed his paws as if grabbing something and jerked his arms upward. The fox's magic closed around the ferret and launched him up into the air like a toy.

Boris turned around to see his friend disappear from sight into the sky; arms and legs waving wildly as his tube like body twisted in mid air.

"Not smart mage, I can crush the boy." Boris muttered, "So

back off and he doesn't get hurt." Boris began edging backward toward the street, hoping to reach the corner before the mage did something stupid.

Trenton cocked his head to the side as a muffle crash and a yelp signaled Carl's descent back to the earth on a nearby roof. "You know, you're right. Strapping young brutes like you could crush my friend. So I'll take him back if you don't mind."

The gag muffled Flint's yelp as Trenton's ring glowed again and his magic snagged the hyena away from the ram. It was a rough pull, because Boris tried to hold on to Flint, but the fox's magic yanked Flint right out of the ram's grasp. The hyena went flying across the alleyway and tumbled to a stop at Trenton's feet, dusty and shaken but unharmed for the most part.

Flint pulled the gag out of his mouth and scrambled to his feet as Boris began to charge down the alley at them. The ram didn't have his axe, but he lowered those big curved horns and barreled down the short alleyway towards Trenton.

The fox dodged to the side, pulling Flint out of the ram's way as well. Flint stayed on the ground as Trenton crouched beside him, hands moving as he wove a spell to fend off the ram. Boris crashed into the wall, then turned, and swung his fist at Trenton as hard as he could. The fox took the blow up side the head, unable to move out of the way without ruining his spell.

The fox grimaced as the ram's punch nearly knocked him over, but he managed to keep control of his spell. The swirling blue aura Trenton was summoning tightened and focused on the fox's paws, turning into a crackling charge around him fists. The ram snorted and tried to back away from the mage when the spell didn't fizzle out, but all Trenton had to do was reach out and tap the ram lightly on his arm.

Flint was probably just as shocked as the ram was that the fox's light touch did so much damage to Boris. The blue energy raced out of the fox's finger tips and coursed through the ram. Boris bellowed loudly and went into spasms as what looked like lightning crawled across his body. The ram fell to the ground unconscious, his wool smoking as Trenton grabbed Flint's paw and pulled him towards the tailor's shop.

The hyena yelped when the fox's paw touched his own, expecting to be shocked just like Boris had. The fox laughed a little and smiled at Flint, who blushed sheepishly at the mage. "It only works once Flint. Now come on, lets go before the ferret gets..."

"Back?" Carl snarled as he dropped from the roof above Trenton and onto the fox's back. Trenton went down with a yelp under the ferret's weight, and Flint reacted before he thought. He rushed the thief and tried to shove Carl off the fox, but the ferret backhanded Flint and sent him sprawling. Carl shoved Trenton back to the ground as the fox managed to turn over, effectively pinning the fox to the ground with his weight. The struggle prevented the fox from casting a spell, and the wiry ferret quickly drew a knife from his belt.

The ferret grinned and his blade made a chilling sound as it cleared the sheath. "I'm going to make your hyena boy pay for the fingers he broke fox." Trenton struggled with the ferret, trying to push him away with his paws or active his magic, but the ferret had the advantage. Carl raised the knife, and Trenton's eyes widened in fear.

Then a loud whip crack echoed through the alley, and the ferret's knife went skittering away from the fight. Flint looked up in surprise as Charles appeared beside him, a heavy bullwhip in the huskies slender paw.

164

Carl pulled his paw back in pain, and then yelped again when Trenton hit him in the face. The fox's paw erupted in another flash of light, and the ferret went flying again. This time Carl crashed into the alley wall beside the husky. The ferret tried to scramble to his feet, but Charles was faster, wrapping the whip around his neck like a noose. Flint flinched as the smiling husky's choked the struggling ferret, the leather whip creaking as Carl twisted back and forth, paws scrabbling at the leather until he slumped into unconscious.

Charles was panting slightly as he let the ferret drop to the ground, still alive but definitely down for the count. Trenton stood up and brushed himself off, grabbing Flint's arms as the hyena rushed too him. "It's okay Flint, they can't hurt you. It's okay now." The fox whispered, petting the panting hyena's head-fur as Flint crouched beside him, shaking in fear.

Charles tossed the whip he was holding away as a couple of the city guards came rushing down the alley, drawn by the sounds of fighting. "Ah the cavalry," Trenton muttered bemusedly. "You're just in time to clean these two up, officers."

"Are you all right Sir?" the German Shepard leading the patrol said, his sword drawn as he stood over the now groaning ram.

"Yes, but these two thugs attacked us." Trenton said casually, as if being attacked in the street was something that happened every time he went shopping. The fox held out his paw, and Flint could see a rather large signet ring on the fox's finger. The dog looked at it, and snapped of a rather formal salute. Trenton smiled at him, "I'd rather like them taken away constable. I'll be by the guard house later to see if they're willing to talk."

The guards nodded, "Very well, my Lord," and the guards proceeded to drag the wounded thugs away with little ceremony, giving Boris a couple thumps to make sure he wasn't any trouble. Flint calmed down considerably once Boris and Carl were gone, standing beside Trenton as the fox rubbed his head and grimaced.

"They left without many questions." Charles said casually once the guards were gone, retrieving his whip from behind a couple barrels.

"Advantages of being a nobleman, Charles," Trenton said happily, patting Flint on the back as he slipped the seal back into his pocket and ushering the hyena back into the shop. "The guards ask a lot fewer questions. Especially about whips and young men."

The husky chuckled heartily and Flint blushed at the flamboyant fox's words, his eyes following the husky's heavy bull whip as they went inside. The hyena couldn't help wondering why in the world a tailor would own a whip like that.

~: :~

Flint's paws were still trembling again as he tried to button a shirt, but this time it was out from fear, not nervous arousal. The hyena sighed and he sat down on the little stool behind the changing screen, the smooth wood cold against his bare rump. His short bushy tail flipped up between his legs into his lap and covered him up, and he pressed his paws against his muzzle. Flint knew Trenton and Charles were out there waiting for him to finish changing, but the hyena had only been able to get the shirt they gave him on.

Flint just couldn't bring himself to go on as if nothing had happened. The other two acted like nothing was wrong, as if being attacked in the street was routine for them. For Flint it was a big deal. He had almost been kidnapped in broad daylight. If Trenton hadn't been there to stop them, and Charles hadn't helped, he and Trenton might be dead now. The hyena was so worked up he jumped when Trenton poked his head around the side of the screen.

"You okay back here?" The fox asked quietly, and the short hyena shook his head, his ears pressed flat against his skull. Trenton disappeared, whispered something to Charles, and then reappeared. The fox knelt down beside the sitting hyena and waited until he heard the sound of Charles leaving the room. "You want to tell me what's wrong?" the fox asked softly, his paw resting on Flint's knee.

"I just..." the hyena lifted his ears up, and licked his lips, "I'm so sorry I didn't stop them." Flint chewed his lip, avoiding Trenton's eyes. "You tried to save me, and I wasn't any help at all." The hyena's green eyes brimmed with tears as he looked up at the fox. "I never expected them to followed me here."

"So you knew those two?" Trenton's ears cupped forward, and he tilted his head to the side a bit. The fox put his other paw on Flint's knee, trying to comfort the young hyena.

Flint shook his head again, "No, not really. They were on the road from East Haven, and they..." the hyena stopped, swallowing nervously as the tightness in his chest prevented him from speaking.

Trenton could see the fear in the hyena's eyes, and he slid his arms around the half dressed hyena. "Did they hurt you before?" Trenton said slowly, "Did they touch you?" the fox asked, his eyes narrowing.

The hyena blinked when he realized what the fox was asking,

and it sent a shiver down his spine. "No, no they didn't. I think they wanted too, but I got away before they could." The hyena brushed his muzzle against the fox's, and he felt better telling someone about what had happened. "They just took my things."

"So that's why you had so little when you got here." The fox said evenly, his paw petting the hyena's mane slowly. "You going to be all right now?" Trenton asked as his finger's tracing the ridge of Flint's forehead.

"I... I don't know. I was so useless. I couldn't even stop them from hurting you. If Charles hadn't been there you could have..." the hyena choked, pausing for a moment to regain his voice. "You nearly died because of me. How do you deal with that?" Flint pulled his head back a bit and looked the fox in the face. "Does this happen all the time?"

"I won't lie to you Flint," Trenton said quietly. "It has happened often enough for me to expect it will happen again." The fox shrugged lightly, his eyes almost devoid of emotion as he talked about how close he had come to dying. "That's what it means to be an adventurer. Things try to kill you. Usually it's some kind of monster in a dungeon, but sometimes it's other people." The fox brushed his fingers across Flint's face again, and the hyena pushed his muzzle into the fox's paw. Then Trenton's face broke into a grin, and he pulled his paw back.

Flint watched as the mage pulled off his ring and held it out to him. "Here, put this on. The next time you get into trouble, think the word "Shanter" really hard and point the ring like I did. You'll be able to move things just by thinking about it."

The hyena's ears lifted up as he slipped the ring on his finger. "Thank you," Flint whispered, holding out his paw to look at the ring. The silver band had a pair of curved ram horns twisting around it, and the hyena felt his paw tingle slightly as the band shrunk to fit his finger. Flint rubbed the silver slowly, looking up at Trenton sheepishly. "I don't have anything to pay you with though."

The fox laughed softly, petting the boy's head-fur. "It's a gift," he said smiling, before a concerned look creased his muzzle. "You don't have to live like this you know. I could take you back to my family's estate. It wouldn't be a great life, but the life of a servant is much safer than the open road."

Flint smiled and hugged the fox, his muzzle tucked against Trenton's shoulder. "Thank you." He whispered softly, and the fox just nodded and held him.

After a minute, Trenton's muzzle shifted from Flint's cheek to his neck. The fox moved closer, so that their chests were pressed together, making the fox's hug much more intimate. Trenton's paws began to rub at his back as he comforted the hyena, and Flint could feel the fox's paws wander slowly up and down his spine, moving just a bit lower each time. Flint started to blush when he felt a slight pressure at the base of his tail, and he tried not to think about being naked from the waist down as the fox hugged him. Then suddenly one of the fox's paws reached all the way down and squeezed Flint's butt firmly.

The hyena yipped in surprise and jumped, his arms tensing around the fox's neck as he tried to move away from the grabbing paw and found himself pressing up against the fox instead. That made Flint's spine tingle a little and his ears instantly pressed against his head as he embarrassed himself.

Trenton pulled back and ducked his head sheepishly. "Sorry," the fox muttered as his ears flicked backwards, a slight grin creeping across his slim muzzle. "I couldn't resist. Your butt was just too cute." The fox punctuated the last word with a squeeze to Flint's knee, and that made the hyena turn his head away and blush.

Flint's ears swiveled back and forth as he tried to say something intelligent, but the words just sort of tumbled out of his trembling muzzle. "I'm sorry, it won't happen again, I just..." Flint's words sort of trailed off and he ducked his head slightly, his rounded brown ears becoming as flat as his black spots were. "I didn't mean to." The hyena muttered lamely, and was genuinely surprised by the fox's unexpectedly humorous response.

The fox put one paw up to Flint's cheek and nearly died laughing. Trenton knew he shouldn't, but the hyena just looked so damn cute as he fumblingly apologized for something that he had not even done. "Oh sweetie, I'm the one who should be sorry. I grabbed you silly." The fox ruffled Flint's hair and the hyena smiled a bit, still blushing as he lifted his muzzle back up. "But, um, you might want to pull that shirt down. I can see how much you enjoyed it."

Flint's eyes flicked down to his lap, and he was mortified to find that the shirt he was wearing had crept upward enough to expose the growing erection the fox's touch had sparked. The hyena's paws quickly grabbed the shirt and covered himself up as quickly as he could, but Flint could feel his face growing hot again as he blushed furiously. "I'm so sorry Trenton."

The noble fox was chuckling hard as he leaned forward and bumped his muzzle against Flint's broader, squarer jaw. "Oh no sweetie, don't be sorry. I quite enjoyed the view." Flint could see the fox's smile widen and he leaned forward, which made Flint lean back until the fox was almost crouching over him. The fox lowered his voice, and smoothly asked, "Would you mind if I had another look?"

Flint's ears drooped and he blushed so hard it made the color of his fur shift slightly red. The fox's eyes seemed to sparkle as he smiled at Flint; his long fluffy tail began to flick back and forth behind him as they crouched in the small space behind the changing screen. It looked like a patch of black fur on a long flag of red. Flint smiled just a bit as the fox's posture took on an excited, hopeful pose. It was like the fox was suddenly a kit asking if he could have a cookie he was so excited. "Please?" Trenton asked softly, and then Trenton's pink tongue flicked out and ran across his lips in what Flint suspected was an unconscious action.

"Okay," Flint said with a nervous swallow, and he let go of his shirt. The fox almost giggled with excitement as his paws pulled the edge of the shirt up to reveal the hyena's growing erection.

"Oh my," the fox said with a smile as his paw slid around Flint's shaft. "A very nice view indeed…" Flint could not help but grin as the fox glanced up at him. "I think I need a closer look," Trenton said with a big grin, and Flint did not stop the fox when the vulpine's slim muzzle descended to his crotch. The smooth red fur on Trenton's cheek rubbed against Flint's shaft as the fox sniffed at his balls. Trenton breathed in deeply as he pressed the hyena's shaft against his face.

The hyena leaned back against the wall behind him as the fox's warm tongue slipped out and lapped at the underside of his cock. It was a strange new feeling for Flint, and he could not help pawing at the fox's head as Trenton's tongue caressed him. Trenton gave a soft whimper of pleasure when Flint's paw tugged at his black tipped ear, and the hyena decided to settle both his paws on the fox's folded back ears and let him do what he wanted.

That seemed to delight the fox because he moaned loudly as

Flint rubbed at his ears. Flint's hips jumped when the fox tipped his cock up and slid his mouth down around his cock, taking the hyena's shaft completely into his muzzle. Flint whimpered along with the fox and his cock throbbed as the fox's thin muzzle enclosed his shaft. It felt wonderful being inside Trenton's muzzle, and the hyena tried to pay attention to what the obviously skilled fox did as he sucked on his cock.

The fox's lips seemed to curve around his teeth, keeping them well away from Flint's shaft. Trenton did not go too deep too quickly, but instead worked up to taking every inch of the hyena, getting the shaft slick with spit as he went. The fox did not fight against the hyena's paws on his head, but he did not let Flint's paws or hips set the pace. He moved in sync with the hyena's bucking hips, letting Flint thrust a little, but keeping it to a minimum by pinning the hyena's legs gently to the stool. That gave the hyena's thrusts resistance, and made Flint's shaft ache as it moved in and out of the vulpine's skilled muzzle.

The best part of all was the fox's tongue.

It danced and slid across Flint's shaft with ease, curling first one way and then the other. The fox's tongue pulled at the hyena's dick, swabbed across the head of his cock and curled around the base. Trenton traced the thick vein underneath, and then teased the underside of the mushroom head of the hyena's glans. Then the warm ribbon flicked across the slit at the end. Trenton's tongue even reached out beyond the fox's muzzle to lap at Flint's balls, cupping them in a warm, spine tingling way as the fox choked him self on the hyena's dick

It quickly became too much for the hyena, and Flint did not even get the chance to warn Trenton that he was going to cum. Flint's hips just bucked up into that warm muzzle, his paws

173

clutched the fox's ears tightly, and he lost control and began to cum inside the fox's mouth. The orgasm was so hard it felt like Flint's whole body would explode out of his cock. Flint gave a short, barking howl as he came, his penis pulsing inside Trenton's sucking muzzle. The hyena's paws forced Trenton's head all the way down on his shaft so he could feel as much of that wonderful muzzle as possible as he fed the fox the results of Flint's first blowjob.

Trenton seemed happy with all of that, because the fox closed his eyes and pressed his muzzle forward, taking the hyena as far into his mouth as he could. A low moan escaped the corners of Trenton's mouth as the fox drank Flint's cum as if he were a man dying of thirst. The noble's tongue lapped and pulled at the pulsing shaft in his mouth, trying to milk the hyena's balls of every drop of seed. Flint was more than a little surprised that Trenton got every drop of cum that spilled onto his tongue.

When Trenton finished trying to suck his dick off by the root, Flint was panting so hard he collapsed into the fox's arms. Flint watched as the fox's tongue slid around his lips, checking for any stray drops of cum he might have missed. It was a weird and arousing sight, and it made Flint's spine tingle when the fox gave him a tender and gentle kiss. The hyena gasped slightly, almost falling backwards off the stool when the fox broke the kiss. "Wow," Flint muttered, clutching at the fox's shoulders. He felt totally drained, as if the fox had pulled all the energy out of him with his skilled muzzle.

"I take it you enjoyed that?" The fox asked happily as he stood up, patting Flint on the head, his fingers scratching between the hyena's rounded ears.

"Yes," Flint muttered. His ears pressed flat against his head as he grinned up at the fox. "Thank you," the hyena said as he hugged Trenton's waist tightly.

"Thank *you*. I've wanted to do that all day long. You really are too cute for your own good, you know that?" the fox said as his paws stroked Flint's cheek softly. The fox's eyes lingered on Flint's face. "It's your eyes. They're so bright and deep…" the fox muttered vaguely, his fingers tracing the hyena's brow. "Like I could become lost in them."

The hyena blushed again and smiled sheepishly. Trenton found it to be a familiar and endearing sight, the way the little hyena's round ears turned back. Trenton kissed Flint softly on the lips and petted the hyena's short mane slowly. "Now put some pants on, before I do something like that again. We need to hurry and get everything before sundown, so we can meet up with Will and get Aldain back." The fox brushed a paw across Flint's chin, and the hyena arched his muzzle up with a smile. "All right?"

Flint smiled happily as the fox disappeared back into the main area of the shop. This time, when Flint buttoned the shirt up all he did was smile. Flint felt safe again somehow, knowing he was with Trenton and would soon be with Aldain again. The hyena finished getting dressed and hopped off the stool.

~: :~

Flint padded his way along the forest trail behind Trenton. They hyena's ears swiveled this way and that as he listened to all the strange sounds of the forest. It was late now, and Flint was becoming more and more worried as the sun began to set behind the trees. Trenton had commented that the sun going down was a good thing, because they would have the cover of darkness on their journey, but it still made the hyena nervous.

The hyena shifted in the new armor and fancy silk clothes Trenton had bought him. It was strange, feeling the smooth, soft material slide across his fur as the heavier leather pads restricted his movement. The silk had been treated with something to keep it from generating lightning in the hyena's fur, but it still felt odd. The whole outfit was not much heavier than the coarse wool Flint was so used to, but it seemed to breath more easily. Flint had to admit; Charles made very fine clothes. The husky's leatherwork was especially fine quality. The dog had grinned and said something about it being his specialty, and the hyena had too admit the leather looked much better any he had seen before.

Flint shifted the backpack carried, and he was glad that the fox had placed most of the things they bought inside the sack from Will's room. Flint had not looked too closely at what was inside the sack the fox was carrying. After his first experience with it Flint was still leery of the magic bag.

Trenton explained that it could hold a great deal more than a normal bag and always weigh the same amount, but Flint still did not like it. The fox and jackal seemed to own many things that were magic. Trenton's clothes seemed to stay impeccably clean, even after the fight, and the long black staff he was using as a walking stick now practically glowed with power. The ruby tip was even beginning to shed a bright light as the sun began to set over the treetops.

"Why are we coming all the way out here?" Flint asked quietly, the strange shadows in the woods making him keep his voice low. It felt as if he was being watched somehow.

"I told you," Trenton said evenly, falling back so he was walking beside the hyena. Slowing his pace was a strange thing for the fox. Usually Trenton's short size meant he had to rush to keep up with his companions, but he found himself quickly outdistancing the shorter hyena at that pace. "We need to get Will's help if you're going to sneak into the castle. He knows all the secret ways inside."

Flint jumped just a bit as a deer exploded out of a nearby bush and raced into the forest. The hyena stared after the fleeing animal, fascinated by it. Even living deep in a forest most of his life, Flint had not seen much wildlife up close. The hyena had rarely left the village. "I know, but why is he all the way out here?" Flint said as he raced to catch up to the fox.

Trenton smiled, patting the hyena on the back before straightening the new silk cloak Flint was wearing. "Because he worships the Goddess and her only temple is out here where the Prophet's followers won't disturb them."

"Oh." Flint said, and for a second they walked in silence together. "Who's the Goddess?" Flint asked, looking up at Trenton with a puzzled expression.

The fox chuckled a bit and his staff tapped across the dirt trail as they walked past tree after tree, each one bigger than the one before. "She's a nature god, worshiped mostly by druids and people like Will who grew up in the wilder places of the world. It's not a popular faith in this land, but you can find a few followers here and there."

"Why isn't it popular? I like nature." Flint smiled at a butterfly that had floated across their path, his paw reaching out for it. The butterfly curved in the air and landed on the hyena's paw, which made Flint giggle as he sniffed at the creature before it fluttered away. Trenton shook his head at the young male beside him. Somehow, the young hyena had a way of making the simplest things seem endearing.

"The Church of the Prophet is why." Trenton explained as they approached the base of a short cliff. A large hill rose out of the woods, and the cliff had been carved into the hill by some glacier long ago. Flint followed as the fox began picking his way along the bottom of the cliff, "Their Prophet declared worshiping all the old gods an abomination, and over the years the Church has driven most of the Goddess's worshipers out of the kingdom."

The fox eventually came to a small cleft in the rock. Hidden from view was a thick, iron bound door set into the stone cliff with a frame of granite carved out of the rock. Flint tilted his head to the side in confusion when he saw it. He had never seen someone build a door into a hillside before. "The temple is inside the hill?" he asked, and the fox just nodded as he knocked on the door.

"How did the Prophet drive the druids out?" Flint asked as they waited for someone to answer the door.

"With fire, Flint. They did it with fire." The fox muttered as the door opened, and a bear in heavy green robes ushered them inside.

᠄᠄

Will knelt at the Goddess's alter, his eyes fixed on a candle that had burned almost to the base. The temple was a massive cave that had been carved into the hillside, and Will had always been impressed by it. It housed an entire enclave of Druids and had yet to be detected by the Church of the Prophet. It was one of the few Goddess temples that had escaped destruction.

The jackal sighed just a little as he waited in the hope that something, some voice or thought from the Goddess would come to him, that the Goddess would bless him with just a hint of what he should do next. Yet there were no voices on the wind, and the flame did not write words in the smoke. Will had often had days like this before, when the Goddess did not send him any signs during his vigils. That was the fickle way of nature, but today Will wanted an answer so badly it was driving him mad.

Part of him wanted to rush back to the inn as fast as he could and find Flint. Just the memory of the hyena's smile and emerald eyes made the jackal want to grab him up and spirit him away, but another part of Will was scared by that desire. The elder druids had assured him there was nothing wrong with being a tail raiser. The jackal had even been surprised that the druids had observed it in normal animals, and that the Goddess obviously did not object to it. Yet the jackal's heart was troubled, because he felt so strongly for the hyena after such a short time. They had only just met, and yet Will was sure he would die defending the young man.

When Trenton arrived, the fox seemed just as troubled. The vulpine leaned on his staff beside the altar with his eyes narrowed and his brow furrowed. "What is it?" the jackal asked quietly, keeping his voice low in reverence for the place he was in.

"You have to promise not to get mad." The fox whispered, his eyes twitching across the room to where Flint was standing. The hyena waved when Will looked over at him, but he stayed near the column where Trenton had told him to wait.

"Mad about what?" the jackal's eyes narrowed and he hissed, "What did you do?"

Trenton bit his lip, his tail swishing nervously "I need to know how to sneak into the castle. You know how right?"

Will turned his head to the side, "Yes, but you've never cared before. Why now? And why is Flint standing over there where he won't hear us?" the jackal's eyes narrowed slightly and the fox sighed a little.

Trenton's ears drooped a little, "Because I did not want that sweet boy hear you get angry. I want to know how to get in the castle because I'm helping Flint get Aldain back."

"What?" Will almost shouted the word, but caught himself just in time and only whispered it angrily, his ears turning forward as if he had not clearly heard the fox. "How do you expect to do that?" the jackal growled, "That wolf is never going to come to his senses and I'll be…"

Trenton cut the jackal off with a wave of his paw. "I know all that, but Flint needs to learn that for himself. He needs to see Aldain one last time or he will never be able to forget about him." The fox's tail flicked back and forth, and he glared angrily at the seated jackal. "And that will prevent whatever you might have planned for the future. Now are you going to help him, or not?"

The jackal's ears flicked backwards and he glared across the room at Flint. "What makes you think I'm planning something?" Will muttered, his voice low. He didn't like it when Trenton read him so easily.

"You're planning to take him away." Trenton said evenly, "I can see it in the way you stand. Last night you were agonizing over the idea, but today you're ready to rush to Flint's side. Just like I am." The fox's voice was quiet, and the way he spoke made Will nervous. "We'd do anything for him, and we've only just met this strange boy. He's a stable boy who has bright eyes, soft fur, and smooth paws? Everyone wants to help him. Don't you think that's odd?" The fox smiled a bit, his voice growing happy again.

"So how do we get him in?"

Will sighed, rubbing the side of his head. "All right," He muttered glumly, knowing he had no real choice but to help.

~: :~

Flint waited quietly across the room from Will and Trenton as they talked. It was strange, standing inside the Goddess's temple. It was built to look as if it were a normal building on the inside, with brickwork and stained glass windows, not a hollowed out cave in a hillside. It was really impressive, and Flint passed the time looking at the walls and detailed carvings.

Flint was also interested in the Druids themselves. A few were milling about the room, speaking with worshipers and going about their daily business. They moved slowly and wore dark green robes tied at the waist with a black cord. One of them, a coyote, seemed to have taken an interest in him. He watched Flint from across the room for several minutes. Eventually the coyote padded barefoot across the stone floor, his robes swishing back and forth through the dust as he came up behind Flint. The hyena turned a little and smiled shyly at the taller man, and the Druid gave him a tense smile back.

"Hello there, little one," the coyote said in an even measured tone that Flint recognized as controlled anger. He had heard it often enough around the inn to realize it meant trouble.

"Hello," Flint responded quietly, going back to watching Trenton and Will talk with another Druid.

The coyote cleared his throat a little, and then stepped in front of Flint so the hyena had to look up at him. "You know little one, we don't welcome servants of the Prophet into the Goddess's home."

"So?" Flint said quietly, his bright green eyes blinking once in confusion.

"So you need to leave." The coyote said quietly. His words were clipped, and while he attempting to conceal it, Flint knew the coyote was furious.

"I don't serve the Prophet." Flint said simply, taking a step to the side so he could see Trenton and Will again.

"Then take that off." The coyote pointed at Flint's chest angrily. The hyena's paw instinctively closed around Aldain's medallion, and Flint stared up at the Druid, his eyes narrowing.

"This was a gift. I won't take it off." The hyena ducked away a bit, expecting the coyote to slap him like the inn's patrons would have, but he kept his eyes focused on the druid.

The Druid's eyes narrowed and he stood up a little straighter. It was a frightening sight for Flint, with the massive stained glass window behind the druid framing the coyote's angry muzzle and green hood. "Who would give you a Knight's Medallion, if you do not serve the Prophet?" he demanded.

Flint felt a smile creep across his muzzle as he though about Aldain. "My lover did."

"Your lover?" the coyote said with a laugh, the green hood falling back so Flint could see his face better. The coyote's face was strangely familiar. "Are you telling me that you, a young boy, are the lover of a Knight of the Cross?" The coyote crossed his arms over his chest, "An order that is exclusively male?"

The hyena did not blink, or flinch at the coyote's mocking laugh. Flint just said. "Yes."

The druid blinked, and then his gaze locked with Flint. For a long moment there was silence, and then the druid laughed so loudly that it echoed through the cavernous room. Several people in the chapel turned to look at what was going on. Flint flattened his ears a bit, his tail drooping slightly because he was suddenly the center of attention. "What is your name boy?" the coyote asked through a fit of laughter.

"Flint." The hyena said with a glare, "and I'm not a boy. I'm nineteen."

"Well then young man, feel free to stay with us as long as you like. My name is Zane, and should you need anything I would be happy to help." The coyote turned and walked away from Flint, who frowned in confusion as the Druid made his way across the chapel's stone floor, all the while laughing to himself.

Will appeared beside the hyena, his ears turned back slightly and his eyes narrowed in concern. "What was that about Flint?" The jackal asked, and his paw rested on Flint's shoulder as he loomed protectively over the smaller hyena.

Flint watched the Druid disappear into the tunnels at the back of the cavern. "I don't know." He said quietly, but he was more than a little startled by the coyote's reaction and the jackal's swift arrival.

"Come on, we've got everything ready." The jackal tugged on Flint's shoulder slightly, and the hyena turned to face Will. The jackal's eyes searched Flint's face, and he crouched next to the hyena so their eyes were level. "Are you sure you want to go through with this?" Will's concern was heavy in his voice. "You don't have to, you know. We can just... Well, leave. No one is making you go after..."

Flint smiled up at the jackal. It was comforting to know that Will cared about him, but it did not change his feelings for Aldain. "I'm going Will. I need to, just like I needed to spend last night with you."

The jackal looked away, his ears turned back as he patted Flint's shoulder softly. Flint suspected the black furred canine was blushing, but there was no real way to tell because the jackal's fur was too dark. "All right, we need to talk about how you're going to do this."

~: :~

Aldain sighed as he slouched in his chair. The holy book "The Chronicles of the Prophet" lay forgotten in his lap. Normally reading passages from the Prophet's most holy book helped the wolf think. Reading about the Prophet and how he spoke of justice and helping others settled the wolf's mind. In the past, just being in his room used to make Aldain feel at peace.

Today, the words were empty and his room simply felt cold. Aldain's thoughts were too jumbled and he could not focus on anything else but the approaching atonement ceremony.

This was not what the wolf had expected to happen, but Aldain could not ignore the chance Father Thomas had provided him. The cat's explanation was a plausible reason for Aldain to be sleeping with a male, but the council had confined Aldain to his quarters all the same until he could be 'cleansed' of the tainted thoughts he had 'acquired' in his fight against evil.

Aldain snorted in anger. It galled the wolf just to think about the way the priests had talked about it. He had always felt this way about other males, even when he was a cub. Aldain was sure he had been born this way, but the council would never have accepted that explanation. Argo would certainly never believe it. The horse would have hunted down everyone Aldain cared about looking for the person who had 'corrupted' the wolf before accepting that Aldain was born a tail raiser.

At least Flint was going to be safe somewhere with Will and Trenton. They would take care of him. Aldain knew they would, but it was a sad consolation for the wolf. He wanted to be part of the hyena's life, but there was no way it could happen now. In a way, Aldain was also glad he would still be a knight. He would be able to keep helping people this way. Aldain might not like the way the Inquisition was growing in power, but the wolf knew he would be doing good things as a knight. That would have to be enough.

The wolf's ears perked up as the lock on his door tumbled into the open position. He wasn't expecting anyone to visit him, and when his door swung open there was no one there, the wolf sprung from his chair and dived for his sword.

Invisibility was fairly common trick among wizards, and Aldain knew too many people who might use it as a weapon against him. Aldain grabbed his sword and had it half drawn when a startled yip of surprise and the sound of someone tumbling to the ground made him stop. The wolf's ears perked up and he glanced around the room in confusion as he recognized the voice.

"Flint?" Aldain whispered in shock, and he nearly dropped his sword when the hyena pulled back a cloak from around his shoulders and faded into view. The hyena was sitting beside the door, where he had fallen backwards in surprise as the wolf leapt out of his chair. The hyena looked up at the startled wolf with a sheepish smile.

"Sorry, I didn't mean to scare you." The hyena said, his muzzle dipping towards his chest as he fanned his ears back in embarrassment. The hyena's cheeks were red as he stood up nervously and closed the door.

"How, how did you get in here?" the wolf stammered, setting his sword back on the table before taking a careful step towards the hyena, still not sure if what the hyena was for real.

Flint's muzzle split into a slightly larger grin as the wolf drew closer. "Will told me about this passage behind a statue, and that let me into the courtyard. Trenton gave me this enchanted cloak so no one would see me, and gave me this to get through any locks…" The hyena held up a small talisman, and when he saw the look on Aldain's face the hyena just sort of stopped talking, his nervousness overtaking him. Flint shifted his weight from one foot to the other, smiling up at Aldain.

"Okay," the wolf said quietly, standing just as nervously at arms length from the shorter hyena. "But why? It's much too dangerous for you to be here."

Flint rubbed his paws together slowly, and his ears drooped just a little bit. "I needed to see you again," the hyena said quietly, his paws spreading apart in desperation. Everything had been planned carefully except for this part, and once again Flint felt as if he were a million miles from the wolf standing in front of him. "I need to know if you really love me," Flint said quietly, looking hopefully up at the knight.

Aldain's face fell, his tail drooped down and the wolf stared at the hyena with fear in his eyes. "You know I do." Aldain whispered, his muzzle barely moving.

Flint crossed the space between them the instant the wolf said the words, and Aldain wanted to die as the boy hugged him around the waist. "Then come with me." Flint's words were muffled slightly by the wolf's chest, as he began to beg the knight to leave with him, "Just leave with me. I can make you happy, I promise. I can make a home for us to live in. Trenton promised to lend me the money for a cabin somewhere and I swear I'll make a good mate. I'll cook and clean, I'll get a job and do everything you need me to. Anything at all." The hyena's eyes stared up at Aldain desperately. "We can go anywhere you want too, just please," the hyena's muzzle moved back and he stared up into the wolf's eyes, the end of his muzzle brushing against the wolf's nose. "Please come with me tonight."

Aldain's head hung slightly and he closed his eyes as the hyena's muzzle pressed up against his own. Slipping his arms around Flint's shoulders and hugging him brought a sense of peace to the wolf Aldain had never expected to feel again. The wolf's voice refused to work, and he struggled within himself to answer Flint.

"I can't." Flint flinched as Aldain spoke the words. It was the most mournful, anguished sound the hyena had ever heard, and it sounded like the words had been ripped from the knight's heart. The wolf's head dipped down and pressed tightly against Flint's forehead as he clutched at the hyena's shoulders. "I want to, Flint. I want to be with you so badly, but I cannot leave the church." The wolf looked into Flint's eyes, "I do good things here Flint, I've helped people. I want you, but I can not leave the life I have here for my own personal desires." The wolf's arms squeezed Flint tightly, and Flint had to fight back tears as the wolf kissed him slowly on the lips.

"But... But I love you," Flint stammered, his chest heaving as Aldain held him close. "I need to be with you." The hyena's paws clutched at the wolf's shirt, and he pressed his face into the small space where Aldain's chest fur showed above the collar of his shirt. The hyena smiled and breathed in deeply, and Flint's heart ached as that earthy, rich wolf musk filled his nose and made his knees weak. "I can't live without you." Flint blubbered into the wolf's fur, just barely keeping himself from breaking down completely.

Aldain sniffed a little, and rubbed his eyes dry. He petted the hyena's head slowly, kissing Flint between the ears. "You have to, Flint. I have a duty to others. If I leave now, I will endanger the Order itself. Worse, I'll endanger you and the others. I do too much good to throw that away on something for myself. Even if that is loving you." The wolf cradled the hyena tenderly, petting the short brown head fur gently.

Aldain's eyes had a haunted look to them, as he looked into Flint's wide green eyes. "If I were not a knight, I would never have been able to save you behind that little inn. I would never have known you were in danger. You would have died there, alone. That's why I have to stay here. You have to go and live your own life. It's the only way."

Flint sniffed slightly, his chest heaving. He closed his eyes and the hyena knew there was no way he could convince the wolf to come with him. Flint's heart broke, and for a moment he pressed against the wolf to feel his embrace and drink in his scent one last time.

"Okay." Flint whispered, his arms releasing the wolf slowly. He reached into his shirt and drew Aldain's medallion out and off his neck. The wolf stared at him with wide eyes as the hyena pressed the gold disk into Aldain's paws. "I want you to have this back so that you never forget me. I... I don't need it to remember you." The hyena looked up at the wolf calmly, his voice weak as he said, "I'm never going to forget you Aldain."

188

The look on the wolf's face told the hyena just how deeply his heart was wounded by those words. "Oh Flint..." Aldain whispered, his paw caressing the hyena's face. "I can't take this back. You have to keep it, and remember for both of us." The wolf's words sounded so hollow and strange that they frightened Flint.

"What do you mean?" The hyena asked quietly, his muzzle gently touching the side of Aldain's.

The wolf swallowed slowly, and stared into the hyena's eyes. "The council has judged me to be corrupted. Tomorrow morning when the sun rises, they will perform an atonement ritual on me to 'cleanse' me of the thoughts that brought me to that point. They think my time with you was a single occurrence, a single act they can clean from my mind." The wolf's face became scared, and he squeezed Flint gently. "But it wasn't my first time. I have always been like this, and so the cleansing will go much deeper then they expect it to. It will change me. All my memories, my desires will be different afterward. I may not remember you or any of the others at all. I will be a completely different person."

Flint winced as if the wolf had hit him in the face. "What?" he gasped, "Why, why would you let them do that?" The hyena clutched at the wolf's shirt again, trembling in despair. "How could you forget me?" The hyena demanded in a desperate voice.

"My choices were cleansing or death." The wolf's voice was hollow, and he had a sad, empty look in his eyes. "At least this way I can protect you. I will be able to help people. To save someone innocent." The wolf's paw caressed the hyena's face, and Flint pressed against the warm paw. "Like I saved you," Aldain whispered, kissing Flint's nose tenderly as the hyena hugged him tightly.

"So, so you won't remember any of it?" The hyena's eyes flicked back and forth, and he stared up at the wolf in disbelief. "Not even tonight?" The wolf shook his head slowly, and the knight's eyes were filled with sadness.

"Then let me stay the night." Aldain blinked in surprise as the hyena's voice lost all its sorrow and fear. Flint's emerald green eyes stared up at him, and Aldain was shocked by the strength he saw in the young man's gaze. "Let me have one night to remember you by. Let me give you, the real you, one last happy moment on this earth." The hyena's paws reached up, and he brushed them across Aldain's face slowly. "No one will ever know but me."

Aldain held Flint tenderly, and those emerald eyes trapped his heart one more time. "No one will ever know," the wolf said with a slight pant, and then he kissed Flint tenderly, their muzzles meshing together for one more passionate kiss.

They held the kiss as their paws tore at each other's clothes, undoing buttons and tearing silk, rendering each of other naked as quickly possible. They moved together toward the bed, kissing wilding as they stripped each other and leaving a trail of discarded clothing behind them. Flint yipped a little as the wolf tipped him backwards, and Aldain switched to kissing the hyena's neck as they fell onto the bed together in a tangle of limbs and bare fur.

Flint began to pant heavily as the wolf on top of him wasted no time. Aldain grabbed some oil, and before he knew it Flint could feel the wolf's body settle between his legs. The hyena spread wrapped his legs around the wolf's hips as Aldain kissed him deeply. Flint put his arms around Aldain's neck, trembling with joy as the wolf's body descended on him once more. He had waited and hoped for this moment so badly that it hurt now that it was finally here. Flint hugged Aldain's hips with his knees and the wolf Flint loved entered him once more.

Both males gasped as Aldain's pushed into Flint, causing their bodies to tense and press closer together. The hyena's tail hole shuddered around the wolf's invading penis, squeezed it, and Flint stared up into the wolf's eyes as the knight hilted himself inside the hyena's body.

Flint clutched Aldain's neck until the discomfort of being taken went away, and then he relaxed into the wolf's embrace. They both sighed in relief, the tension seeming to flow out of their bodies as they joined together, as if both males had been holding their breath until that moment. The wolf pressed down on Flint with his body. Aldain began to mate his young lover slowly, their bodies shifting across each other as they made slow love to one another. They were one body again, one flesh, and it made them both whole again.

It lasted forever. Flint could feel every inch of the wolf's shaft as it pushed deep inside him. The hard pillar throbbed inside the hyena as the wolf made Flint's body his. Flint could feel it this time. The sense of completed belonging filled him as Aldain took his body again. The feeling Flint had searched for with Will, and even hoped to find in Trenton's touch now filled Flint completely as the wolf made love to him.

The hyena was home here, underneath this wolf. His body and soul belonged to Aldain. The wolf owned Flint and loved him and it made the hyena complete. Flint could feel it in the way Aldain's hips bucked and drove the wolf's cock into him, pounding against the spot inside the hyena that made his back arch and his body tingle. He could feel it when Aldain kissed

him. The wolf's passion made everything he did a possessive act. The way the wolf's paws moved across Flint's body confirmed it, as the wolf tried to touch every inch of Flint's fur with his paws. Flint closed his eyes and reveled in the feeling of completeness that filled him as he clung to the wolf's body. Aldain held the hyena tightly and felt the same way.

The two men were in heaven for a long, long time. Aldain took things slow, his thrusts measured to prolong the mating for as long physically as possible. Flint did not complain one bit; all that mattered was that the wolf was inside him again. He was home. Eventually Aldain flipped Flint over onto his stomach, his body spooning the hyena from behind as he pushed into the smaller male beneath him. Flint yipped and panted, squirming as he desperately pushed back against the invading cock inside him. He could feel the wolf's thrusts speeding up. Flint could feel them grow shorter as Aldain's knot began to press against his tail hole, swelling wider than the hyena's tail hole quickly. Flint panted, and he groaned Aldain's name when the wolf slipped one paw down and took hold of Flint's cock. The hyena's hips bucked, and his jaws snapped shut as his cock throbbed, his tail hole tightened down hard on the invading wolf's dick as he came across Aldain's bed with a stifled howl.

The wolf's knot bumped and thrust against his tail as Flint came, and the wolf's teeth gripped the back of his neck. Flint shuddered and collapsed under the suddenly hard, rough thrusts from the knight. Aldain's body tensed and Flint felt that thick, hard knot stretch him open so wide it made the hyena cry out in pain. Aldain's muzzle came down next to his own, and Flint pressed his muzzle against it, kissing the wolf hard as their eyes meet. With a sudden jerk forward the wolf popped inside, tying them together with his thick canine knot.

Aldain and Flint both moaned together, their bodies shaking as the wolf's nature joined them together as. For one, long moment, they were only one person locked together in pleasure as they came together. Their muzzles pressed against each other, their eyes stared into the others and they breathed in unison. Their bodies were as joined together as their hearts were in bliss. For that long moment, each was in heaven in the arms of the other. Aldain even whispered, "I love you" into Flint's ears, which made the hyena so happy he nearly came a second time.

Then slowly the feeling passed, as their panting fell out of sync and became erratic. Aldain lifted up off Flint's back, running his paw through his short head fur. The knight remained tied inside the young hyena for only a little while longer, his knot deflated quickly as the foolishness of their mating became apparent to the knight.

They were in the heart of the Prophet's castle, surrounded by a hundred members of the Church. If they discovered Flint here, especially like this, there would be no way Aldain could save him. Aldain hugged Flint tenderly, holding the hyena as long as he dared.

"You," the wolf panted, kissing Flint quickly. "You should go. If someone were to finds you here in my room, they might…"

"I know." Flint whispered quietly, his muzzle pressing back against Aldain's in a tender kiss. The wolf's paws traced Flint's back as the hyena touched his face with one paw, and his fingers traced the wolf's features slowly as they stared into each other's eyes. "I love you." Flint whispered, and he kissed the knight's neck tenderly, pressing his face to the wolf's shoulder.

"Flint." The hyena's head jerked back and he looked at Aldain with hope in his eyes. Aldain's heart broke as he kissed the hyena tenderly one last time, and looped the gold chain around his neck, letting his medallion fall over the hyena's heart. "Never forget me Flint," The wolf said sadly, "but never forget this either." The wolf drew back a little, his paws on Flint's shoulder. "I want you to be happy, Flint. I saved you so you could be happy, and if you find someone else I want you to be..." The hyena's eyes began to water, and he hurriedly kissed Aldain before the wolf could finish his sentence. He could not bear to hear the wolf tell him to find someone else.

"I'll never forget you." Flint said it like a solemn vow, and the wolf knew he would live on in some part through this young man. The knight nodded silently, as for a moment they held each other again.

Flint's eyes watered and his chest heaved as he got up and pulled on his shorts. Then he hugged the wolf one last time until he could stand it no longer, and then raced from the wolf's room and into the night.

Aldain hung his head as the young hyena left with tears streaming down his muzzle. The wolf hung his head and quietly began to dress, readying himself for daybreak. The wolf pulled on his boots and buckled his belt, and his eyes began to tear up. Aldain cursed his own foolish weakness as he began to cry.

Aldain's ears shot up as a yip of terror echoed through the castle outside his door. It was a barking, laugh-like cry of pain that could only have come from Flint. The knight grabbed his sword and ran from his room as fast as he could.

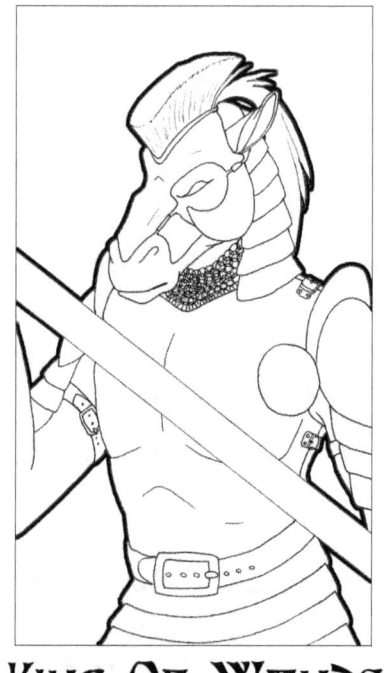

King Of Wands

Chapter VI

Tears raced down Flint's cheeks as he ran from Aldain's room. He jogged down the hallway outside the knight's room towards the castle courtyard, his bare feet slapping on the stone tile floor, because in his haste the hyena had forgotten his shoes. When he reached the arched doorway leading to the courtyard Flint stumbled to stop. The short hyena stood in the moonlight, his arms and legs trembling as his body simply refused to go any farther.

The hyena bent double as his sobs turned into heaves, full body convulsions so powerful they practically drove him to his knees. His heart ached so terribly, Flint was sure it would burst inside his chest and no matter how hard he tried not to he could not help but sob openly. Flint stared at the ground, gasping in fright when a shadow fell over the hyena. He looked up and found a tall horse in shining metal armor staring him in the face. Emblazoned on his chain mail was the Prophet's cross, and his face was twisted into a dark scowl.

"What are you doing here?" The horse knight demanded. Flint sputtered, his mind racing. Flint had forgotten more than his shoes. The cloak that made him invisible lay discarded on the floor of Aldain's room. The hyena glanced back and forth and tried to run, but his legs refused to obey him.

"I, I just…" the hyena stammered, but his mind froze as the knight drew his sword. The long steel blade glimmered in the moonlight.

"You are trespassing," Argo Steadfast said evenly, "You have five seconds to tell me why you are here…" the knight's eyes fell onto the gold medallion around Flint's neck, and his nostrils flared.

The horse felt his chest tighten in anger as he stared at the medallion around the boy's neck. Argo's nostrils flared as the scent of sex reached his nose, and he snorted in disgust when he recognized reek of Aldain's musk on the boy. A young hyena, wasn't that what Father Tully had said? The horse's anger boiled into rage.

Aldain had lied to him. The hyena had been just as willing in their sodomy as he had been, and the wolf had even betrayed the memory of his father by giving his Knight's Medallion to a damn tail raiser.

"So," Argo snorted, "You are the one Aldain has betrayed us for. You think you can just corrupt a Knight of the Cross and get away with it?" Flint raised his paws and tried to explain, but Argo gave him no opportunity too. Flint's words became a strangled cry of pain as the knight ran him through.

~: :~

Aldain raced from his room and towards the sound, but he staggered to a stop after only a few feet. The wolf's tail went limp and his sword hung from his hand as his ears swiveled back-

198

wards, splayed out wide as his muzzle fell open in shock. The world seemed to fall away from Aldain, and all the wolf could do was stare at the sight before him.

At end of the hall, framed in the archway and backlit by the moonlight, was Flint. He was cowered in front of a large, equine knight. Argo Steadfast, leader of the Order of the Cross, stood proudly over the hyena with his arm extended and sword thrust out, right through Flint's midsection and into the wall behind him.

The hyena's paws clutched at the blade, the pads sliced open as the knight withdrew his sword in a smooth, almost triumphant motion. Aldain watched blood pour from the wound as Flint sagged against the wall. The hyena looked up as the horse raised his sword to cut Flint's head from his shoulders, and Aldain howled in rage.

The wolf could see nothing but Argo's face as he rushed the horse. The other knight turned just in time to block Aldain's sword blow, but he took Aldain's fist right between the eyes. The wolf forced Argo away from Flint, hurling the larger knight to the ground as Flint slumped towards the wall behind them. The horse began to stand, blocking Aldain's next swing with his larger sword. Aldain howled at the horse as he staggered to his feet, their blades clashing.

"How could you?" Aldain shouted, his blade sending sparks flying as it slid along Argo's sword. The wolf's teeth flashed as he tried to catch the horse off guard with a bite, but the older knight stepped back quickly. "He was only a boy!"

The horse snorted and shoved the shorter wolf back, using his height and reach to his advantage. "How could you Aldain? How could you sully your father's memory with your debauchery?"

The horse swung his sword up, caught the wolf's blade, and then shoved hard, trying to trip Aldain with an outstretched hoof. The wolf and horse struggled, their bodies pressed close and their swords useless as they fought to push each other down.

As they clashed, Flint let out a loud whine that was filled with pain. Aldain's eyes widened at the sound, he growled loudly, and shoved Argo back as hard as he could. The horse toppled to the ground, and Aldain swung his sword in a wide arch at the fallen horse's head. The flat of the blade struck the Cardinal alongside his head and he went down, knocked out cold. Only chance and the wolf's rage saved the man from being beheaded.

Aldain did not waste another moment on the horse. The wolf rushed to Flint's side, sheathing his sword in a practiced motion as he brought his paws to the hyena's wound. Flint grunted in pain as the wolf's touch made the wound burn, but the wolf's muzzle pressed against Flint's and the hyena's wild eyes calmed when he recognized the wolf. "It's okay Flint, I'm here, and I've got you." The wolf smiled weakly as he summoned his power to heal, staring the hyena in the eyes. "I can heal you remember? Remember our first night?"

The hyena's muzzle twitched, and he grinned weakly at Aldain. "Yeah…" he muttered quietly, blood beginning to leak from one corner of his muzzle. The hyena's blood was everywhere, covering the wolf's paws as he tried to heal the young man he loved.

Nothing happened. Aldain furrowed his brow and summoned the magic he had used so many times to save so many lives, but the power did not come. The knight's magic failed him. The wolf could feel where his divine strength had once been inside him, but now it was gone. Aldain knew in that instant, deep in his heart that the Prophet had refused to heal Flint.

The wolf began to panic as he looked back up at Flint's face, but the hyena's eyes were already glazing over. The wolf pulled off his shirt, tying it quickly around the hyena midsection in an attempt to bind his wound, but it was nearly hopeless. The wound went right through him, and he was loosing too much blood. Aldain picked Flint up off the ground and carried him as fast as he could towards the main chapel.

~: :~

"I need a priest!" Aldain shouted as loud as he could, bursting through the main doors backwards so he did not hurt Flint any worse than he already was. "Father I need healing," the wolf shouted again, and he spotted a calico cat priest rushing towards him. The knight held Flint still as the young priest moved his slender paws, summoning the Prophet's mercy. The cat's paws glowed a brilliant blue and he reached out towards Flint's back as another door in the chapel burst open again.

"Stop right there, Brother! By the authority of the Inquisition, do not heal that boy if you value your soul." Father Tully raced toward them from the back of the cathedral, and the old otter's sandaled feet slapped on the stone floor as he jogged up to them.

"What are you doing out of your rooms Aldain? Why is that thing here?" The otter pointed at Flint accusingly, "How could you bring someone so unclean into our house of worship?"

"He needs help!" Aldain shouted at the old priest. "He's been stabbed, help him." The wolf's cries turned desperate as the cat priest backed away from the wolf and hyena, and the otter stepped between them. "That's what we do," Aldain pleaded.

"Then why have you not healed him yourself then?" The otter spat back, the fire returning to the old priest's eyes. "Or have you tried," the otter's tone became measured, and he turned his muzzle up at the wolf, "and failed?"

Aldain stared at the otter and his eyes narrowed dangerously as realization struck. "You revoked my knighthood? You took my powers away from me, and you did not even warn me?"

The otter's gaze remained neutral as he placed his paws behind his back, "You gave me no choice. Until your atonement is complete, your knighthood is forfeit." Father Tully did not even look at Flint. "And that heathen will find no help here."

Aldain stared at the otter in dumbfound shock. "If you will not help him, then I was never a knight to begin with." The wolf turned and raced from the chapel, and the otter's paw reached out to stop the calico cat when the younger priest tried to follow after him.

"No," Father Tully said coldly, a smile dancing across the otter's lips as Aldain disappeared through the castle gates and into the city. "The fool has made his choice. Go and summon Lord Argo."

~: :~

Aldain held Flint tightly, cradling the boy against his chest as he raced out of the castle and into the city streets. The wolf panted and ran as fast as he could, his hind paws skittering on the cobblestones as his grip on Flint began to slip because of the hyena's blood. He had to find a healer. Fast.

Aldain searched desperately for a temple, but the knight could not remember where any of the rival faiths were located. The Church allowed only a few inside the city walls, and he had never needed to go to them before now. The wolf cursed himself and ran harder, keeping Flint as close to his chest as he could in the hopes of staunching the blood flow with his grip alone. The wolf just had to hope that one of the outer parishes did not know of his transgressions yet and would heal Flint without asking many questions.

The streets flew by as Flint's breathing became labored, and the few people left on the streets scattered out of Aldain's way as he ran. The people of Newcastle had learned a long time ago to stay out of a knight's way, but for the first time Aldain wondered if they moved out of respect or fear.

Aldain turned down a small alleyway to cut between two busy streets when Flint's paw pressed unsteadily against his face. Aldain could feel hyena's paw smear blood across the gray fur on his face, and then Flint's face came into view as he pushed himself up so he was sitting up in the wolf's arms instead of lying against his chest. The hyena had a big, goofy grin on his muzzle and leaned forward awkwardly, his muzzle bumping sharply into Aldain's as the wolf ran. The wolf was startled by the rough attempt to nuzzle him and he stopped running, clutching Flint tightly to keep from dropping him.

The hyena's eyes twitched back and forth as he looked at Aldain's face, and the wolf looked back in stunned silence. The young male looked at him with nothing but love in his eyes. There was no anger, no sadness, and no pain in Flint's face. Just a happy smile as he stared into the eyes of the one he loved. Flint's smile twitched and he whispered, "I love you Aldain," in the wolf's ear, and it almost made Aldain cry. The words were so tender, so caring that they frightened Aldain to his very core. Aldain smiled as Flint's breath passed over the wolf's ear, and he stared into the hyena's big green eyes. Aldain had never seen the complete devotion or love that looked back at him from Flint's eyes.

Aldain's chest tightened when that love drained from the hyena's eyes. Flint's muzzle was still twisted into a smile and pressed against Aldain's own in a tender nuzzle, but it no longer moved as the hyena breathed in and out. Flint's ears remained perked up, but the hyena's eyes were now lifeless emeralds, without any of the love or innocence Aldain had come to cherish. Flint was dead.

"Flint?" the wolf whispered in disbelief, his paw caressing the hyena's face tenderly. The knight stared into the boy's emerald green orbs, but this time there was no one there to look back at him.

Aldain stood perfectly still, unwilling to believe the boy had just passed away in his arms like that. He held the hyena tightly so Flint's now limp body would not move, trying to stand perfectly still. It felt as if moving would somehow make it all real. No matter how hard Aldain tried, the wolf could not keep his ears from pressing against his head or his tail from sliding down between his legs. "No..." the wolf muttered, choking on his words. "No, this can't be happening." The wolf felt so horrible he wanted to scream. It felt like a hole had been ripped in Aldain's heart as he stared into the hyena's hollow, emotionless eyes. "You can't die Flint." the wolf whined, almost begging. "You can't." he pleaded, but to no avail. The hyena was gone.

Aldain moved his paw across the boy's face, carefully closing Flint's eyes. The slight movement made the hyena's muzzle tilt forward, and it rubbed against Aldain's cheek as the weight of

hyena's body made him slump forward against the wolf's chest. Flint's arms gave the wolf a limp mockery of a hug as his body settled lifelessly into the wolf's arms. Aldain cradled the boy's body against his chest and began to cry. The wolf just stood there in street, dumbstruck as the hyena's lifeless body pressed against his throat and chest. The warmth of Flint's fur rapidly escaped into the cold night, and a chill settled into Aldain's fur as the hyena's blood soaked through his clothes and pelt to the wolf's skin and turned cold in the night air.

Aldain's chest ached and his legs trembled as he continued to hold the dead hyena in his arms, unwilling to move an inch even though he knew Flint was gone. The weight of Flint's body began to make the wolf's arms burn, and he struggled to hold the hyena up just a little bit longer, but there was no way the wolf could fight gravity. With a sharp cry of sorrow and pain, the knight's knees buckled and Aldain fell to the ground.

The wolf ignored the pains of his body as best he could, still cradling Flint's body in his arms. Aldain stared down at the young hyena's face, his small features and slight frame making Flint seem so fragile even though there was no way to hurt him now.

Aldain could feel the tears begin to well up in his eyes as he stared at Flint's still form. How could he have let this happen? How could he have failed the boy so completely? Aldain couldn't even protect Flint from just five feet away. Aldain tried to wrap his mind around what had happened, but he just couldn't believe how totally he had failed Flint.

Aldain had used the boy back in East Haven, and then pushed him away not once but twice. Then the wolf had let him die, right in the middle of the abbey. On the sword of another knight!

Argo had killed Flint without a second thought. Aldain balled his fists, his chest heaving as his sorrow turned to rage. All Flint had wanted was the wolf's love and company. How much was that to ask? Even Flint's last breath had been a declaration of love. A single, deadly thought entered into Aldain's brain, wedged there like a steel spike.

The boy did not deserve this. Flint did not deserve to die, and there was only one thing he could do now.

"I will not let this happen to you," the wolf whispered, staring intently at the young hyena's still face. Aldain cradled Flint's head against his shoulder and picked Flint's body up carefully. The hyena's blood covered Aldain almost from head to toe now. The wolf began to jog into the night, carrying the dead hyena in his arms, his destination fixed firmly in his mind.

~: :~

Father Tully waited in the empty chapel for Argo to arrive, reading a passage from the Chronicles. The otter's muzzle broke into a mean smile when Argo came into the room, his hooves echoing on the tile floor. The tall horse rubbed the side of his head, and he looked as if his spirit had been broken.

"So Lord Argo," the otter said casually. "Are you are ready to admit you were wrong about your favorite knight? That he has been corrupted of his own free will?"

The horse flicked his ears back with a snort. Argo's eyes were smoldering with anger as he watched the otter smile at him. "Yes," the horse muttered, "but Aldain's actions do not prove the Order itself has been corrupted."

"That may be true," the otter said, closing his book. "Luckily, you have the opportunity to prove the Order is still loyal to the Church." The otter stood up and walked over to the taller horse, looking him over slowly. The otter touched his collar, tapping the Inquisitor's pin slightly to indicate that Argo's pin was out of place

Argo blinked and reached up to the small medal he wore as well, his scowl darkening for a moment. The otter wasn't acting as a priest tonight. Tonight he spoke for the Inquisition.

Father Tully smiled as the horse fixed the pin. "Good. Now, my sources in the guards say that Aldain has left the city, heading west carrying his heavily wounded hyena friend." The otter sneered the last word, his whisker twitching as Tully look up at the horse. "There is only one place he can go for help in that direction, and that is to the druids. If you slay Aldain tonight, then I will report to the Grand Inquisitor that your Order is indeed loyal to him."

"I cannot kill a fellow knight," Argo protested, "He must stand trial..."

"Aldain is no longer a knight. I have rescinded the Prophet's favor from him, a power that the Grand Inquisitor has bestowed upon me," the otter narrowed his eyes, "to use as I see fit. You will kill Aldain tonight Argo, and the boy he was with. Or else I shall find you to be in collusion with corrupted beings, Lord Argo, and someone else will become the leader of the Order of the Cross."

Silence filled the room as Argo breathed slowly in and out for a few moments. The horse knew this was a test, that the otter had likely caused all of this to happen just to force Argo to follow the Inquisition's orders. If he did this, there would be no going back. The Order would become a sword for the Inquisition.

Argo nodded once, and left the room without a word.

Father Tully tossed his book onto the table, bowed once to the altar, and left as well. Neither man noticed the slim tabby cat watching them from the shadows of the temple, kneeling in the back row of pews where he had been praying for forgiveness for most of the night. As Father Thomas stood up, his striped paws trembling, and he knew in his heart what he had to do.

~: :~

Trenton wandered towards the front of the chapel, drawing close to where Will was kneeling beside the altar of the Goddess. The jackal's black fur drank in what little light the candles shed, and the moon outside did not make the black furred male any easier to see. Trenton leaned on his staff and sighed softly, watching as the jackal prayed. The jackal's ear's twitched, and he turned to glare at the fox. "You don't have to stay here, you know. Go back to the inn. I'll wait for Flint to return."

The fox's tail flicked back and forth, and he huffed just a bit. "Like I would be able to sleep," The noble muttered.

"We should never have let him go," Will muttered quietly, and then silence returned as Will went back to praying.

The fox twitched his left ear and looked down at the floor. "I know."

"Flint would never have stayed, even if you had tried." Zane made his way into the chapel. His green robes flowed behind him as the druid moved silently across the stone floor. "I saw the look in that young man's eyes," the coyote said quietly, as Will and Trenton looked up at the druid. "There was no way you could have prevented him from going."

"Maybe," Will muttered, "but we should have tried harder..."

A loud bang on the main doors made everyone turn towards the door. The metallic clang sounded again, and again as someone began to beat relentlessly on the door with something metal. Zane almost made it to the chapel doors before the wooden bar holding them closed splintered under the repeated blows. A wolf in the armor of a knight shouldered the door open.

"What is the meaning of this? You cannot barge into this house, even if you are Knight of the Cross." The coyote shouted, but when the stranger turned around the coyote's anger turned instantly to concern. The wolf was covered from head to toe in blood, and he carried a grievously wounded hyena.

"You the Head Druid? Fix him," the wolf demanded, his voice offering no hint of compromise.

The coyote did not even look at the knight; he had eyes only for Flint. "Oh little one, what have you done?" Zane whispered, and the druid's paws began to glow a soft blue color as he summoned a healing spell. When the coyote's paw touched Flint, the power of the Goddess had nowhere to go, and the coyote knew the truth in an instant. The hyena was already gone.

"He is already dead, knight." The coyote looked up into the wolf's eyes, and he knew that this wolf had to be the knight that Flint had claimed to love. "I'm sorry."

"I know that," The wolf snapped as Will and Trenton came running towards them. "And I told you to fix him."

"Oh my god," the fox muttered, staring at Flint's lifeless body. The fox cradled the boy's head as Aldain held him, and tears began to form in the noble's eyes.

Will took one look at the hyena and shouted, "What the hell happened Aldain?" The jackal's hackles were up and his teeth bared, but Aldain just shoved Will out of his way. The wolf grabbed Zane by the collar of his robe and dragged the Druid bodily towards the altar, wading through his friends like a storm.

"Stand aside, Will. Now," the wolf rounded on the coyote. "Let me get the little things out of the way. Yes, I know where your temple is. No, the Inquisition does not, and they are not coming here tonight. I don't care that you hate us, all I care about is that you," the wolf hurled the coyote against the alter, where Zane came to a stop with a shocked look on his muzzle, "can bring the dead back to life."

The coyote said nothing at first; he just closed his muzzle and stared passively at Aldain. The wolf ignored his companions as they began to talk over each other, demanding to know what happened to Flint. The wolf just clutched Flint tightly to his chest and stared the druid down. Eventually, the coyote's eyes flicked away from the wolf's gaze.

"I can restore him to life," Zane said quietly. "But there will be a price."

Will and Trenton stopped talking and stared at the coyote. "What?" The fox and jackal muttered together. "Wait, really?" Trenton shouldered his way between the knight and druid, "You can you bring him back as in back to life? Not just as a zombie or something?"

The coyote nodded slightly, his eyes nervously watching the knight. "Yes, the Goddess can restore your friend to life, but she will demand a high price. There is a balance in nature that must be maintained."

"I will pay it." The wolf said simply as he moved towards the altar.

"Do you realize what that means knight?" Zane said, "Will you really give up your life for his?"

Aldain laid Flint out on the stone slab, his paw caressing the dead hyena's face. "He already did for me."

The druid lowered his head, "It will be a few hours before I can have the ritual prepared." The coyote looked at Will and Trenton, and they stared at each other at a loss for words. The fox and jackal moved towards the altar and the bloody wolf, and Zane went to fetch the materials he needed for the ritual.

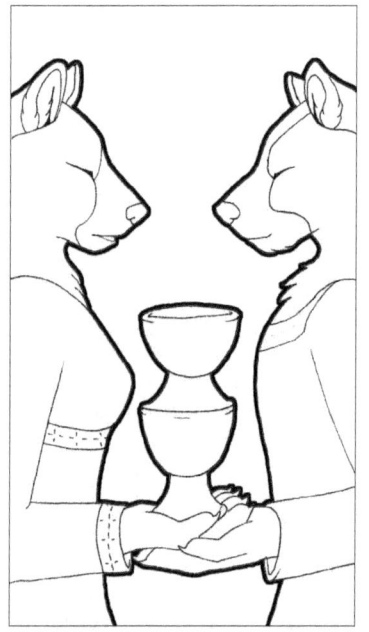

Two Of Cups

Chapter VII

B
lack sand ran between Flint's fingers as he closed his paw. The presence of sand made no sense to the hyena, because moments ago his paw had been clutching Aldain's face. His fingers should be sliding through the wolf's fur, touching the soft skin beneath as he hugged the knight. Instead, fine grains of sand slipped through the hyena's fingers and it felt like he was lying face down on the ground. Flint struggled to understand what was happening to him. The world seemed to spin wildly around him, as if he were falling endlessly, but Flint knew that he was laying face down in the sand. Flint opened his eyes and tried to stand up, but all he could do was roll over onto his side. The pain in his stomach was gone, but every movement he made took so much effort. Flint opened his eyes, and what he saw made the hyena's legs curl against his chest in fear.

The black sand formed a vast desert that stretched out as far as the eyes could see, a rolling sea of blackness shifting slowly in the wind. In the distance, jagged mountains rose up against a sky filled with unfamiliar stars. There were no plants or animals, no life at all; just endless sand glittering in a soft light that had no source. "Hello?" Flint shouted, his ears folding back in fright as the sound came out as a whisper. "Aldain!" Flint tried to shout again, easing himself onto his knees as he looked around panic. The desert swallowed the hyena's words, turning them into a whisper only barely audible above the gentle howl of the wind and shifting sand.

Flint staggered to his feet and looked around slowly, trying to figure out how he had gotten here. He could remember the castle, and the equine knight that had stabbed him. He remembered Aldain carrying him through the streets. The wolf had been holding him tightly and crying as he ran, but after that everything was a blank. It was like he had fallen asleep. Flint stood up slowly, his limbs aching and his paws trembling. Then Flint saw something move.

It was a sliver of color on the edge of his vision, just a flash of white in the monochromatic landscape. Fear grabbed hold of Flint, freezing his legs and tail as he turned his head to look. There, coming over the rise of the nearest dune, was a dalmatian dressed in black robes. The dog's white fur stood out against the black sands, his tattered robes shifting in the wind as he came over the ridge of sand, a long black scarf fluttering behind him in the breeze.

A black plume of dust rose into the air as the dog slide down the side of the hill, the sand drifting in the air lazily as the dalmatian came towards him, one arm raised in greeting. "Hello there, little one." the dog called out. It looked like the dog had shouted the words, but the silence of the landscape suppressed the sound somehow, making the words echo as if the dalmatian were miles away from Flint.

"Hello?" Flint called out, and the word was nearly drowned by the quiet wind. "What's going on?" Flint could see the dog better now.

The man's robes were torn around the bottom, and his scarf was whipping in the breeze, but the dog was smiling happily. It was a charming smile, and he waved at Flint a second time. "Hello young man, my name is Bayon. Are you alright?" the dog said with another smile. The way his words became whispers frightened Flint, but the dog's smile was very disarming.

"I, I don't know," Flint stammered, his eyes scanning the sand dunes. "Where am I? What is this place?"

"This is the land of the dead," the dalmatian said, calmly holding his paws behind his back. "I'm afraid you've died young man."

"Dead?" Flint yelped his voice pitched quite high. The dalmatian smiled slowly, and pointed down at Flint's stomach.

Flint touched his stomach, afraid of what he would find. The short brown fur on his stomach was matted with blood. Flint looked down at himself and the dried blood that covered his paws. He could see the stab wound from the knight's sword, but there was no pain. Flint began to gasp, his chest heaving in fear as he stood in the black dessert, and then he realized something. Until now, he had not been breathing at all. Flint stopped, holding his breath in fear until he realized that it didn't matter.

Flint crossed his arms over his belly defensively. He wanted to cry, but it wouldn't do anything would it? He was standing in a desert of black sand, in only his underwear and medallion, and he was dead.

Bayon patted the young man on his shoulder, "Yes, I'm sorry Flint, we're both dead," Bayon said smoothly. "But as you can see, that is not the end of the world."

The dalmatian smiled brightly, his mind working fast. He had been dead for weeks now, and the experience had not been what he had expected. To say that Mak'tchen had been angry with Bayon for failing in life did not do the Devourer's rage justice. The terrible, badger-like beast he had worshiped in life frightened the dalmatian beyond words now, but his master had given him one, very final, opportunity to serve before he entered Mak'tchen's afterlife. If Bayon could still complete his task and deliver Flint to the Great Devourer in death, then he might be forgiven for his failures in life. At least, he would be allowed to remain in Mak'tchen's service as something other then a meal. There was a pause as the hyena seemed to think of something, and Bayon grinned broadly at the young man, "So, why don't you come with me Flint?"

Flint's brow creased in confusion. Even in life, he had never met this dalmatian. "How do you know my name?" Flint said, and then made the mistake of looking into the dalmatian's eyes.

Bayon's eyes flashed red and his voice had a strange echo to it. "Follow me," the dog commanded, and Bayon's dog's gaze seemed to fill Flint's thoughts with cotton, making it impossible for the hyena to think clearly. The dog tugged on Flint's paw and Flint did as he was commanded, following the handsome dog across the dessert.

~: :~

Will sat just outside the main chapel, pretending to pray for guidance. In reality, the jackal was just brooding, his thoughts whirling as he waited for Zane to prepare the ritual. The jackal was roused from his thoughts by a knocking at the outer door.

He glanced around, and got up to see who it was. He stared out the slot in the door, and then pulled the iron bolt back. "What are you doing here?" the jackal said gruffly as he opened the door for Father Thomas.

The tabby cat flared his whiskers in surprise, but remained calm. "William. Good to see you again," the tabby said quietly.

"Make it quick Father, tonight it not a good night," The jackal growled.

"No it is not," the tabby said quietly, smoothing his whiskers with his paws. " A band of knights is coming for Aldain and his hyena friend. They believe he is here, and will attack the druids in less than an hour."

The jackal blinked, and his frown darkened into a scowl. "And you have come to warn us then?" Will snapped, "Or are you here to ask us nicely to turn him over?"

"To warn you. Hello Trenton." Father Thomas said sadly as the fox came up behind Will. "I cannot let the Inquisition start a holy war over this, and if this temple burns then there will be a war between the old faiths and the Church again." The tabby lifted his chin a bit, licking his nose as Zane came to the doorway to the main temple, "Too many people died in the old wars, and I do not want to see that happen again."

"Then you are not very good priest, Father Thomas." The coyote said darkly, and the tabby cat averted his eyes from the hooded man's glare.

"Perhaps not," the cat said haughtily, "but I do not believe the Prophet…"

"How many were there?" the jackal barked, and Trenton jumped at the jackal's outburst.

Thomas did too, his fur fluffing out under his robe. "Five," He said quietly, smoothing himself down with his paws. "All are well trained knights."

"A war party." Trenton said evenly, "At least we have time to prepare. I can ward the main doors and perhaps buy us the element of surprise. Go and tell Aldain, we'll need his help for this."

The jackal shot Trenton a sharp look. "Aldain can't fight them," the jackal growled. "The Order will try to kill him on sight. Where will that leave Flint?"

The fox stared at Will, the emotion gone from his voice as he readied himself for battle. "Then unless you still want to take his place, we need to make sure that doesn't happen."

~: :~

The foyer of the temple was deathly silent. The waiting made Father Thomas's tail twitch and his fur stand on end. The tabby cat stood on the far side of the room from the main door and away from the tunnel leading in from the surface. With the cold, stone wall at his back, the cat waited with his tail and claws twitching in anticipation.

Eventually, the sound of men approaching reached the cat's ears as heavy hooves stepped onto the stone floor. Two armor-clad knights, an imposing bull and lion with crosses emblazoned on their chest plates and shields, edged their way into the foyer with their swords at the ready. They glanced at Father Thomas in surprise, unsure what to do.

Thomas waited as they looked him over, glanced at each other, and motioned for someone to come forward. Argo strode into the room as if it were a council meeting instead of the temple of an enemy faith. The horse glanced around the room once, and snorted. "Father, what are you doing here?" the horse said with a flat tone in his voice as two more knights flanked him. The fox and mouse knights looked like fast, wiry fighters, and did not have the heavy armor on that the others wore.

The tabby cat cleared his throat and said, "I am trying to stop you from making a mistake. You shouldn't be doing this Argo." The cat's confidence grew as several of the knights looked at each other with worried expressions on their faces and Argo closed his eyes. The horse was gritting his teeth so hard the cat though he might crack a tooth. "This situation needs a delicate touch, Argo," Thomas said smoothly, taking a step towards the knight, "I know Father Tully has…"

Everyone watching the two men gasped as Argo spun towards the tabby cat and swung his sword, nearly cutting the priest in two. The knight's heavy sword sliced the cat from hip to neck and threw blood across the wall as Thomas collapsed. "I will not be corrupted by listening to more traitors," the horse said coldly. The horse looked at his knights with a fire in his eyes. The bull and lion seemed pleased, but the fox knelt beside the priest to heal him.

"No one touch him," the horse snapped. "Whatever has poisoned his mind may be contagious." The fox knight flattened his ears and looked at Thomas's eyes as the cat struggled to speak, blood pooling around the cat as his eyes closed. The priest's breathing grew shallow as the fox held his paw over the dying priest.

"Break down the door," Argo commanded, "and kill anyone you find inside." The horse pointed to the temple door with his sword, and very nearly clipped the little ball of fire that came flying out from between the barely open doors with the blade. The fireball struck Argo in the chest and erupted into a brilliant explosion that flooded the room with light and scorching flames.

~: ~

"Here they come," Trenton yelped as he pulled his fingers back as Will closed the door and barred it. Painful bellows and the crackling sound of fire filtered through the heavy door as the knights outside dealt with Trenton's fiery spell.

"That was pretty harsh Trenton." Zane muttered, warily watching the fox take up a position in the back of the room. "I did not like Father Thomas much but he was never..."

"Argo killed him." The fox muttered, readying several magic wands and potions for the battle. There was a moment of silence, as the party members and Zane bowed their heads slightly. The silence was broken by Trenton's voice as the fox began casting spells to strengthen the group, shielding them in magical armor and quickening their movements in the vain hope of giving them an edge against the knights outside.

Will smiled slightly, readying one of his throwing knives as he glanced at Aldain, who was standing shoulder to shoulder with the jackal now. They were standing in the main aisle of the temple, preventing anyone who entered the door from reaching the altar. "At least this way we've forced them to use up their healing powers," the jackal muttered, "We'll only have to kill them once."

Then the door gave a massive shudder as someone struck it from the outside. "Small blessings..." the wolf muttered, his eyes emotionless as they waited for the door to give way.

There was a second, and third heavy thud before the bar broke and the door splintered inward, allowing the hot air and scent of burned fur to fill the temple. The knights made for an impressive sight, because although they were all panting and surrounded in scorch marks, none of them were burned. Only the fox knight in the back looked the least bit singed. Every man clutched his weapon close, knowing that at this point combat was inevitable.

Argo bellowed a battle cry, and the knights charged, two heading for Zane and Trenton as the rest rushed to surround Aldain and Will together.

Zane roared in response to the attack, a deep primal bellow rolling out of the smaller druid as the lion slashed at him. Zane's sleek coyote form shifted and grew as the knight's sword drew blood along his shoulder and forearm. The wound would have seriously hurt the coyote had he still been a normal man. As a huge feral coyote larger than a riding horse, the druid shrugged the blow way as if it were nothing. The lion did not react as well too the massive set of jaws the druid closed around his shoulder. Zane's jaws jerked to the side, sending the knight tumbling to the ground where the huge coyote proceeded to maul him.

Will and Aldain spun towards the charging knights, moving together to force the knights to split around them like water around them. Each of the adventures blocked blows meant for the other, their years of adventuring together allowing Aldain and Will to move in concert with each other, keeping their backs together and preventing the knights from surrounding one of them to gain an advantage. They traded blows with the knights, who began to circle around the pair like sharks. Argo was strong and the fox was swift, while the mouse weaved and bobbed as they fought, ducking every blow the adventures tried to land.

The disgraced knight and rogue weathered the knight's attacks fairly well, waiting for their chance. It came when the mouse bobbed away from the other two knights, and the two canines launched their attack. They spun sideways, forcing the shorter mouse between them. Aldain lashed out at the mouse with a sweeping blow to the head, and the mouse deftly avoided the blow by ducking and stepping away from the wolf. Aldain felt sorry for the mouse as Will grabbed him from behind. The mouse's eyes widened in pain as Will's daggers plunged deep into gaps in the knight's armor. The mouse gave a pained squeak and collapsed, likely dying, as the two canines turned to face the horse and fox on even terms.

Trenton did not fare was well the others had. As the bull charged at him, Trenton used his position at the back of the room to launch a spell meant to paralyze the charging bovine. The spell made the bull falter for a moment, but he shook off the effects, and Trenton did not have the chance to cast again before the bull crashed into him. The taller knight used his shield like a battering ram, sending the slender mage tumbling to the ground with a yelp. Trenton's tail and legs flailed as he tried to stand up, but the bull stomped on the fox and held him down, sword raised to strike him dead. The blow would have likely landed, had Will had not caught sight of the fox's plight and rushed to aid him.

The thief leapt over the fallen mouse, rolled beneath the knight's blow, and caught the bull's blade with crossed daggers. The jackal put everything he had into turning the blow aside, but the bull was much stronger than the lithe jackal, and the heavy blade slammed down into Will's shoulder. The bull laughed, smashing his shield into the jackal's black muzzle. Will cried out in pain and fell to his knees, stunned.

224

Trenton watched in horror as Will fell and the knight raised his sword again. The bull brought the blade down in a powerful chopping motion and slashed the jackal across the chest with enough force that the blade sliced right through his armor and fur to the bone. The bull even laughed as the jackal collapsed at Trenton's feet, and he stepped over Will's groaning form to kill the fox as Trenton scrambled backwards. The fox squeezed his paws together and gathered up a spell, his fingers moving as he wove a powerful spell fueled by his anger.

There was sharp intake of air as Trenton's cupped his paws around his muzzle, his magic focusing on the fox's voice. "LEAVE!" the fox bellowed, and the force of his rage combined with the spell to form a deadly wave of sound. The wave passed over the Will and slammed into the bull's chest, lifting him off the ground and flinging him across the temple. The bovine knight slammed into a row of wooden pews that shattered like kindling as the knight struck them. The bull came to a stop in a heap of broken wood and twisted armor, where he lay unmoving. The wave of sound spread out from the fox's muzzle, washing over everything in the temple.

The sound splintered the church pews, shattered the stained glass windows, and flattened everyone standing in its path. Aldain gasped in pain as the sound wave flowed over him. The wolf dropped his sword and covered his ears, opened his mouth and tried to relax as the sound shook his body. The wolf had been caught in this spell before, and Trenton had told him how to avoid the deadlier effects of the spell. The other knights in the room were not so prepared.

The spell flattened the fox knight outright and killed the wounded mouse on the ground. Argo's bellow of pain was lost in the sound of the spell, which drove the horse down to his knees. The spell rattled everything the horse wore, cracking the gems in his sword hilt and fracturing the metal plates of his armor just like the stained glass windows.

Even Zane and the lion knight were caught up in the spell. The druid was flung against the far wall, his larger body providing a bigger target for the spell's outer edge. The lion Zane had been tearing apart was knocked unconscious as the fox's spell washed over his mauled body.

As Trenton's spell faded, silence filled the temple. Everyone but Will and Trenton had been deafened by the spell. Aldain grabbed his sword and stood his ground, weaving a bit as the ringing in his ears faded into silence. The only person with the strength to get to his feet to face him was Argo.

The battered horse staggered backwards away from the wolf, trying to get some distance between him and the mage before the fox decided to kill him outright. The horse looked around the room for a moment, weighing his chances. At least two of his knights were dead, and the other two would join them soon if they weren't dead already. There was probably no way he could take Aldain in his condition before the fox tipped the scales in the wolf's favor. His healing powers were exhausted, and the monstrous druid would be getting to his feet soon. With a snort the horse turned and retreated from the temple, cursing as he was forced to leave his fellow knights to die at heathen hands.

Trenton staggered to Will's side, cradling the thief as he lay on the floor, trying to hold Will's wound closed to stop the bleeding. The fox's paws fluttered across the jackal's face, and he was gasping in fear as he looked into the eyes of his closest friend as the jackal bled across the floor. "Zane! Zane, help me!" the fox yelped hoarsely as he rubbed his face against the jackal's muzzle. Will's muzzle turned into a pained smile as the fox caressed his face, their muzzles pressed together.

"You can't leave me," the fox whispered to the only other person who could hear him, his ears folded back against his head as the fox looked into the jackal's eyes and nuzzled his wounded friend's face, "You can't leave me Will." Trenton muttered again as a shadow passed over the jackal's face. Someone knelt by his side and healed the wounded rogue.

Will gave a bark as his wounds closed, and Trenton sighed in relief as the huge gash across Will's closed. "Thank you, Father," Will muttered, and Trenton looked up in surprise to see Father Thomas standing over them.

Will and Thomas both smiled as Trenton threw his arms around the tabby's neck. "You're alive!" the fox barked happily, "But how?" Trenton asked, pulling his head back. "I saw the horse cut you down."

The tabby cat smiled, "That young fox knight was not willing to follow Argo's orders and let me die. I owe that young fox my life," the tabby raised his eyebrows at Will, "and so do you. I hope he is still alive."

"I think so," Will muttered as his paw rubbed the fox's head-fur. "Unless this loudmouth finished the job."

"You're horrible William." Trenton muttered as he looked back at Will and hugged his neck tightly. "I'm so glad you're alive," The fox muttered, tears choking his voice this time. The jackal seemed to blush under his dark fur as the fox hugged him, but it was hard to tell. The tabby cat turned away so his presence would not embarrass the jackal further, seeing to the wounded and dead knights.

Zane stood guard over the fallen knights, healing them just enough so that they would not pass into the next life. Thomas got the young fox healed well to stand, but the lion was still badly wounded and remained unconscious. The gashes and puncture wounds he had received tussling with Zane's monstrous form seemed to resist the tabby's magic.

Then the cat performed last rights over the mouse and bull, and asked for a cart to carry them home in. The druids did not speak to the priest; they simply went and got a horse and buggy. When the cart was hitched up and ready to go, the tabby cat came up to the coyote that had stood watching them the whole time. Thomas nervously coughed as he brushed his paws clean on his burned robes, patches of blood staining the cotton.

"Please accept my apologies for this unprovoked attack," the tabby muttered, his eyes moving across the men he had once adventured with. "I wish I could have persuaded my fellows to follow a more peaceful course."

Zane snorted, "Your faith has never followed the peaceful course Thomas. You are a good man. For years, you led a simple flock of good people out here in the countryside. You lived in peace with us because you are a sensible, kind-hearted man, but your Prophet carved his way into heaven with a sword and earned his purity by putting others to the fire. I doubt our two faiths will ever know peace, unless you do something to change yours." The coyote turned his back on the priest, moving toward the altar to continue his ritual.

Will shrugged slightly, working his newly healed shoulder. "You had better go, Thomas. Tell your fellow council members that Aldain has left their service for good. Anyone who comes back looking for revenge over what happened tonight won't walk away like these two." The jackal jerked his head towards the fox and lion. "Not even you." The jackal spoke the words softly.

Thomas's paws tightened into fists at the threat, and the tabby slipped them into his robes to hide that fact. The tabby met the rogue's eyes, and he knew that the jackal regretted having to say those words, but he would not regret carrying them out. Thomas nodded once and said, "Well then, this is goodbye Will. Aldain. If either of you need me, I will be in my parish. I doubt I will be serving on the council after this." The tabby cat turned his back on the temple and made his way outside.

It was quiet outside the temple where the cart was waiting. Trenton sat in the seat beside the vulpine knight, talking quietly with the man. "You sure you won't reconsider?" Trenton said quietly, and the fox shook his head.

"Your family may be nobility, but I won't leave the church. Not yet." The fox looked back at the bed of the cart, which was filled with the bodies of two knights and the unconscious form of a third. "If I can change them from the inside, perhaps this sort of thing won't happen again." The knight cast his eyes to the ground as Thomas approached, and Trenton patted his shoulder gently.

The fox carefully slipped a piece of paper into the knight's paw, out of the tabby's view, and whispered, "Come to this address if you need help. My family could always use a loyal servant who doesn't believe their lord is perfect."

The fox nodded once as Trenton got down and Thomas climbed up beside him. Trenton looked up at the tabby, and for a second they looked at each other without speaking. Trenton had always found the tabby to be stuffy, finicky, and tough to deal with, but a fine man who always did the right thing. They had always been at odds with each other, but always on the same side. "Goodbye Thomas," the fox whispered. "You should come to Irena some day for the festivals."

The tabby nodded once. "I'll try." Then the knight snapped the reigns, and they drove their fallen brothers home.

Aldain watched everything without moving away from Flint's body, just standing in a daze in the center of the ruined temple. All around the wolf, broken wood and shattered glass crunched under the returning druids paws. Aldain looked up at the walls, where the stain glass windows had once been. They had given the cavern the appearance of a building, making you feel like the druid's temple was above ground in the sunlight, where it belonged. Now, bare rock was visible though the broken windows. They had been an illusion, and just like his old life, they were beyond repair. Aldain closed his eyes and simply knelt down beside the altar where Flint's body lay, and waited for his fate to claim him.

~: ~

Flint staggered a bit as he trailed across the sand dunes beside Bayon. The dalmatian was still talking, or at least sounds were coming out of his mouth. It was hard to hear him properly, not because of what the desert did something to sound, but because of what he was saying. If the guttural sounds were words, then they were a language Flint did not understand. The problem was, the dalmatian's words made it so hard for the hyena to think. Every time he got his thoughts into line and tried to do something other then follow the dog, the dalmatian's words got in the way. The dog's voice was a smooth whispering, curling around Flint's thoughts as the dog lead him across the sands, talking but saying nothing as the two males made their way across the black desert.

As they walked, the landscape of the desert changed slowly. The black sand dunes grew shorter, and there were bits of scrub and bare trees from time to time. The landscape was turning into a flat plain of dust instead of rolling dunes, and just here, there was a line where the sand of the desert gave way to broken, rocky ground. It was a definite line, a border that stretched to the horizon on either side. It was a border Flint was about to cross. Somehow, the change did not make Flint feel better. In fact, it frightened him all the way down to his tail.

Flint stopped walking when he reached the divide and looked down. He could feel the sharp rocks under one hind paw, biting into the pad of his foot. His paw nervously closed around the Prophet's cross medallion, his fingers rubbing the emerald gingerly. The medal made him think of Aldain, and the thought of the wolf's warm smile calmed his thoughts. Suddenly the fog in his head rolled back and he could think clearly again. Why was he doing this? What was he doing, following this stranger? For the first time, Flint really looked at the landscape in front of him. There was a deep, shadowy canyon not far away, and a smooth path running down into the depths. Instead of simply being black like the dessert, the canyon had hints of blood red in the deeper shadows. The path down even looked suspiciously like a tongue.

"Where are we going?" Flint said. He pulled back so that he was standing firmly on the sand of the dessert.

"We're going to the afterlife that has been promised to me," Bayon said simply, his words echoing a little, as if he were in a deep cave. The dog was standing on the sharp gravel rocks, and his white fur stood out even more in front of the canyon. "This is the underworld after all. Don't you want your final reward?" Bayon's whispered words were sweet and normal sounding, but they set off alarms inside Flint's head.

Flint squinted, trying to see what was inside the canyon, "But this isn't what the afterlife is supposed to be like," he mumbled, taking a step backwards. "There is supposed to be a castle, not a canyon, and the Prophet," Flint gasped in pain, his wrist aching as Bayon's paw leapt out and grabbed hold of him.

Flint looked up at the dalmatian as the dog twisted his arm. Bayon was smiling broadly at the look of pain on the hyena's face. "Ah yes, that's what the Prophet's little book says, doesn't it? Well I don't think a filthy tail raiser like you has much chance of getting into the Prophet's afterlife. I can see it in your eyes. You just let me lead you along without asking any real questions. I bet that's what you would have done even without the spell. It's what you've always done. Running after your little knight and his fellow murderers." Flint cried out as Bayon's fingernails dug into the skin of his arm. It was surprisingly painful, even thought he was already dead.

A sharp wind rose up, whipping the strip of black clothe away from the dalmatian's neck. The makeshift scarp disappeared into the canyon, which seemed to be breathing in deeply as Bayon spoke. "I read other books, you little fool, and I know about a far better afterlife. One with feasting and ravaging, and I intend to be sitting down for dinner, not the main course." Flint tried to twist away from Bayon's face as the dalmatian leaned in close to him, his smile bright and terrifying. Flint could see the second smile underneath Bayon's muzzle, where the red wound was a sick mockery of the dog's grin. "You are my way inside," The dog hissed, "A sacrifice to appease Mak'tchen, one he asked for specifically."

Flint tried to pull away from the dog, but Bayon was far stronger then he was. In desperation, Flint struck the dalmatian with the paw holding his medallion, the holy symbol slapping the dog across the face. The medallion was lightweight and Flint didn't put much into the punch, but Bayon jerked back screaming as if he had been burned. The dalmatian released Flint, clutching at his face howling in pain, and Flint could see the livid cross mark branded on the dalmatian's cheek. The hyena turned ran as fast as he could away from the dog and the horrible canyon.

Bayon howled in agony, smoke curling from underneath the paw holding his cheek. The dog growled and raced after Flint, jaws open wide. The hyena's paws slipped and slid on the sand as he ran as fast as he could. The dalmatian had the look of a wild man now, a beast with jaws open wide as he lunged at Flint with madness in his eyes and the Prophet's cross burned into his handsome face. Flint twisted to the side and flung himself to the ground, diving out of the dog's way just in time. The dalmatian's clawed hands slashed at the sand as he landed, barely missing the hyena's leg. Flint tried to scramble to his feet and run, but the desert sands shifted under Flint's paws and he stumbled against a dune. The dalmatian was almost on him, when a swirl of gray rushed past Flint.

There was a flash of steel and a muffled bark of pain, as someone threw himself between Flint and the dalmatian, knocking the now feral dog away. Flint yipped in surprise, staring in shock at the hyena that was now fighting with Bayon. It was his father Samuel.

The dalmatian howled and threw himself at Flint's father, and while Flint knew that the dog's howl was a battle cry of pure rage, the sound was so quiet Flint could barely hear it. "Dad!" Flint screamed at his father, but that sound died too, swallowed by the sands. Another hyena rushed at him, grabbing him around the stomach and hauling Flint into the air. Flint grunted as he was flung over her shoulder, and he stared in shock at his mother's face as he was carried away across the sand.

"Mom?" Flint yelped, and his mother only smiled at him and ran. Flint clung to her, staring back at his father. Behind them, the dalmatian was on his feet again. Samuel circled the dog, sword at the ready. Flint watched in shock at his father as they clashed, fought for a moment, and separated again as Samuel shoved Bayon away from him. That was when the bull appeared.

The bull did not burst into being or rise up out of the sand. One moment he was just standing between the two men where he had not been the moment before. The bull was wearing a long black robe roughly the color of the sand that obscured most of his body. It made the dark brown fur on his head and his long white horns stand out even more against the black landscape. The dalmatian paused, staring up at the robed figure as if he were frightened of him. Flint's father turned and ran after his mother, racing up the side of a sand dune and away from the newcomer. The bull's arm left the folds of his robe, and Flint could see he was holding a long, double headed executioner's axe. The last thing Flint saw before he was carried over a sand dune was the dalmatian turning to run, as the heavy axe swung through the air.

The dalmatian's howl sent a shiver down Flint's spine and he clung to his mother as he was carried over the dunes, the sound ringing in his ears as it died away.

Flint clutched at his mother, his arms encircling her neck. He pressed his face to the short mane of fur on the back of her neck and breathed in, letting the old, familiar scent of his mother flooded his nose. A feeling of belonging enveloped Flint, the fuzzy memories of home and how it had smelled calming him down. After a minute or so of running, Flint's mother slowed down, and set Flint down against a sand dune. She crouched beside her son and patted him down, making sure he was all right. That was the first time Flint had been able to see her face properly, and Flint nearly started crying when he looked into the dead, gray eyes of his mother Julia.

"Are you okay honey?" Julia said, her words mere whispers like every other sound in this place. "Gods, how you've grown," she muttered, a paw ruffling the hyena's short mane. "But you're still my little boy aren't you?" Her voice sounded like it was about to break, and she stared at Flint with a sad smile on her muzzle. Flint stared at his mother in shock, his paw reaching up to touch her face.

The woman Flint had called mom for too few years looked at him, her face broken by a huge grin. It was his mother, there was no doubt about that, but everything about her was gray now. Even her eyes had changed, as if the sand had leeched the color out of her. Only her smile seemed alive.

"Mom?" Flint blurted out, his paws trembling. She nodded once, her smile breaking into a huge grin as Flint's paw touched her face, the hyena's fingers brushing across the short fur as she touched noses with him, and then hugged Flint tightly. Flint stammered, too shocked to say anything as he hugged his mother back. "How, how can you be here? Dad! Dad was back there we have to…"

"I'm right here son." The masculine voice was quiet, but it sent shivers down Flint's spine. The short hyena glanced up at his father, a tall and proud looking hyena who had just come around the nearest sand dune. He was dressed in strange armor that Flint had never seen him wear before, and he looked drained of color just like Julia was. Flint was almost on the verge of tears when his father hugged him. "It is so good that we found you when we did," Samuel said, and Flint looked up at his father with fear in his eyes.

"Dad?" Flint babbled, "What's going on? You and mom, you're both," Flint swallowed, unable to go on. He knew that his parents were dead. Flint had buried them both back in East Haven. He had kept the headstones clear for nearly ten years.

"Dead," Samuel said softly, and the deep masculine voice of his father sunk into Flint's thoughts, and the whispered words made Flint's heart skip. "We're are all dead son."

Flint looked down at himself again, staring at the wound on his stomach for a second time. The dry blood flaked off Flint's fur and fell to the sand, forming red dots in the sand. Then the color faded away, and the blood became merely a few more grains of black sand. Flint crossed his arms over his chest, looking up at his parents as the truth hit him. He was dead. He had died in Aldain's arms, and now he was with his parents again, just like the village preacher used to say he would be. Flint sniffed, his chest heaving as he began to cry. His mother held him close, cradling her son gently as he sobbed, his tears turning to dust in the wind before they even had time to fall.

Flint wasn't sure how long he cried on his mother's shoulder, there was no way to tell time in this horrible place. He only knew that his eyes hurt from the dusty tears and that his parents were still here, their fur and clothing the same colorless gray as the light.

Flint rubbed his nose with his paw, the aching pain inside his chest draining away. Now he just felt cold and empty. Julia was petting his mane slowly, her face carefully blank as she lowered her muzzle to nuzzle her son softly. Flint's father knelt down beside them uncomfortably, his eyes scanning the dessert around them as if he were keeping watch. Samuel reached out a paw tentatively, touching his son's shoulder gingerly as his brow furrowing in concentration. "I'm sorry son," Samuel said, his gruff voice still quiet as a whisper. "Your mother and I..." Flint's father paused, his eyes avoiding Flint's. "We should have been there to protect you son. Whatever killed you, we should have stopped it." Flint looked up at his embarrassed father. He was never good at talking to me when he was alive, Flint thought, and now he isn't any better.

"No," Flint muttered, his voice stronger now then it had been before, "There's nothing you could have done. You both died years ago." Flint muttered, remembering the night the village elders had come home instead of his parents. "Bandits killed you in the fields. There was nothing you could do." Flint caught the look his mother and father gave each other when he said that.

"You're right, we shouldn't talk about it. Nothing we can do now right?" Julia said, his voice taking on a forced brightness. "Tell us what's happened to you, how you've lived your life. How you," she stopped, her eyes flicking to the wound on Flint's stomach. "What brought you back to us?" she finished, trying to make it sound like a happy question.

Samuel coughed, his paw patting his son's shoulder gently

"We... Well you see, we don't know what happened to you after we left. We just knew where we would find you." Flint looked at his father, and he could see the desperation in the old hyena's eyes. "Have you been alright?" he asked, his voice a distant and painful sound.

"I... I've been okay." Flint said as he rubbed the grit from his eyes. He wanted to cry, his chest ached from the sobs he was holding back, but he couldn't do it anymore. He felt to empty to cry. "I've missed you both so much," Flint whispered, hugging his father gently. Flint closed his eyes as his father gently rubbed between his ears. The sensation made Flint's eyes water again. He had missed that.

Samuel smiled a bit, holding his son awkwardly until the hug ended. "We've missed you too, Flint, but you seem to have grown up to be a fine young man." Flint smiled a bit as his father patted his shoulder. "Did you keep the house and farm in good repair?"

Flint's face fell, and his ears turned backwards. It had been along time since he'd seen his father. He had forgotten how much their home and the little farm he worked had meant to the old man. "The village elders said I was too young to live by myself. I had to move in with Tongish, and they sold the farm to pay for my upkeep." Flint felt horrible as his father's face fell, but he had to tell him. Lying to his father now, in this place, was inconceivable. Samuel looked down at his paws and fell silent.

His mother patted him gently, guiding Flint to sit back cross-legged in the sand. "I'm glad he took you in. At least the village didn't send you to an orphanage, they are horrible places. Did you get married?" Julia asked hopefully, her voice quiet even though she was right beside Flint. "I know you... were still young, but love can happen any time. Maybe Tongish's daughter took a fancy to you? She was a sweet girl when I worked there."

Flint shook his head, his thoughts jumbled by everything that was happening. The attack, the calm way his parents were talking, the alien landscape, all of it made it hard for Flint to think. "No, no, she never liked me much. She was never very nice either, I don't know why. I did find love though. Aldain was..." Flint stopped, his throat closing up as he thought about the wolf. He wanted to see Aldain again so badly it hurt.

"Aldain?" Samuel said cautiously, looking up at his son. Flint could see the suspicion in the older hyena's eyes. "That's not a very lady like name son. Was she a foreigner?"

Flint blinked away his tears before looking up at his father. Again, the truth was all there was. "No, he's a Knight of the Cross."

For a moment, only the wind of the desert made any sound, until eventually Julia coughed and patted her husband on the shoulder. "Well, like I said, love can happen at any time," she said carefully, her hushed voice edged with worry. Flint looked up at his father, his stomach turning as the older hyena stared at the horizon.

The older male chewed his lip, glancing at his son out of the corner of his eye. "Did he love you back?" the hyena said finally, his spotted forehead wrinkled in thought.

Flint's ears turned backwards, and he smiled sheepishly. "Yes," he muttered, folding his paws in his lap. Samuel and Julia watched as their son ducked his head and blushed, his open face making his feelings for the wolf easy to read.

Samuel nodded once, sighing. "Then I supposed I shouldn't make a fuss. It's all in the past after all." Flint's father stared out into the distance, watching the dunes. "Besides, there's no time to worry about things like that."

Flint stared at his father as the older hyena stared at the horizon. There was something wrong. They were dead now, why was there no time? Flint looked back and forth between his parent's faces. They were acting very strangely; as if they were frightened something could happen at any moment. His mom held him close, her eyes searching the sand dunes when not staring at his face. His father was watching too, his eyes sweeping the landscape in between words. "Where are we?" Flint asked, his voice growing louder as he focused on speaking, "That dalmatian said this was the afterlife, but I don't remember the priests saying anything about a dessert in their sermons. They spoke about a castle paradise where you worshipped the Prophet all day. Not this."

"We are in the afterlife," Samuel said calmly, "just not in heaven." Then he cleared his throat and said in a monotone voice, as if he were quoting from memory, "And the Prophet spoke again, saying, "There shall be a desert where the unfaithful will wander for all eternity, their voices silenced and their tears turning to dust in the wind. They shall wander there until the day of reckoning comes, when they shall be judged and found wanting. From chapter three, verse nine, of the book of the First Day." Samuel blinked when he finished the quotation, and shook himself, as if the words had sent a chill down his spine. "That is where we are now son. The desert of the unfaithful." Flint just stared at his father, his bright green eyes wide as he tilted his head in confusion.

Flint's mother straightened up a little and pointed across the sand dunes to the horizon. "Look over here son. Do you see the Prophet's castle?"

Flint looked where his mother pointed, and at first he saw nothing. There was only black sand, rolling on forever until it met the sky. Then, as if it were growing closer by the second, Flint could saw the hazy shape of a castle on the horizon. The longer he looked, the clearer the castle became as if it were rushing towards him. There was a border where the dessert became green grass, the castle ramparts growing closer and closer as the banners of the Prophet unfurling in the wind. Flint stared at the castle, his heart filling with fear and guilt as he looked, as if the Prophet himself were judging Flint. Julia shifted, blocking Flint view, and the terrible feeling of guilt faded away. The image of the castle retreated back to the horizon.

"It, it moved," Flint whispered, his tail curling between his legs as the fear lingered in his mind, "Like it was coming for me somehow. He was watching me."

"Yes, the Prophet watches everyone here," Samuel said evenly, "The desert is where your soul goes to be judged. If you followed his teachings in life, then Prophet allows you into his paradise. If not, as the scriptures say, then you must walk these sands for eternity." Samuel said, his eyes watching Flint's face as fear crept into his voice. "You didn't you go to the Church much after we died did you son? You were supposed to learn the Prophet's ways. We always tried to teach you his ways."

Flint was staring into the middle distance, the fear caused by the vision of the Prophet's castle beginning to fade slowly. "No, no... I never went to the church. I had to work on Sundays because Tongish always took his daughter, and someone had to stay at the inn." Flint looked at his parents, their faces filling with concern as he spoke. "Neither of you went to Sunday services either, there was always too much work to do on the farm. I never had time to read the Testaments after you died. What happens if I didn't follow his laws?" Julia and Samuel looked down without speaking, their eyes avoiding their son's face. "I never followed the Prophet. I..." Flint blinked once, surprised at his own words, "I hate him."

"Then as your father said, you can never leave the desert." Flint jumped at the sound of the words. They were normal sound, rolling over the black hills like the wind did. After having to strain to hear everything his parents said to him, hearing real words booming over the black sand filled Flint with a primal fear. It was the kind of fear everyone is born with, a fear that comes from the back of the brain that tells you to run from the darkness. The hyena looked up, and standing behind his father was the robed bull, his axe and white horns glimmering against the black sky.

The bull's fur was a creamy brown, a smooth warm color that made Flint think of rich earth, while his horns were a bone white color. He was tall, much taller then any of the hyenas, and his robe was the same dull black color of the sky and sand dunes. He still held the heavy executioner's axe on one hand, the heavy axe head dripping blood onto the sand. The only other color on the bull was the deep green cord wrapped around his waist that held his robes closed. Julia looked up at the robed figure, her voice still muffled by the dessert as she pleaded with him. "You said you would wait, that we would have time with him. We did what you wanted us to, and we've stayed here for so long..."

The bull raised a paw for silence, and Flint swallowed when his mother stopped speaking. Julia was clearly terrified by the huge bull. "You have had your time with your son. Now he must go."

"Who are you?" Flint whispered, staring up at the robed man.

Fear clutched at Flint's chest as the bull's eyes fell on him. The milky white, pupil less, eyes bore into the hyena's soul.

"I am Dommun, god of death," the bull said, and Flint flinched at the word. Here, in this silent dessert of black sand, the bull's cold voice sounded like the last noise you would ever hear.

"What did you do to that dalmatian? The one who attacked me?" Flint looked at the blood dripping off the axe, and reached a paw out and to his father, squeezing it tightly in case this was the last time he could ever do so.

"He was a heretic, a worshiper of Mak'tchen the devourer. I took him to be judged by the Prophet, as all souls must be if they remain in the desert," the bull said, his axe moving slowly as he turned it over once. It made a soft whistling sound started as if the edge was cutting the wind. "He was found guilty of interfering, and now it is time for you to go as well."

"To be judged?" Flint whispered softly, but Samuel shook his head.

"No son. You're not going to be judged, not yet. That's why Lord Dommun," Samuel nodded towards the tall bull beside him, careful not to look him in the eyes, "let us stay in the desert so long. We had to wait here until you died, to make sure no one interfered with you spirit while it was here." Samuel smiled at his son, his voice soft and sad.

"What do you mean?" Flint muttered, his voice rising in alarm even as the dessert crushed the sound.

Julia stroked her son's face gently, brushing her fingers across his short fur. "That man who attacked you? He was taking you back to his god. Mak'tchen would have eaten your soul and spat you back out a twisted mockery of the person you were. You would have gone back as something horrible." Julia smiled, her paw cupping Flint's face gently. "We couldn't let that happen to you."

Flint looked at his mother, then his father, and then at the massive bull. "What do you mean, go back?"

"Someone is going to bring you back to life." Samuel said softly, his muzzle turning up in a sad smile. "Perhaps that knight of yours has found a way."

Flint blinked in surprise, his chest heaving. "I'm, I'm going back? Aldain is…" Flint's voice broke, his words failing as he hugged his mother tightly. He was going back. Aldain was going to save him. Flint clung to his mother, crying with relief, until he saw the pain in her eyes. Flint looked into his mother's eyes, and then up at his father. They were happy, but so terribly sad at the same time. His parents had spent nearly ten years here, in this terrible black dessert, waiting for him.

Then the hyena looked up at Dommun, and the emotionless gaze made Flint's blood burn. "Why would you do this? Why didn't you just stop the dalmatian before he got to me? Why keep my parents here, in this horrible place, for all these years?"

"Because I cannot interfere," Dommun said coolly, his horns dipping towards the hyenas as he bowed his head. Flint's fur prickled as the bull's blind eyes stared at him. "I am bound by the laws of heaven, just as all the gods are. The Prophet has decreed that I must lead the dead to his judgment, and not interfere in the fate of any soul. I can take no action that will change a person's fate, not even one of my own worshipers." Flint's face was a mask of confusion, and he glanced back and forth at his parents for some kind of explanation.

The white horned bull let out a rumbling sigh, "You are an innocent one, aren't you?" Dommun said, his muzzle turning up at the corners as Flint looked at him. "The old gods have been forbidden by the Prophet to interfere directly in the world like we once did. We can act only through those who choose to follow us. I could not stop one of Mak'tchen's servants from affecting you even though I desired to." The bull's head tilted to the side, indicating Flint's father with the point of a horn. "So I told your parents what would happen when you died, told them where that man would lead you, and delayed bringing them to their judgment. Nothing more. They have made their own choices."

Flint felt the tears welling up again, and he hugged his mother tightly. He had so many questions that they came tumbling out all at once. "But, who was that man, and why did you stop him from following us? How am I going back?"

The bull's brown lips pulled back in a wicked smile, and his white teeth gleamed in the gray light. "The man's name was Bayon, and he was not aware of another rule the Prophet has made. Once you enter the afterlife of an old god, you cannot come back to the desert. You must remain there forever, no matter what happens to your soul there. If you do, then I must take steps." Dommun turned his axe again, the red blood gleaming on the axe heads as they spun once. "As for why you are going back?" The bull's smiled softened considerably, and for the first time Flint could see a bit of kindness in the god's face. "I would suspect your young lover is unwilling to give you up just yet, and love makes men do very foolish things," the bull said smoothly. Flint colored, his ears turning a bright red as the god of death smiled down at him.

Dommun turned his back on the three hyenas, as if he were standing guard over the. As the black robes moved, Flint caught a glimpse of a little green pouch on his belt with the symbol of an acorn on the side as the bull set the head of his axe in the sand and put his hands on the handle. "You three have very little time left to be a family. I would not waste it wondering why I have given you the opportunity." Flint squeezed his mother's paw again and looked up at his father, who hugged his son tightly one last time.

~: :~

It seemed like Aldain waited by the altar forever, his paw gently petting Flint's lifeless face. The blood in the hyena's fur had begun to congeal, and Aldain could feel his own fur beginning to mat together as the hyena's blood dried in his clothes.

Trenton and Will lurked around the edges of the temple, compelled to stay and watch even though they were both desperate to avoid looking at Flint's still form for their own reasons. Aldain however, could not bear to look away from the young man's still face.

After organizing the druids to deal with the wreckage created by the battle, Zane returned and began to prepare the spell. The coyote inscribed a large circle around the knight and the altar before positioning Flint's body so he was laid out flat on the altar, his muzzle pointed skyward with his hands clasped over his chest. Aldain just watched, kneeling beside the altar on bruised knees as tears washed away the blood on the wolf's face. Once, Aldain would have thought of this place as a blasphemy, an affront to his God. Now the wolf had no faith left in the Church's teachings. The Prophet and the Church were dead to him the moment they allowed Flint to die.

Eventually the druid was ready and Zane stood across the altar from Aldain with Flint's still body between them. "Are you sure you wish to do this, knight?" The coyote's eyes watched Aldain's face warily, searching for any hint of doubt in the wolf's tear stained gaze. "There is no breaking this vow once it is taken. The Goddess will hold you to this oath much tighter than the Prophet ever did."

The wolf's face darkened and his ears splayed outward. "Do not taunt me Druid. I do not care what the price is, only that you bring him back." The coyote nodded slightly in the face of the wolf's cold stare. There was no arguing with the wolf's words. This was what Aldain wanted.

"All right, then lift up your palms like this and lean over him," the coyote muttered, holding his paws, palms up over the altar. Aldain did the same, his elbows resting on the altar beside Flint's body. The Druid reached out and ran his paw through Aldain's head fur. The coyote's paw came back damp with the wolf's sweat, which he rubbed across Flint's forehead. Next, the Druid brushed his fingers across the wolf's cheeks, gathering up the tears that had been flowing for nearly an hour on the ends of his fingers. Aldain's tears anointed Flint's eyes, and then the coyote lifted the ceremonial knife into view.

Aldain stared at the blade. It was carved from a horn and had a sharp curve to it. The wolf could see his friend's reactions out of the corner of his eye as the druid lifted the blade. Across the room Trenton covered his eyes, and the wolf was sure the fox was fighting back tears. Will just stared at him, a look of sad admiration on his face as he watched the wolf. Aldain looked back at the Druid as the knife glinted slightly in the low light and he could not stop his tail from drooping between his legs at the sight of his own death.

This was it. There was no turning back now. Aldain was going to die betraying his faith with his soul unclean. His damnation was certain. There was no way the Prophet would forgive this kind of sin, or any of the others Aldain had committed since meeting Flint.

Flint. The wolf looked down and his mind latched onto the thought of the hyena's voice and the innocence that had once filled the young hyena's eyes. Flint would live again, and the others would keep him safe. They would make sure Flint was happy and safe, Will had promised too. In the end that was all that mattered.

Aldain closed his eyes and nodded before lifting his chin, exposing his throat, and waiting for the cut that would end it all.

The wolf gasped in pain and surprise as the coyote's knife cut across his palm instead. Dark red blood welled up from the deep wound and the druid grabbed Aldain's paw, forcing him to clench it into a fist. The wolf hissed in pain as his blood dripped onto Flint's bare chest as the Druid spoke the last words of the incantation.

"Then with the sweat of your brow, the tears of your soul, and the blood of your heart, the bargain is made."

A flash of green light erupted from the altar, and the light suffused the hyena. With a terrible howl, Flint's body jerked back to life.

~: :~

For Flint, the world went from being a black dessert of silence to a world filled with pain, color, and sensation. Every sense Flint had was overloaded in one horrifying second as the world rushed back to him in a blurry, dancing spiral. The sounds and scents of life erupted back into his brain like a thousand painful needles jabbing into his skin and eyes, and it made the hyena howl in pain.

Flint grabbed hold of the paws that reached out to him, desperate for any anchor in this maelstrom of sensation and thought. When Aldain's familiar scent reached Flint's nose, the hyena clung to the wolf desperately. Aldain seemed to be the only real thing in the world, the only solid object Flint could hold on to. Flint closed his eyes and pressed his face against the wolf, burying his muzzle in Aldain's fur with a sob as his mind burned from the pain. He was home.

The wolf's arms closed around Flint and the world slowed down, returning to a normal pace as Aldain held him close. The hyena sobbed loudly as his body shook uncontrollably, and his head was cradled by the wolf's gentle paw. Aldain stared into Flint's eyes, and smiled slowly as the hyena held him back. Flint could not speak; he could only react as the wolf kissed him passionately. The hyena threw his arms around the wolf and hugged him as tight as he could. The pain was over and everything was right in the world.

The hyena was still trembling when Aldain broke the kiss, and the hyena yipped as Will and Trenton hugged him just as fiercely. The hyena laughed a little, his body trembling as he hugged everyone. Flint was so happy to be back to be out of that horrible darkness it made it impossible to speak. He was happy, they were happy, but he could tell there was something hanging in the air. Something darkened the faces of the adventurers. Aldain beamed, but he was sad. Will held him close, but in a protective way as if to keep him from going somewhere. Trenton stood

close by, but he had tears streaming down his cheeks. Everyone's smile was half hearted.

Aldain hugged Flint again, holding him tightly to his chest for a while until the coyote standing beside the stone altar cleared his throat. "It's time. The sacrifice must still be made soon or else the spell will be undone."

Flint looked at Aldain in confusion, "What's going on?" Flint managed to whisper, his throat aching. Aldain's paw brushed Flint's face, caressing him tenderly. The hyena breathed in the wolf's scent and smiled, his eyes half closed as he pressed his muzzle against the knight's paw. Their noses just touched.

The wolf stared into Flint's eyes for a long moment and smiled. "I love you," the knight said quietly, Aldain's breathe passing over the hyena's lips just before they kissed. Then the wolf pulled away and stood beside the altar. "All right, do it." Aldain said quietly. The coyote looked at him carefully, and then glanced at Flint.

"Are you sure? You can still back out. The balance could be restored to the way it was." The coyote's tone was measured, and Flint felt he was testing Aldain somehow.

The wolf bristled, his hackles rising and his teeth flashing as he snarled at the druid. Flint jumped in the jackal's grip, startled by the wolf's violent reaction. Will held him steady as Trenton stepped between him and the altar so Flint could not see well.

"Kneel before the altar and give me your sword." The coyote intoned, and Flint's heart skipped a beat as Aldain did as he was told. The wolf pressed the side of his head on the blood covered stone, his face turned towards Flint. The wolf's smile was so sad, and Flint's heart stopped when the coyote raised the sword.

Flint struggled and tried to shout, but no words came out. Trenton looked away and even Will closed his eyes, but the jackal held the hyena firmly in place. The coyote's arms seemed to move in slow motion, and all Flint could see was the knight's sword arching slowly towards the wolf's neck. Flint watched Aldain's eyes close just before the sword struck, a smile on his lips.

The coyote tapped the sword lightly on Aldain's neck and said, "By the power vested in me by the Goddess, I knight you Sir Aldain, Protector of the Land. Rise, and serve the Goddess for the rest your days as payment for the life of Flint."

Everyone sort of froze in place as a collective moment of confusion washed over the group. Aldain's head snapped up and he gaped at the coyote while Flint fell still in the jackal's arms. The Druid turned the sword around and presented it to the wolf hilt first. Aldain took his back sword with a shaking paw.

Will regained his voice first. "What sort of sick game are you playing?" the jackal shouted at the druid, and Flint took his chance to slip out of the black canine's grasp and race to Aldain's side.

The wolf almost fell over when Flint tackled him, hugging him so tightly it was hard for the wolf to breathe. The knight blinked once, twice, and then closed his arms around Flint protectively and stared up at the druid.

The coyote smirked and put his hands behind his back. "Yes, that's it. I'm sorry, but I had to be sure his intentions were true."

"You put him, put us, through that just to test his resolve?" Will shouted as he advanced on the coyote. Trenton blocked his path and quieted the jackal, covering Will's mouth with a paw. The fox looked down at Flint and Aldain, letting them have a moment of peace together.

"You're... you're serious?" The wolf stammered, his grip on Flint tightening.

The druid's smug muzzle split into a big grin. "Yes I am. So long as you serve the Goddess faithfully, then Flint's life will continue. If you cease to walk with us, he will die in an instant. That is the bargain you have struck, knight." The coyote smirked at the wolf, enjoying the moment a great deal. "Is there something wrong with the arrangement?"

Aldain looked away from the coyote as Flint kissed and rubbed against the wolf's face, both of them covered in blood and dirt but happier than anyone the druid had ever seen before. "No, no there isn't," The wolf said with a grin, and he hugged the hyena tightly.

~: :~

Flint lay in a warm bed beside Aldain. The hyena was on his side, curled up in the crook of Aldain's arm, his head resting on the wolf's shoulder. Flint had one arm draped over the wolf's belly in tender hug, and the wolf's paw pressed against the small of Flint's back. Flint smiled, his chest heaving slightly as the wolf shifted his naked body into a more comfortable position, bringing himself closer to Flint. The hyena murred softly and pawed at the wolf's chest, and Flint was delighted when the wolf's arm pulled him even closer. Flint smiled, laying his head on Aldain's chest again. Flint was amazed at how wonderful the night had become. They had collapsed into this warm bed a few minutes ago, their paws roaming each other as they began to mate for the third time tonight.

Flint blushed, his ears turning backwards as he watched the knight's chest rise and fall. The first time had been a surprise. The druid's had provided them a place to clean the blood from their fur, and after they finished washing in the temple's underground stream and climbed into a warm bath the wolf made love to Flint. Aldain had taken Flint from behind, holding the hyena tightly in the warm bath water. Then they had mated again as they dried their fur, Aldain taking him on all fours this time. Flint could feel his face growing hot as he remembered how wantonly the wolf had pressed against him, never straying more the a few feet from the hyena's side. Once they got to the room, the third mating had happened almost instantly. Flint had enjoyed that time most of all; because the wolf had made love to him in the same way that Flint had lost his virginity to the wolf back in East Haven. Face to face, their gazes locked as their bodies joined in passion.

Just thinking about that brought a stirring to the hyena's sheath, but Flint didn't know if he could handle a fourth time with the inexhaustible knight. The wolf seemed to be filled with an energy that refreshed him each time, while Flint felt drained by everything that had happened. The hyena grinned, his fingers playing with the wolf's fur. It didn't matter how tired Flint was, he had never felt this good in his life.

"I can feel your heart beating." Aldain whispered, and Flint turned his head to smile at the wolf.

"I can feel yours too," the hyena said, placing his paw over the wolf's heart. Flint smiled, his fingers rubbing the wolf's chest gently. It seemed like their hearts were beating in sync with each other.

"No," Aldain whispered as he took Flint's paw in his own. "I can feel you inside here," the wolf muttered, pressing Flint's paw against his own chest. Aldain's muzzle rubbed at Flint's forehead, kissing the hyena as the wolf breathed in deeply. "And you smell so wonderful... So strong," Aldain muttered, his lips brushing against the hyena's forehead.

Flint blinked, his eyes meeting Aldain for a moment. The wolf's eyes seemed distant, as if he were lost deep in thought. "Can you hear the wind in the trees?" the wolf asked quietly, his fingers stroking the hyena's short mane. Flint blinked and looked around the small room they were in. There was no sound but the steady beating of their hearts. They were underground, in the hollowed out center of a hill. No trees, and certainly no wind, were anywhere nearby.

Aldain sat up slowly and turned toward the door, his eyes still far away. Flint wrapped his arms around the wolf's waist, clutching at Aldain so he could not leave. "Where are you going?" Flint asked quietly, his voice filled with worry.

Aldain smiled down at his lover, and the wolf's paw slowly caressed the frightened hyena's face. "I don't know." The wolf said, his voice a little dreamy as he grinned at Flint. "But you're coming with me," the wolf finished happily. The wolf got up, pulled on his pants, and walked to the door without anything else. Aldain smiled back at Flint, his gray tail wagging back and forth as he gripped the doorknob and waited for the hyena to follow. "Come on Flint," Aldain said happily, and the hyena got up with a nervous smile and followed after him.

~: :~

Argo stumbled through the forest, every part of his body aching. Blood was still trickling from his ears and the horse feared he might be permanently deaf from the fox's spell. The cuts and gashes Aldain and William had inflicted burned, and large parts of the horse's armor had been destroyed and fallen away in his flight from the temple. Argo could barely see, and he recognized the way his vision blurred as a concussion. The horse had suffered a lot of punishment in the service of the Prophet, but Argo knew he was in very bad shape right now.

The worst part was, Argo knew that his fellow knights were dead. He had failed them, and the Order as a whole. Even if he could survive to morning and find a way back to town and the safety of the castle, Argo wasn't sure if he would live long enough to defend the Order from the Inquisition. Everything the horse had done tonight turned his leadership of the Order into a failure, and the horse looked up at the heavens, begging the Prophet to forgive him. Argo cried as his prayer fell only on his own deaf ears.

Then the horse looked up into the night, and like a sign from the Prophet, Argo saw a chance for redemption.

~: :~

Trenton looked up from his book when someone knocked on his door. The fox hurriedly grabbed his robe and pulled it around his waist as he got up to open the door. He tied the robe closed around his waist, silently glad that the only armor he ever used doubled as a nightgown. He would just have to hope whoever it was would not notice the bulge the robe barely covered. "Yes, yes I'm coming," the fox called as the visitor knocked again. "Will!" the fox said happily as he opened the door, "What brings you to my room tonight?" he asked, leaning against the doorframe with a smile.

The jackal's eyes narrowed slightly and he licked his lips unconsciously as Trenton swished his tail back and forth playfully, actually loosening his robe so it almost fell open. "I just needed to talk with someone," Will muttered as he looked away from the fox's slim muzzle. The jackal would normally have smirked at the way Trenton came on to him so blatantly, but now it made Will's stomach tighten into uncomfortable knots. It did not help that they close enough for the jackal to smell the fox's arousal.

"Well, why don't you come in," Trenton said smoothly, opening the door all the way and moving into the room. Will lurked by the door as the fox poured a glass of wine for him, picking up the glass he had been drinking before the jackal arrived. "You going to join me, or wait in the hall for someone else to talk too?" The fox said playfully, "I'm sure that Aldain will be free in a few hours."

Will rolled his eyes at that, and closed the door.

~: :~

Flint followed Aldain through the druid's temple, and the wolf seemed much happier once they were outside. The wind rushed through the wolf's fur and he breathed deeply, holding Flint's paw tightly as the hyena walked beside him. Flint kept close to the wolf, his eyes darting back and forth as they made their way through the dark forest. The hyena did not feel comfortable being out here half naked, but the wolf seemed to love it.

Aldain made his way through the forest easily, and Flint could not see any path that the wolf was following. The hyena flinched as branches scrapped across his muzzle, his yip of pain bringing Aldain to a sudden stop. The wolf was suddenly close to him, his finger's brushing across Flint's muzzle slowly as the knight checked for a cut. Flint blushed, mumbling an apology as Aldain smiled at him. The wolf kissed Flint gently on the cheek, his larger paw squeezing the frightened hyena's paw. When they began to move again, Aldain was careful to hold the plants and trees out of the hyena's way, guiding him through the undergrowth as the hyena kept glancing around in fright at the darkness around them.

Aldain wasn't worried. He could tell Flint was frightened, but somehow the wolf knew there was nothing in the forest tonight that could hurt them. The most dangerous thing within a mile of them was a feral bear asleep in his cave. Aldain wasn't sure how he knew that, he just knew that Flint was safe right now. He knew it in the same way he could feel the hyena's heart beating with his own.

Eventually they came to the top of a hill, where a tall black stone rose up out of the ground like a tower. The bluff over looked the forest, where a low bank of fog had seeped in between the trees. The half moon illuminated the landscape better here, and it looked as if the two were standing on some forgotten shoreline, and the trees were bobbing on an ocean of mist. The wolf stood beside the stone, his paw squeezing Flint's tightly as the hyena stood beside him.

"Where are we?" Flint said quietly, his muzzle pushing under Aldain's arm so the wolf would wrap his arm around the shorter hyena's shoulder. It felt cold out here to the slim hyena, but the wolf's arm kept him warm like a blanket.

"I don't know," Aldain said with a smile on his face. "But I like it." The wolf hugged Flint tenderly, but not for warmth. He wasn't cold at all. Aldain felt so alive it frightened him. The wolf could feel the power seeping out of the stone, a tingling natural energy that flooded his body and made his fur stand on end. It was like the power Aldain had felt in the holy temples of the Prophet. Only this time, the presence felt peaceful and relaxing instead of overbearing and sharp.

"So do I," Flint said absently, and then he looked around curiously. "Does this place feel odd to you?" he whispered, instinctively keeping his voice down as if he were inside a church.

"No," Aldain said happily as he sat down beside the stone, his back pressing against it. "It just feels right." Flint blinked and looked down at the wolf that was smiling up at him. Flint's muzzle twitched, and then broke into a shy grin as the wolf squeezed his paw. "Sit with me?" the wolf asked innocently, and the hyena blushed as he slipped into the wolf's lap. They sat there together, and Flint felt his heart swell as the wolf hugged him to his chest.

Flint smiled at Aldain nervously. The wolf was acting so strange. Aldain's smile was dreamy and his eyes flicked back and forth unsteadily, as if he weren't quite awake. The wolf's paws were constantly touching the hyena, his fingers tracing Flint's spots or running through the hyena's short fur. The constant touching made the hyena blush in arousal, his muzzle dipping as the wolf caressed him. Flint could not believe how much passion the wolf poured into everything he did now, and still Aldain seemed to be full of energy. Flint licked his lips in trepidation, the feeling of straddling Aldain's lap making the hyena hard in his silk pants. Aldain's muzzle rubbed against his face, and he reached down to caress the outline of Flint's erection. "Can I make love to you one more time?" the wolf whispered before kissing Flint tenderly.

The hyena whimpered, his muzzle dipping down under Aldain's as his body tensed at the wolf's touch. "Yes," Flint whispered, and he kissed Aldain slowly before standing up. They both pulled of their pants, and Aldain sat back down on the grass, his back against the standing stone. The wolf was grinning like an idiot as he looked up at Flint's naked body. Flint blushed, looking down at the handsome wolf. Aldain's muscular body seemed to glow in the soft moonlight, and the wolf was fully aroused as the naked hyena descended back into Aldain's lap.

Flint kissed Aldain deeply, turning his muzzle to the side so their mouths meshed together. The hyena lifted his tail up and reached back to guide the wolf inside him. Their kiss broke when Aldain pressed himself up into the hyena, both males clutching at each other in pleasure as the wolf slipped past the hyena's resistance. Both of them groaned, their paws squeezing hips and shoulders as their bodies trembled in shared pleasure. Flint whimpered and squeezed down on Aldain as the wolf pushed up into his smaller lover.

Flint's forehead rested on Aldain's neck as they began to make love. The wolf had one paw wrapped around Flint, and the other on his hip, guiding the hyena as Flint began to move himself up and down in the wolf's lap. Aldain moved his hips in concert with the young male, the wolf's muzzle rubbing and bumping against the hyena's head as Flint rode him slowly. Their breathing was slow and they moved together as they made love surrounded by nature.

Aldain could not believe how good it felt to push up into the tight hyena. The wolf pressed his muzzle against the boy's neck and mated him wantonly, the hyena's weight on his hips making it hard to push up. That resistance felt good, and every time he pushed into Flint made Aldain's heart burst with pleasure. The wolf kissed Flint hard, his paws holding the hyena's hips tightly as his arousal continued to grow, the wolf's knot growing and pulling at the hyena's insides.

Flint yipped when he first felt the wolf's knot pull at his tail. Flint felt like he was flying as he mated the wolf, his body shaking as Aldain moved inside him. The hyena barked, squirming and pushing himself down onto the wolf. Flint was trembling all over as the wolf touched him inside and out, Aldain paw rubbing at Flint, as they both drew closer and closer to losing themselves in each other. Flint opened his eyes and stared into Aldain's face. "I love you," the hyena gasped, his eyes watering as he felt the wolf tie with him.

Aldain leaned up, kissed Flint hard and thrust fully inside him. The hyena gasped into the wolf's mouth as the wolf took him completely, the wolf's nature locking them together. "I love you too Flint." Aldain whispered, his muzzle rubbing against the hyena's face and his body trembling as he lost himself inside the hyena.

Flint watched the wolf's face as his lover peaked inside him. The wolf's nose wrinkled, his eyes closing tightly and his mouth opening in a moan. Flint stared into the wolf's face, a mask of pleasure as he filled Flint's body. The hyena trembled, biting his lip as the wolf continued to pleasure him. Flint tensed, his body shaking as he joined his lover in heaven and emptied himself across the wolf's chest with a loud moan.

Aldain came for a long time, much longer than normal. He trembled and barked, his body tensing as he thrust weakly into Flint. The hyena pressed his paws to the wolf's face as the knight howled. Flint clung to the wolf's shoulders as he went through a powerful and draw out orgasm. It felt good holding him like that, their bodies pressed together. Flint felt connected to the wolf. Flint felt alive as Aldain's pressed deep inside him.

For Aldain, the experience could only be called divine. The wolf climaxed so hard he almost blacked out. Aldain could feel every inch of his body tingle with pleasure, as if he had been set on fire. He felt connected to the grass and trees around him, to the bird soaring high overhead, and especially to the hyena he was inside. Oh, how Aldain connected with Flint! Before, all Aldain could feel was Flint's heartbeat in time with his own. Now he could feel everything the hyena did, the way the young man's lungs expanding as he panted, and the sensation of his tail squeezing around the wolf inside him. Aldain's body trembled as he shared everything with the hyena, experiencing the hyena's climax with him. Flint's joy at making his lover climax and the hyena's tender concern flooded through Aldain's thoughts. Aldain's body shook in the grip of shared ecstasy, aching as he emptied himself inside Flint. Aldain gripped the young man he loved just as tightly as Flint clung to him.

Then with a gasp it ended. Aldain and Flint clutched each other, their bodies heaving, and their fur steaming in the night air. Aldain felt the connection with Flint flow away, the hyena's thoughts and sensations fading away until all that remained was the steady, shared heartbeat. Aldain smiled up at his lover, kissed him, and then held the hyena tightly in his arms until sleep claimed the young man.

Aldain's eyes began to droop as well, and he could feel the exhaustion overwhelming his body as he slipped out of Flint. He smiled, holding the warm hyena close to his chest as he listened to the forest for the first time in his life, and found it was singing him to sleep. As Aldain stroked Flint's mane gently, the wolf realized he had no regrets. This moment, in this place, with this young man, felt more right than anything else he had ever done before in his life.

Just before the wolf lost consciousness, the wind changed. The trees rustled and the song of the forest became a warning instead of a lullaby. The crack of branches being stepped on and rush of small creatures fleeing under hoof thundered in the wolf's ears, startling him awake before the attack came. Argo was coming.

On pure instinct, Aldain rolled to the side and hurled Flint away from him and out of danger. The hyena yelped in fright as he skidded to a stop, but the wolf's swift action caused Argo's sword to cut through air instead of the hyena's body.

Aldain tried to stand and face the horse on his feet, but he had no time to move and no armor to block the wounded knight's sword. Argo's sword flashed in the moonlight, glowing with the Prophet's blessing as he prepared to cut Aldain down.

"No!" Flint screamed as the horse raised his sword. The hyena threw out his paws as the horse struck, and Aldain was blinded by flash of white light as the blade descended towards him.

When Aldain could see again, Flint was straddling his lap, the hyena's head pressed against Aldain's neck as he cried. The hyena's muzzle was streaked with tears, and his paws caressed the wolf's face. Aldain blinked in surprise, and smiled as Flint kissed him almost desperately between sobs. "Hey," Aldain said slowly, his paw brushing Flint's face. "It's okay. I've got you," the wolf muttered, his arms encircling the sobbing hyena. "It's okay, we're both okay." Aldain whispered again, patting Flint's head gently.

Flint shook his head, glancing over his shoulder to the right. Aldain followed his gaze, and his grip on the hyena tightened a bit as Flint said, "No, no it's not all right." The hyena sobbed, his fingers fumbling as he tried to pull a ram headed ring off his finger. "I didn't mean to do it, I just pushed him too hard. I didn't mean to do it," Flint cried, pressing his face into Aldain's fur.

Aldain petted Flint's head gently, holding the young man so Flint's face was turned away from where Argo lay. The horse was propped against a nearby tree, and the force of his impact had splintered the trunk. Just like it had splintered the bloody stub of a branch protruding from the horse's chest plate. The wolf closed his eyes and cradled Flint, praying to the Goddess that the old horse would rest easily.

~: :~

Sunrise brought a nervous energy to the Prophet's followers in Newcastle as Father Tully began to prepare his Sunday morning sermon. The otter continued to act shocked and amazed as each new messenger came rushing in to tell him what was happening. The prisoner had escaped in the night and the ceremony to cleanse him was being canceled. Four knights were missing, and Lord Argo could not be located by any of the other priests. No spell could reach the horse, or even locate him. Some of the townsfolk had seen Argo and the other knights leaving the city under cover of night, and rumors were running rampant that they had fallen in battle during some secret mission, or worse, betrayed the Order just like Aldain had.

The otter smiled to himself, smoothing his naturally oiled fur down with a paw as he looked into the full-length mirror Father Tully kept in his study. The otter carefully brushed out the whiskers that formed his bushy mustache and straightened the satin robes he was wearing

In a few minutes, Father Tully would walk into the main temple and announce to the largest congregation in the surrounding lands that the Order of the Cross had been corrupted, and that their leader had returned to his heathen ways and had to be hunted down for his crimes. The otter would be handing the Grand Inquisitor everything he needed to break the Order and force the Knights into serving the Inquisition. It would be a more painful transition than if Argo had survived, but in the end the Knights would be under the authority of the Inquisition and doing the work the Prophet had intended them to do. Rooting out and destroying all those who were unbelievers

"Perhaps one day," the otter mused to himself as he turned away from the mirror, "I will be able to thank that deviant of a wolf for giving me this opportunity."

Tully walked away from the mirror, and a shadow followed him across the room. The old priest reached for his copy of the Prophet's Chronicles that was sitting on his desk, and his paw twitched in pain. The otter would have screamed as the knife plunged into his back, right above where his tail joined with his spine, but the black paw clamped over his muzzle kept Father Tully from speaking.

Tully struggled to move, his arms flailing as William held him upright by the grip on his muzzle. The otter's finger's clawed at the jackal's strong arm, but Father Tully's lower half had gone numb. The old otter could not even his get his tail to respond to his commands. Tully's scream of agony came out as a muffled whimper as Will pulled his curved knife out of the otter's back and held it to the old priest's throat. "I warned you to leave us alone, old man," the jackal hissed in the priest's ear, and then the jackal did exactly as he had promised he would.

Will was outside the castle walls by the time someone found

the otter's body, and well out of the city before the knights could mobilize themselves to catch him.

~: :~

A week later, Aldain sat beside a large oak tree and watched as Flint and Trenton played in the grass of a large meadow near the Goddess's temple. It was strange to see the fox acting half his age, but the hyena seemed to bring out that side of the noble. Aldain watched with a smile as they tumbled together in the grass, until the fox ended up on top and began to tickle the hyena without mercy, sending Flint's sharp, happy laughs echoing across the field. The wolf shook his head, his fur shifting slightly as the breeze sang through the tree above him.

The past few days had been unlike any he had ever lived before. The wolf found himself in touch with the forest in a way he never would have imagined. Most of the powers he had used as a Knight of the Prophet had returned to him. He could feel the good and evil in the hearts of men again and heal with a touch, but he could also hear the wind whisper things in his ear and the birds sang real songs now instead of just chirping. The wolf sensed Will's approach long before the jackal reached his side, as the grass whispered to him that the jackal was coming towards him. That was something he had never been able to do while serving the Prophet.

Will stood beside Aldain and watched their friends playing in the grass like cubs. Then the jackal stared down at the knight in his new, green tinted armor with a sad, slightly angry look on his face. "You don't deserve him." The jackal's voice was hollow and bitter. "You know that right?"

The wolf tore his eyes away from Flint as the hyena raced across the meadow and he looked at the thief with a sad smile. "I know. Sit down, Will." The wolf patted the grass beside him and Will sat down beside him, crossing his legs tightly in a way that reminded the wolf how limber the jackal was. Will brooded for a moment, until the wolf said, "You don't deserve him either. So can we just be happy he's alive?"

Will laughed slightly, the edges of his muzzle turning up into a big grin. "Oh no, I didn't say I deserve him." The jackal looked out across the meadow, where the fox was now racing on all fours away from the hyena. "I don't deserve Trenton either."

The wolf chuckled slightly. "Neither did I, and he's happier with you anyway." Aldain grinned, nudging the jackal in the ribs. "I saw you two together last night. Out by that standing stone on the bluff? He seemed to be enjoying your attentions more than he ever did mine."

The jackal's ears flattened against his muzzle and he ducked his head, grinning slightly. "Oh Goddess, you saw us?"

The knight nodded slightly. "I did, and I must say it was quite a sight. I didn't know the fox could take it from behind so quickly, or that you could..."

The jackal laughed, throwing up his paws in embarrassment, "All right, fine. Lets change the subject." The thief grinned slightly, picking up a rock and tossing it from one paw to the other. "It's bad enough we have the same deity now, do we have to compare our sex lives as well? We will have nothing left to argue about." The jackal tossed the rock at the wolf, who caught it easily and joined Will in a dark chuckle.

"All right," the wolf said. "What are we going to do about Flint when we head off on our next journey? Zane has been hearing things from the south, and I will have to leave soon." The wolf tossed the stone back to the jackal, and Will caught it, staring at the small stone in thought.

The jackal looked out across the field, as Flint chased after Trenton trying to get his shirt back. "He can't come with us. He's too inexperienced, too trusting." The jackal licked his lips slightly, his eyes watching the hyena in worry.

"He adjusted well to what happened with Argo," Aldain mused. The truth was the wolf didn't want to leave Flint behind. "He's wearing Trenton's ring again."

"He would be in too much danger." The jackal passed the rock back to the knight.

"Agreed," Aldain muttered, "but where do we send him? The church may begin looking for me again, and they will find him easily if he stays here or with Trenton's relatives." The wolf tossed the rock back at Will, and the jackal was about to say something when a soft cough and the shuffle of paws announced the appearance of Zane.

The Druid stood quietly beside the two adventurers for a moment before saying, "I think I might have the solution."

"You, sir, are much too quiet." Will muttered as he tossed the rock at the Druid, who caught it easily, looked at it oddly, and then let it fall to the ground. Aldain nodded in agreement. The Druid was indeed far too quiet, even to the wolf's improved sense of hearing.

"Yes well, do you think I could teach Flint to be that quiet? The boy is strange. There is something about him, an..." the coyote turned his paw over as if he were grasping at something as he searched for the right word.

"Innocence." Aldain and Will said it together, and then smiled at one another.

"Yes, that's it." The druid looked out over the field, where Flint and Trenton now lay in a heap on the far side of the clearing, panting and laughing together. "He is innocent in a way I have not seen before, and I think that he could become a fine Druid if you would let him."

The coyote looked at the two canines, and Will and Aldain glanced at each other. The jackal shrugged slightly, and Aldain smiled, looking at Flint as the hyena walked across the meadow towards them, a big smile on his spotted muzzle. The hyena's short brown mane fluttered in the breeze, and his tail wagged back and forth as he jogged, bare-chested towards the wolf. "I think that might work out nicely." The wolf said, and got up to meet his lover halfway.

www.ingramcontent.com/pod-product-compliance
Lightning Source LLC
Chambersburg PA
CBHW071822020726
47502CB00004B/1198